Chapter 1: F

The first time I meet him, it's in the bustling, rain-soaked streets of New York. I'm darting through Midtown, minding my own business, when he nearly plows me down in his rush to some appointment that must surely be more important than anything else. His suit is sleek, tailored to perfection, hugging his broad shoulders and narrowing at the waist in a way that suggests he spends far too much time in front of a mirror. As he strides past me, a whirlwind of confidence and arrogance, he barely spares a glance. The dismissive glare he tosses my way makes it clear he doesn't care that he's nearly upended my morning. "Watch it, lady," his eyes seem to say, "the world doesn't stop for you." I'm left drenched in more than just the rain, feeling a mix of annoyance and a strange flutter of intrigue.

I think I'll never see him again, but fate, as it turns out, has other plans. Later that evening, when I attend a gallery event for work, there he is across the room, a veritable statue of sophistication amid the chaos of clinking glasses and idle chatter. He's transformed somehow, his laughter echoing through the space like music, effortlessly drawing the attention of everyone around him. The way he throws back his head, eyes sparkling with mischief, suggests that the entire night exists solely for his amusement. I can't help but feel a twinge of irritation as I watch him mingle, a crowd of admirers orbiting his gravitational pull. Who does he think he is?

"Isn't that the guy you nearly collided with this morning?" my colleague Jenna whispers, nudging me with her elbow. She sips her wine, her eyes alight with excitement. "He's quite the catch, isn't he?"

"Catch?" I scoff, crossing my arms as I take a sip of my sparkling water, pretending it's a drink worthy of the occasion. "More like a hazard."

"Come on, he's gorgeous! Look at that jawline," she insists, her voice lilting with playful mischief. I can't deny he's handsome, with sharp features that would make any sculptor weep. But that arrogance? It's a major turn-off.

"You mean the jawline that's attached to a heart of stone? No, thank you. I'll take my chances with the art rather than the man." I roll my eyes, but I can't resist glancing back at him. He's now deep in conversation with a well-dressed woman who looks equally charmed and oblivious to the world around her.

Before I can divert my attention back to the art on the walls, he catches my eye. For a split second, our gazes lock, and the room fades away. I'm suddenly acutely aware of the thrumming pulse of my heart, the faintest blush creeping into my cheeks. But then he smirks, a confident, cocky smile that doesn't reach his eyes, and the moment is gone, replaced by a familiar irritation. I quickly look away, focusing on a painting that depicts a chaotic swirl of colors, mirroring the tempest of emotions brewing within me.

"Be cool," I mutter under my breath, chastising myself. "It's just a guy. A rich, arrogant guy, who probably doesn't know the difference between a landscape and a portrait."

As the evening unfolds, I try to navigate the sea of pretentious art enthusiasts and brokers, but I can't shake the feeling of his presence looming in the background. Each time I glance over, he's there, mingling, laughing, and every so often, casting another glance my way. The smirk has morphed into a curious expression, and I find myself wondering what exactly he sees when he looks at me—just another face in the crowd or something more?

I decide to make my rounds, hoping to distract myself from the enigma that is him. I mingle with a group discussing the significance of brush strokes in contemporary art, forcing myself to engage in conversations about the pieces adorning the gallery walls. But every laugh, every opinion I share feels hollow, as if I'm merely playing a role in a production where the spotlight is fixed on someone else.

Delicate Pursuit

Alina Ford

Published by Alina Ford, 2024.

DELICATE PURSUIT

First edition. November 5, 2024.

Copyright © 2024 Alina Ford.

ISBN: 979-8227503763

Written by Alina Ford.

"Lydia!" Jenna calls, drawing my attention. "Come on, let's take a picture by that massive painting!" She motions excitedly toward a vibrant mural that consumes an entire wall, a riot of color and form that could only be described as chaos incarnate. I smile at her enthusiasm, allowing her to pull me away from the heaviness that has settled around me.

As we pose, arms linked, her camera clicks, capturing the moment. I feel a little more at ease until I sense his presence again, lurking just outside the frame. Glancing to my left, I find him standing nearby, arms crossed, watching me with a mixture of amusement and intrigue.

"Your friend's very photogenic," he comments, his voice smooth like silk. I can't help but notice how it sends a shiver down my spine.

"Not nearly as photogenic as your ego is inflated," I retort, crossing my arms defensively.

He raises an eyebrow, clearly entertained. "Touché. I'm curious, though—what's a girl like you doing here among the elite?"

I can't help but smirk. "I'm not here to socialize with the elite, just trying to keep my job." I take a sip of my sparkling water, the bubbles dancing in my mouth, wishing it were something stronger.

"Ah, the tragic artist's assistant, living for the art and suffering for the sake of aesthetics," he muses, a twinkle in his eye. "Very poetic. But surely there's more to you than just canvas and brushes."

Before I can muster a sharp comeback, he's already stepping away, leaving me flustered and questioning whether I should have taken the bait. I watch him disappear into the crowd, my heart racing in a way that feels strangely thrilling and infuriating all at once. I might just need a drink after all.

The air inside the gallery buzzes with a concoction of laughter, the clinking of glasses, and the faint sound of a jazz quartet playing in the corner, casting a warm glow over the gathered crowd. I navigate the sea of vibrant paintings and sculptures, feeling the energy ripple around me. But amidst the lively conversations, my attention is repeatedly drawn back to him. He's a magnet, and despite my best efforts to ignore him, I can't help but steal glances.

He leans against a wall, a glass of scotch in one hand, his casual posture suggesting he owns the place—or perhaps the city itself. There's something effortlessly charming about the way he engages with others, his laughter infectious, the kind that makes the world feel a little brighter. It's infuriating. I can't decide if he's a social butterfly or just a particularly skilled chameleon, blending seamlessly into every conversation, all while remaining slightly aloof, a mystery wrapped in a tailored suit.

"Lydia!" Jenna's voice pulls me back to the present, her eyes wide with excitement. "You have to meet this artist! She's amazing, and her work is all about the intersection of dreams and reality. You'll love her!"

I force a smile, nodding as she tugs me toward a petite woman with a wild mane of curls, each lock bouncing with enthusiasm as she speaks animatedly about her latest piece. As I listen, I can't shake the feeling of being watched. Sure enough, when I chance a glance over my shoulder, there he is again, watching me with an amused expression, like I'm the punchline to a joke only he's in on.

"Great. Now I have an audience," I mumble under my breath, forcing myself to focus on the artist's story about a painting that supposedly depicts her late-night dreams. "Very inspiring," I say, plastering on a sincere smile.

When Jenna nudges me excitedly to ask my opinion on the artwork, my mind wanders back to the stranger. Why can't I shake him from my thoughts? Maybe it's the way he seems to command a room, or perhaps it's that flicker of recognition in his gaze that both annoys and intrigues me. With a deep breath, I excuse myself, claiming I need to check on something.

I find myself wandering toward the back of the gallery, where the artwork is quieter, more contemplative. The subdued lighting casts an ethereal glow over a series of monochromatic photographs, each depicting the fleeting moments of life—an old man feeding pigeons in the park, a child laughing as she leaps through puddles. I'm lost in the images when I hear footsteps approaching, the soft click of heels on polished wood echoing through the space.

"Nice, isn't it?" comes a voice, smooth as velvet, pulling me from my reverie.

I turn to find him standing beside me, the faintest hint of a smile dancing on his lips. "These are breathtaking. They capture moments that are often overlooked."

I force a smile, determined not to let him rattle me. "They are. I suppose some people just know how to look deeper."

He tilts his head, genuinely intrigued. "Touché. I'm starting to think you might be full of surprises."

"Or maybe I'm just trying to avoid becoming another face in the crowd," I shoot back, my heart racing despite myself.

"Is that what you think I am? Just another face?" His voice drops to a conspiratorial whisper, and for a moment, I can see a flicker of something genuine behind the charm—a hint of vulnerability that I wouldn't expect from someone like him.

"Honestly? Yes. Just a guy in a suit with a hefty dose of self-importance." I can't help but laugh, the tension between us shifting. "Is it too much to hope that there's more to you?"

His laughter is deep, infectious, and it stirs something inside me that I thought I'd tucked away beneath layers of practicality and professionalism. "You're bold, I'll give you that. Most people wouldn't dare challenge me, let alone with such wit."

"Then I must be doing something right," I reply, surprised at the ease with which we're talking. "But I'm not looking for a fight. Just trying to navigate this event without getting swept away by the tide of sycophants."

"Believe me, I know the feeling. They flock to me like moths to a flame." He takes a sip of his drink, the amber liquid catching the light, and I can't help but admire the way he holds himself—confident yet casual, as if he's just an ordinary guy enjoying an ordinary evening.

"What do you do?" I ask, intrigued despite my better judgment.

"Investment banking," he replies with a shrug, as if it's no big deal. "And you?"

"I'm an artist's assistant. It's a far cry from banking, I know. But I appreciate the arts, even if it's not always glamorous."

"Not glamorous?" He chuckles, his eyes twinkling. "You're surrounded by creativity, passion, and beauty. I'd call that glamorous. You must have stories."

"Only the ones I can tell without getting fired," I quip, and he laughs, the sound rolling over me like a wave.

As our conversation flows, I start to see layers beneath his polished exterior. There's a depth to him that contradicts the image he projects—a hint of vulnerability that piques my curiosity. I find myself wanting to peel back the layers, to discover who he really is beneath the tailored suits and charming smiles.

"Let's make a deal," he proposes, leaning in closer, the scent of his cologne—a mix of cedar and something citrusy—enveloping me. "I'll tell you a secret if you promise to share one in return. It could be fun."

I'm tempted to say no, to keep my secrets locked away, but there's something in his gaze that suggests he's genuinely interested. "Alright," I say, my voice steady despite the flutter in my stomach. "You first."

"Alright, here goes. I hate art shows." He grins as if he's just dropped a bombshell. "But I can't resist a good scotch, and I like to know what everyone's talking about. It's a networking thing, you see."

"Why am I not surprised?" I reply, shaking my head with mock disbelief. "Alright, my turn. I once fell asleep in a gallery, drooling on a priceless painting. Not my finest hour."

He bursts into laughter, the sound reverberating through the gallery. "I'm sure they were flattered to be so close to such a masterpiece as yourself."

I roll my eyes, fighting back a smile. "Yes, because I'm a real work of art."

"I bet you are," he says, his tone suddenly serious, and the air between us thickens.

The moment stretches, a delicate tension crackling in the space that surrounds us, and I wonder if perhaps we're both a little more than the labels we wear. In this lively gallery filled with creativity and dreams, it feels as though we've just begun to tap into something deeper, something worth exploring.

The air thickens with anticipation as we stand amid a sea of vibrant artwork, the vivid colors and shapes swirling around us like the thoughts racing through my mind. I can feel the weight of his gaze, an almost tangible force, and it prompts a flurry of emotions I wasn't prepared to confront. There's something unsettlingly magnetic about him, the way he leans in just slightly, as if sharing a secret with the entire world.

"I can't believe I'm admitting this," I say, breaking the silence that has stretched between us like a taut string. "But I actually fell asleep at an art opening once. Just laid down on the floor and zonked out, right next to a sculpture. It was a bold move, especially when everyone was dressed to the nines."

His laughter dances in the air again, and I relish the warmth it brings. "Now that's a power move. The ultimate statement: 'I'm so cultured, I can nap among the masterpieces.'"

I roll my eyes, the banter igniting a spark of playful energy. "If only I'd thought to add a touch of flair to my outfit. I could have made headlines as the 'Sleeping Beauty of Contemporary Art.'"

"Beauty indeed," he quips, his voice smooth as silk. "But I'm not sure it would have been a flattering portrait in the gallery brochure. Can you imagine? 'Please enjoy our exhibit, but watch where you step—there's a woman in a red dress catching Z's.'"

"Next time, I'll bring a pillow and an eye mask. Maybe a sleeping bag for dramatic effect," I retort, grinning as I lean against a nearby wall, feeling more at ease than I have all evening. There's something intoxicating about this unexpected connection, a spark that I can't quite articulate but can certainly feel.

"So, if art isn't your whole life, what is?" he asks, his curiosity genuine as he leans against the wall, mirroring my relaxed stance. "What makes Lydia tick?"

I hesitate for a moment, unsure how much to reveal. "Well, aside from enduring the trials of fine art, I'm pretty much just trying to keep my head above water in this city." I gesture around the room. "It's easy to get lost in the noise here, don't you think?"

"Absolutely," he replies, his expression softening. "But I think you're the kind of person who finds a way to stand out, even in a crowd. I respect that." His compliment catches me off guard, igniting a flutter of warmth in my chest.

"Are you flirting with me?" I tease, trying to keep the tone light, even as a part of me wonders if he might actually mean it.

"Maybe," he says, his eyes glinting with mischief. "But that depends. If I am, does that mean I get to take you out for coffee sometime? Or should I settle for a classic New York slice?"

"Only if you promise to let me pay for my half," I counter, raising an eyebrow. "I don't want to go down in history as another damsel lured by a knight in shining armor."

"Fair enough. But I have to warn you, my idea of a great date includes pizza, a bit of banter, and maybe a heated discussion about art. You might regret that decision."

"Regret is not in my vocabulary, unless we're talking about eating too many carbs," I laugh, and just like that, the air shifts again, the chemistry between us crackling like static electricity. I can't ignore it, and it terrifies me in the best way.

Suddenly, the room feels smaller, the light dimmer, and for a brief moment, it's just the two of us caught in our own world. But then reality intrudes, as Jenna appears at my side, her expression a mix of excitement and urgency.

"Lydia! We need to—" she starts, but her words falter as she registers the tension between me and my enigmatic companion. "Oh! I didn't mean to interrupt. I just... can we talk?"

"Sure, what's up?" I ask, reluctantly breaking my gaze from the stranger.

Jenna leans in, lowering her voice. "I just overheard some people talking. There's a big buyer here tonight, someone with deep pockets and an eye for talent. I think we should try to get in front of them."

"Is it anyone I should be worried about?" I glance back at the man who has captivated me, but he's already slipped back into the crowd, effortlessly charming another group with his magnetic presence.

"No, but I heard he's looking to invest in new artists and emerging talent. This could be a great opportunity for both of us," Jenna says, her enthusiasm palpable.

"Okay, let's find him," I say, feeling a rush of adrenaline at the prospect. "But first, I need to—"

Before I can finish my thought, I feel a sudden shift in the energy around me. A loud crash echoes from across the gallery, a jarring sound that makes the room go still. Everyone turns, eyes wide, as a massive painting—one of the main attractions of the exhibit—teeters precariously on its frame before crashing to the ground, shattering the tension with an unsettling thud.

"Oh no!" Jenna gasps, her hand flying to her mouth. "What happened?"

I make my way through the crowd toward the fallen artwork, heart racing. As I draw closer, I notice something strange—a scuffle among the attendees. Voices rise in panic as people jostle to see what's happening.

Then I spot him, the man from earlier, standing at the epicenter of the chaos, his face a mask of confusion. He's scanning the crowd, looking for someone, and the way his expression darkens sends a chill up my spine.

"Lydia, wait!" Jenna grabs my arm, but I shake her off. I need to know what's happening. The atmosphere is charged with anxiety, and instinct pulls me forward.

Just as I reach the edge of the throng, I hear him shout, "Get back! Everyone stay where you are!" The urgency in his voice cuts through the noise, drawing everyone's attention.

A sense of foreboding washes over me as I catch his gaze again, a flicker of something unnameable passing between us. Before I can process it, another crash reverberates through the gallery. My heart sinks as I realize that whatever is happening, it's far from over.

Suddenly, there's a loud bang, and the lights flicker ominously. A sense of dread unfurls in my stomach. "What the hell is going on?" I whisper, feeling the ground shift beneath me.

In that moment, I realize that my night has taken a turn I never could have anticipated, a twist that promises to unravel everything I thought I knew. As chaos ensues, the last thing I see before everything spirals out of control is his piercing gaze, filled with urgency and something akin to fear. Then the lights go out completely, plunging us into darkness.

Chapter 2: Unexpected Encounters

The conference room hums with the low murmur of chatter, a sea of blazers and pressed shirts swimming around me like school fish, all eager to avoid the sharp eye of the predator lurking at the head of the table. Lucas Morgan leans back in his chair, his gaze fixed intently on the presentation slides projected on the wall, but I can feel the weight of his scrutiny. The man radiates an intensity that nearly vibrates the air. He's not merely observing; he's dissecting, and it sends a shiver of both trepidation and defiance racing down my spine.

I shift in my seat, clenching my hands together to steady the tremors threatening to reveal my discomfort. The meeting drags on, each speaker fumbling to impress him, their voices blending into a monotonous drone. I attempt to concentrate, but the magnetic pull of Lucas's presence is impossible to ignore. His hair, dark and perfectly tousled, catches the overhead light, making him look every bit the enigmatic art patron that he is. But it's those eyes—cool and calculating—that draw me in like a moth to a flame. They bore into me, making me hyper-aware of every shift in my body, every beat of my heart.

Finally, the time comes for me to present our project. My team has poured countless hours into developing a sustainable initiative that aligns with our company's core values. I rise, plastering a confident smile on my face that feels more like a mask than an expression of genuine assurance. The projector flickers to life, and I launch into my carefully rehearsed speech, my voice steady but my pulse racing.

As I weave through the details, I can feel Lucas's gaze on me, sharp and unwavering. I describe our innovative approach to reducing waste, highlighting the partnerships we've forged with local artisans to promote a circular economy. I finish with a flourish, believing I've captivated the room. A small part of me relishes the satisfaction of having held my own, at least until Lucas leans forward, his interest piqued, a sly smile creeping across his lips.

"Impressive," he begins, his voice smooth as velvet, yet edged with something more biting. "But tell me, how do you plan to scale this initiative? Surely you don't expect it to remain a small-town project forever. What happens when the numbers start to rise, and you're faced with real financial pressure?"

The room holds its breath, and I feel the heat rise in my cheeks. I open my mouth, words spilling forth like water from a broken dam, and the initial rush is exhilarating. "We're already preparing for that eventuality. Our projections indicate a significant increase in demand, and we're exploring options for broader distribution while maintaining our commitment to sustainability."

He raises an eyebrow, an expression that communicates both skepticism and intrigue. "But isn't that the crux of the issue? In order to grow, you'll have to compromise your values, won't you? It's a tricky balance, maintaining your principles while pursuing profit. It often leads to...unexpected encounters with reality."

The way he emphasizes the last two words makes my stomach knot, a cold flash of irritation lighting up my chest. I meet his challenge head-on, the fire in my gut igniting. "If we sacrifice our values for profit, what's the point of any of it? Isn't the goal to create something that matters, not just something that sells?"

His expression shifts, amusement dancing in those striking blue eyes. "Ah, the idealist speaks. Tell me, how do you reconcile the beauty of your vision with the brutal truth of the market? Because it's a dangerous game, and the odds aren't in your favor."

The tension in the room escalates. My colleagues glance between us, clearly entertained by the sparring match unfolding. I take a deep breath, grounding myself in the belief that I can navigate this confrontation. "I believe there's strength in integrity. If we stand firm, we can attract investors who share our vision. We're not just selling a product; we're advocating for a change. If that isn't worth pursuing, then what's the alternative?"

His laughter, rich and resonant, fills the room. "You have passion, I'll give you that. But remember, passion alone doesn't pay the bills." He leans back, folding his arms, the picture of a man who enjoys watching others squirm. "Let's see if your vision holds up when the stakes are raised."

Something in his tone both infuriates and intrigues me. It's almost as if he's testing me, challenging the very core of my convictions. The sensation is electric, swirling with an unexpected exhilaration. I can't allow him to intimidate me; I refuse to show any weakness.

"Maybe it's time you learned that not all battles are fought with a ledger," I retort, my voice steady despite the turmoil inside. "Sometimes, the most valuable outcomes come from the most unexpected places."

His eyes narrow slightly, a flicker of respect passing through the sharpness. "Interesting perspective. I'll be watching closely to see how your idealism fares against reality. But mark my words—this industry has a way of chewing up and spitting out the naive."

The meeting continues, but my mind is racing, trying to comprehend the unexpected thrill of our exchange. Lucas Morgan isn't merely a consultant; he's a formidable adversary, a storm cloud looming over my plans. His smooth arrogance, combined with that tantalizing hint of challenge, leaves me craving more. I feel alive in a way I haven't in years, dancing on the edge of something exhilarating and terrifying all at once.

As I sit down, the room buzzing with conversation, I can't shake the feeling that this encounter is just the beginning. Lucas and I are bound for a tumultuous journey, one that will test not only my professional aspirations but also the limits of my resolve. The stakes are high, and the unexpected twists are just beginning to unravel.

The tension in the conference room crackled like static electricity, the air thick with a mix of frustration and unspoken challenges. Lucas Morgan leaned back, arms crossed over a tailored suit that screamed both wealth and authority. I could feel his gaze like a spotlight, illuminating every one of my flaws as I nervously fiddled with my notes. The projector hummed softly behind me, its glow casting sharp shadows that mirrored my unease.

"Let's not pretend that the numbers are in your favor," Lucas remarked, his voice dripping with a condescending charm that made my skin crawl. "You've presented a compelling vision, but visions don't build businesses, do they?"

I took a deep breath, determined to maintain my composure. "True, but without vision, what's the point of business? I'd rather aim for something meaningful than simply chase profit."

His expression flickered for a moment, a hint of amusement dancing at the corners of his mouth. "Ah, the romantic idealist. It's a charming perspective, but I assure you, the business world is less forgiving than you seem to think. If you want to play in this arena, you'll need to sharpen those claws."

With each word, I felt the fiery embers of my frustration simmer into something more potent, a resolve hardening within me. "Maybe it's time for the business world to change," I shot back, my voice steady, though my heart raced. "We can create something that's both profitable and socially responsible. The two aren't mutually exclusive."

The room buzzed with whispers, my colleagues glancing between us like eager spectators at a prizefight. Lucas raised an eyebrow, his lips curling into a wry smile that made my stomach twist. "You have guts, I'll give you that. But guts don't pay the rent."

As if he could sense my irritation morphing into something bolder, he leaned forward, his tone shifting to something more probing. "Tell me, do you really think your vision can withstand the pressure of reality? It's one thing to have ideals, and another to see them through."

My heart raced not just with indignation but with an unexpected thrill at the prospect of standing my ground. "If I didn't believe in the possibility of change, I wouldn't be here at all. I'm willing to put in the work to prove that integrity can lead to success."

A low chuckle escaped him, smooth yet underlined with a hint of challenge. "Proving it and doing it are entirely different beasts, my dear. I'm curious to see how you handle the inevitable pitfalls. The world has a way of testing those who dream too brightly."

I didn't have time to consider how his words dug at my insecurities. The meeting ended with the usual pleasantries, but I felt Lucas's gaze on me as I gathered my materials, an invisible tether of competition pulling me back into his orbit. I wasn't ready to let him dismiss me so easily.

As I stepped out into the hallway, the chaotic swirl of colleagues parted for me, their murmurs still buzzing with the remnants of our exchange. I felt exhilarated, yet unsettled, my mind racing with thoughts of Lucas. There was an intensity about him that was both intimidating and strangely intoxicating.

"Nice work back there," a coworker, Jenna, called out, falling into step beside me. "You really held your own."

"Thanks," I said, trying to downplay the warmth creeping into my cheeks. "I just couldn't let him walk all over me."

"Still, you might want to be careful. He's known for his... aggressive negotiation tactics."

"Is that what they call it?" I scoffed lightly. "I'm not afraid of a little challenge."

"Oh, it's more than a challenge," she replied, rolling her eyes as we approached the elevator. "Lucas Morgan is a force of nature. People either love him or fear him."

"Sounds like someone I know," I muttered, thinking back on my recent encounters.

The elevator doors slid open, and I stepped inside, still processing the whirlwind of emotions from the meeting. Lucas Morgan had turned what should have been a straightforward work presentation into a battleground. The thrill of conflict, however, was a feeling I hadn't anticipated.

As the doors slid shut, I caught a glimpse of Lucas standing at the end of the hallway, watching me with that same calculating gaze. A flicker of annoyance ignited in my chest, but it was tempered by something else—curiosity. What drove a man like him? What shaped the fierce intellect beneath that polished exterior?

Later that evening, I found myself in my small but cozy apartment, the walls lined with colorful art and photographs that reflected my love for creativity. I poured a glass of wine, hoping to unwind, but my mind kept drifting back to Lucas. Why did he rattle me so? What was it about our verbal sparring that made me feel alive?

After a long, contemplative silence, I pulled out my laptop, determined to dig deeper into the enigmatic world of Lucas Morgan. I wasn't one to back down from a challenge, and I wanted to understand the man behind the smirk. My search led me through articles about his philanthropic ventures, interviews revealing a sharp wit that matched his business acumen, and snippets of gossip about his notorious reputation for cutthroat deals.

The more I read, the more layers I uncovered. Lucas was a paradox—an art lover with a business mindset, a man who claimed to support creatives while simultaneously dismantling their dreams with a single glare. I couldn't help but admire the contradiction; it was compelling, intoxicating.

In the midst of my research, my phone buzzed. A message from Jenna popped up: Hey, are you free tomorrow? Let's grab lunch! I'll fill you in on all the latest office gossip, including what's brewing with Lucas.

I smiled at the thought of a casual lunch, a reprieve from the storm of my thoughts. Sure, I'd love that! What time?

Noon? The usual place?

Perfect! Can't wait.

As I finished my wine, the anticipation of tomorrow lingered in the air, wrapping around me like a warm blanket. I still had questions about Lucas, and I was more determined than ever to figure him out. He might be an intimidating presence, but there was something more beneath that polished exterior, a spark of challenge that fueled my resolve.

Tomorrow would bring new encounters, and I was ready for whatever twists the day might hold. The office might be a battleground, but I was prepared to navigate the treacherous terrain, one confident step at a time.

The next day unfurled in a typical, bustling New York morning, the city vibrating with the energy of ambition and caffeine. I arrived at the café where Jenna and I agreed to meet, its warm, inviting aroma of freshly brewed coffee mingling with the sweetness of pastries. As I entered, the bell above the door chimed softly, welcoming me into a world that felt comforting and familiar, a stark contrast to the tension I'd experienced in the conference room.

Jenna was already seated, animatedly gesturing as she recounted the latest office drama. "So, you won't believe what happened at the last staff meeting. Carla tripped over her own feet while trying to present. It was like watching a slow-motion train wreck!" Her laughter was contagious, and I found myself chuckling along, the weight of yesterday's encounter with Lucas momentarily lifted.

"Did she at least recover gracefully?" I asked, taking a sip of my coffee, the warmth spreading through me.

"Graceful? Hardly! She just stood there, red as a beet, while everyone pretended to check their phones," Jenna replied, shaking her head, her eyes sparkling. "But enough about Carla. Tell me about you and Mr. Morgan. You two were practically having a duel up there!"

I rolled my eyes, the memory of our clash still fresh. "It wasn't a duel, just a heated discussion. He's... infuriatingly charming and annoyingly perceptive. He knows exactly how to push my buttons."

"Charming? You mean ruthless. The man eats idealists for breakfast." Jenna leaned in closer, her voice dropping to a conspiratorial whisper. "He's known for making or breaking people's careers with a flick of his wrist. I hope you're ready for that kind of pressure."

"Oh, I'm ready," I said, an edge of determination creeping into my tone. "If he thinks he can intimidate me, he's sorely mistaken. I won't let him—no matter how many cutting remarks he throws my way."

Jenna grinned, clearly enjoying my fire. "I like this new attitude. You should keep it up. Just remember, there's a fine line between confidence and reckless ambition."

As we continued our conversation, my mind wandered back to Lucas, a man who blended elegance with danger like the finest art—an intricate puzzle I felt compelled to solve. The allure of his intellect was undeniable, even as I resented the way he made me question my convictions.

After lunch, feeling rejuvenated by our banter, I returned to the office, ready to tackle the day. The atmosphere was charged, and I could sense the murmurs of my coworkers as I walked by. I caught snippets of conversation that made my ears perk up: "Did you hear? Lucas is coming back this week for another round of meetings."

I tried to brush off the unease that crept in. He was just a consultant, I reminded myself. Nothing more. Yet, the thought of facing him again stirred a whirlpool of nerves and excitement.

Later that afternoon, the project team gathered in the conference room, the air thick with anticipation. Lucas arrived promptly, his presence transforming the room. He wore a tailored navy suit that seemed to have been crafted just for him, projecting an aura of authority and charisma. He offered a casual nod, his eyes gliding over the assembled team before settling on me, igniting a spark of electricity that danced along my skin.

"Shall we dive in?" he asked, his voice smooth like whiskey, coaxing us to engage.

I took a deep breath, reminding myself of my earlier resolve. "Yes, let's. We've made some adjustments based on your feedback." I launched into the presentation, the numbers and projections flowing from my lips with newfound confidence.

Lucas listened intently, his expression a mask of contemplation. But just as I was feeling encouraged, he interjected with a single question that sliced through my enthusiasm. "What happens if your assumptions are wrong? What's your contingency plan?"

A wave of frustration washed over me. "We have a solid plan in place that we can adjust as necessary. Flexibility is key in any business strategy, especially one this ambitious."

He leaned back, a playful glint in his eyes. "Ah, flexibility—such a lovely word. But are you truly prepared to pivot when the market inevitably shifts? Or will you dig in your heels and watch your dreams crumble?"

The room went silent, every pair of eyes on me, and I felt heat flood my cheeks. "If I have to pivot, I will," I declared, my voice steadying despite the storm brewing inside. "But I refuse to back down from what I believe in. You're wrong if you think I'm here to compromise my values."

Lucas's gaze bore into me, and for a moment, the world outside faded away. "Perhaps I'm wrong. Or perhaps you're simply naïve." His words were a challenge, and the edge of my frustration morphed into something sharper, more daring.

"We'll see who's naïve when this project succeeds," I shot back, my pulse racing.

Just as the tension reached its peak, the door swung open, and in strode the head of our department, Mark, a jovial man with an air of authority that was impossible to ignore. "Ah, good to see everyone engaged! What's the topic of discussion? I hope I'm not interrupting."

Lucas's demeanor shifted, the competitive gleam in his eyes dimming to a cool professionalism. "We were just exploring the potential challenges of our current initiative."

Mark nodded, oblivious to the undercurrents swirling between us. "Excellent. Let's keep that dialogue open. Collaboration is key!" He beamed at the team, then turned his attention to Lucas. "I trust you'll continue to provide invaluable insight, Lucas."

"Of course, Mark," Lucas replied, though his gaze flicked back to me, a silent acknowledgment of our earlier skirmish lingering in the air.

The meeting moved forward, but the energy felt fractured, tension still palpable. I could sense Lucas's presence like a weight pressing down on me, a constant reminder that our battle was far from over. The spark between us crackled with an unexpected intensity, igniting both my ambition and my irritation.

As the meeting wrapped up, I caught a glimpse of Lucas's fleeting smile, the corners of his lips curling in a way that sent my heart racing. There was something magnetic about him—something that pulled me in and made me want to unravel the mystery he presented.

As everyone began to filter out, I hesitated, my feet rooted to the spot. I turned to Lucas, who was packing up his laptop with an ease that belied his earlier demeanor. "You know," I began, hesitantly, "you don't have to be so abrasive all the time."

He paused, looking up with a mix of surprise and amusement. "And you don't have to be so stubborn. But where's the fun in that?"

Before I could respond, a sudden commotion erupted outside the conference room—loud voices, followed by the unmistakable sound of glass shattering. Panic washed over me as I exchanged a glance with Lucas, who immediately sprang into action, rushing toward the chaos.

My heart pounded in my chest as I followed closely behind, curiosity and dread intertwining. As we rounded the corner, the scene unfolded before us: a crowd had gathered around a broken window, shards of glass glistening on the floor like dangerous confetti. But it wasn't the shattered glass that caught my attention; it was the figure slumped against the wall, a flash of red staining their shirt.

"Call an ambulance!" someone shouted, and I felt a chill race down my spine as I caught Lucas's eye. The tension that had simmered between us now felt like a distant memory, eclipsed by the urgency of the moment.

"Stay back!" Lucas barked, shoving his way through the throng of onlookers, his voice steady even as chaos swirled around us. I hesitated for just a moment, my instincts screaming at me to run, but the magnetic pull of the situation was too strong.

What had just happened? And who was hurt?

In that instant, everything shifted, the world teetering on the edge of something I couldn't quite comprehend. Lucas's intense gaze locked onto mine, and in that brief moment, an unspoken connection formed between us—one that bound us together in the face of uncertainty.

And as I stepped closer to the unfolding drama, I knew that whatever came next would change everything.

Chapter 3: Breaking the Ice

The office was a labyrinth of glass and steel, the stark lines of modern architecture often mirroring the tension that buzzed in the air between Lucas and me. On this particular night, the fluorescent lights cast a sterile glow over the scattered papers and half-empty coffee cups that cluttered our shared workspace. The clock on the wall ticked relentlessly, each second a reminder of the late hour, yet neither of us seemed inclined to leave. I was hunched over my laptop, fingers dancing over the keys in an attempt to weave together our chaotic project into something coherent, while Lucas leaned against the edge of the conference table, arms crossed, the very picture of displeasure.

"Your approach is far too optimistic," he remarked, his voice laced with that all-too-familiar cool disdain. "This isn't a fairy tale, Emma. We need data-driven decisions, not wishful thinking."

I shot him a glare, my irritation sparking like a live wire. "And yet, here we are, stuck in this 'fairy tale' because your so-called data isn't doing much to inspire our team. Maybe if you actually let people feel a sense of ownership in this project, we wouldn't be drowning in spreadsheets."

His brow arched, a flicker of amusement breaking through the tension. "Ownership? This isn't a playground, Emma. It's a business. We can't afford to coddle anyone's feelings."

"Coddling? Is that what you think I'm doing?" I shot back, my heart racing as I leaned closer, the adrenaline of our verbal sparring pushing me forward. "You think passion is coddling? Maybe you should try it sometime. It could open your eyes to the world beyond those cold statistics you cling to."

The words hung in the air, a palpable challenge, and for a moment, I thought he might retaliate with that biting sarcasm he was known for. Instead, his gaze flickered away, a muscle in his jaw tightening as if I'd hit a nerve. A moment of silence stretched between us, charged and thick with unspoken words. I hadn't anticipated this shift, this crack in his polished exterior.

"Passion can be reckless," he finally said, his voice quieter, the sharpness dulled. "Sometimes it leads to failures that we can't afford to make."

I studied him, my anger giving way to curiosity. There was a vulnerability there, a glimpse of the man beneath the carefully constructed façade. "Is that why you push everyone away? Because you're afraid of failing?"

He straightened, the sudden defensive posture signaling the end of that moment of honesty. "I push people away to keep the business afloat. Emotions complicate things, Emma. I can't afford to get distracted."

"But you're distracted now," I pointed out, taking a step closer, emboldened by the fleeting connection. "You're here, arguing with me about project details at ten o'clock at night, and that's not just about business. You care, even if you won't admit it."

The air crackled, and I could see the gears turning behind his eyes. He wasn't just a cold businessman; there was depth there, a tangled web of experiences that shaped him. For the first time, I saw the glimmer of something beneath the arrogance—perhaps regret, perhaps a longing for something more than this relentless grind.

"Tell me something, Lucas," I ventured, leaning against the table beside him. "What drives you? What are you really trying to achieve?"

His expression darkened, and I could almost see the walls rising back into place. "I don't think that's any of your business."

"Maybe not," I admitted, "but you've already shared more than you intended. It's just us in this office, and I'm not going to pretend that I don't see the effort you're putting in."

He sighed, the weight of his frustration palpable. "I guess it's easier to fight with you than to admit that sometimes I don't know what I'm doing."

I blinked, momentarily taken aback by his admission. The air shifted once more, this time laden with honesty. "You? The infamous Lucas Morgan, who always has the right answer?"

A slight smirk curled his lips, the moment of vulnerability dissolving back into his usual composure. "I've made mistakes, Emma. This project—everything about it—is important. It represents everything I've worked for, everything I've sacrificed."

"Sacrificed?" I echoed, my voice softer now, probing. "What did you sacrifice?"

He glanced at the floor, the bravado slipping. "Relationships. Happiness. A life outside of work. It all fell to the wayside the moment I stepped into this role."

I couldn't help but feel a pang of sympathy. Beneath the cool exterior, he was a man grappling with the enormity of his choices. "And what if you don't have to choose between your dreams and your life?"

He met my gaze, an intensity flaring in his eyes. "You make it sound so simple."

"Maybe it is," I countered gently. "You're allowed to dream, Lucas. You're allowed to have both. It doesn't have to be an either-or situation."

As the words lingered, I could see him reconsidering, the walls beginning to crumble. There was a flicker of hope in that moment, a chance for connection that felt rare and exhilarating. The night wore on, and while the battle over our project continued to simmer, we were no longer just adversaries. We were two flawed individuals, standing on the brink of understanding, each wrestling with our own ambitions, our own dreams, and the lingering specters of failure that haunted us both.

As the hours slipped away, the fluorescent lights overhead flickered like stars caught in a cosmic dance, illuminating the shadows of our heated debates. Lucas paced the office, a restless energy radiating from him as he flipped through documents with an intensity that suggested more than just a desire to get the project done. I watched him, caught between irritation and an unexpected curiosity. This man, this formidable opponent in our project, was clearly battling something deeper than mere corporate strategy.

"Honestly, Lucas, if you spent half as much energy on collaboration as you do on criticism, we might actually get somewhere," I said, trying to keep my tone light despite the growing tension. "I mean, are you always this negative, or is it just when I'm around?"

He halted, turning sharply to face me, eyes narrowed like a hawk sizing up its prey. "Negative? I'm being realistic, Emma. This project is a reflection of our entire department's future. A slip-up could mean layoffs, budget cuts—"

"Or an opportunity to innovate!" I countered, crossing my arms defiantly. "You act as if every idea outside your carefully structured plans is a death sentence. Maybe what we need is a bit of chaos to shake things up."

He studied me, the corner of his mouth twitching in what I dared to interpret as amusement. "Chaos, huh? Perhaps you've been spending too much time in the creative department."

"Don't underestimate creativity, Lucas," I replied, a grin creeping onto my face. "It's the spark that ignites change. You should try embracing it before you drown in your own spreadsheets."

"Touché," he admitted, the humor glimmering in his eyes, but the seriousness quickly returned. "But let's not forget: the real world doesn't care about sparks. It's about outcomes."

"Outcomes are great, but without passion, they mean nothing," I said, my voice softening as I took a step closer. "You know that, right?"

The charged silence that followed crackled with unspoken words, and I felt the walls we'd been building around our conversations begin to falter. His expression shifted, revealing something raw beneath the polished exterior—the flicker of vulnerability that had surfaced earlier. "You think passion will save us? You think it's that simple?" he asked, his tone turning serious.

"Sometimes it is," I replied, emboldened by the honesty we were sharing. "What if we took a chance? What if we poured our hearts into this project, let it become something more than just a number on a report?"

Lucas ran a hand through his hair, the gesture revealing the fatigue and frustration simmering beneath the surface. "You're asking for a lot," he finally said, his voice barely above a whisper. "I can't afford to care too much. Caring leads to complications, and complications lead to disappointment."

"You think I don't know about disappointment?" I replied, my heart aching at the openness of his admission. "You think I just skip through life, sprinkling fairy dust everywhere? I've been there, Lucas. We all have. It's what makes us human. It's how we grow."

He glanced away, his jaw tight, as if my words had struck a nerve he wasn't ready to acknowledge. "You're young," he said finally, a hint of resignation in his voice. "You'll learn the hard way that passion can burn you. Trust me."

"Maybe I'd rather burn than live in a cold, gray world," I said, feeling my resolve strengthen. "At least burning means I'm alive."

A moment stretched between us, and I could see the flicker of a new understanding igniting in his gaze. There was a softness in the air, a shift that made the late hours feel less oppressive and more intimate. "I admire your tenacity," he admitted, his voice low and sincere. "It's refreshing, even if it's infuriating."

I couldn't help but smile at that. "Infuriating? Or just what you need?"

"Maybe a little of both," he replied, a hint of a smile breaking through his stoic demeanor.

With a newfound sense of camaraderie, we turned back to the project, but the dynamic had shifted. As we bounced ideas off one another, our laughter punctuated the air, lightening the atmosphere that had once been thick with tension. I could feel the barriers crumbling, the walls of formality collapsing under the weight of our honesty.

Then, as if the universe had conspired against our fragile connection, the fire alarm blared, a shrill, jarring sound that shattered our moment. Lucas jumped, startled, and I couldn't suppress a laugh at his reaction. "You're not exactly the heroic type, are you?" I teased, rising from my chair.

"Right now, I'd rather be a heroic type than the guy stuck in a burning building," he shot back, heading for the exit with purpose.

We tumbled out into the dimly lit hallway, the air thick with confusion as our colleagues rushed past us, eyes wide and expressions panicked. The alarm echoed around us, a cacophony of chaos. Lucas's presence beside me was grounding amidst the mayhem, a steady force in the storm of bodies.

"Is this how you typically celebrate a breakthrough?" he asked, raising his voice above the din, a teasing glint in his eyes.

"Only when I get to see you flustered," I replied, matching his playful tone. "What's next? A dance-off in the parking lot?"

He shot me a skeptical look, but there was a hint of a smile lurking beneath his bravado. "If it keeps you from jumping into a flaming inferno, I might just take you up on that."

We made our way outside, the cool night air a refreshing contrast to the chaos behind us. I could see the stars twinkling above, a vivid tapestry against the dark sky. For a brief moment, we stood together, breathing in the coolness that enveloped us. The laughter we had shared felt like a shield against the uncertainty ahead, a promise that perhaps our partnership could evolve into something more.

"Maybe we should keep the fire drills to a minimum," I suggested, glancing sideways at him, my heart racing with the exhilaration of the unexpected connection.

"Or perhaps we should embrace the chaos," he replied, a playful smirk returning to his lips. "You never know when a little fire might spark something extraordinary."

As the crowd began to disperse, I felt a warmth bloom within me, a flicker of hope for what lay ahead. The night had transformed into something more than just a work obligation; it had morphed into a possibility—a crackling fire of potential ignited between us, and I was ready to see where it might lead.

The chaos of the fire drill had temporarily subsided, leaving a peculiar calm in its wake. As I stepped outside, the night air brushed against my skin, carrying with it the sharp scent of freshly cut grass and the distant hum of city life. I could hear the chatter of our colleagues, some still animated by the adrenaline of the alarm. My heart raced, not just from the excitement of the evening but also from the fleeting moments I had shared with Lucas—our sparring transformed into something deeper, a connection that left me both exhilarated and perplexed.

Lucas stood beside me, his hands shoved deep into his pockets, the shadows of the night framing his profile. "So, what now? We wait for the all-clear or do you want to sneak away and grab some coffee?" He glanced sideways, the corner of his mouth twitching in a half-smile that sent an unexpected thrill coursing through me.

"Coffee sounds good. Let's pretend we're not running a multi-million dollar project and instead are just two people enjoying the night," I replied, matching his playful tone. "Besides, I could use a caffeine fix after our 'intense brainstorming' session."

As we made our way to the nearest café, the atmosphere shifted from professional to almost conspiratorial. The streets were alive, lights flickering like fireflies as we passed bustling bars and restaurants. It felt refreshing to step out of the confines of the office and into the world, where laughter and music filled the air, a stark contrast to the sterile environment we had just escaped.

In the café, I opted for a cappuccino, while Lucas settled for a simple black coffee, his usual choice, I noted. We found a quiet corner table, the hum of conversation creating a comfortable backdrop for our newfound rapport. The warmth of the espresso cup cradled in my hands grounded me as we navigated the conversation from work to life.

"So, what do you do for fun when you're not drowning in spreadsheets?" I asked, teasingly raising an eyebrow at him.

He chuckled, the sound rich and warm. "I think I might have forgotten what fun is. My schedule doesn't exactly allow for spontaneity."

I couldn't help but smile. "Seriously? The notorious Lucas Morgan, devoid of fun? You're pulling my leg."

"Maybe I have a few surprises up my sleeve," he replied, his eyes dancing with mischief. "But you'd have to convince me to let them out. What about you? What do you do when you're not saving the world one project at a time?"

"Oh, I have a flair for the dramatic," I said, feigning seriousness. "In my spare time, I host tea parties for my cat, Mr. Whiskers. He's quite the critic."

Lucas laughed outright, the sound drawing the attention of nearby patrons. "A cat critic? I'd pay to see that."

"Trust me, it's a riveting affair," I said, leaning in conspiratorially. "He gives me one paw for 'good' and two for 'great.' Anything less than stellar gets a hiss and a flip of his tail."

"Sounds like Mr. Whiskers has high standards," he said, the laughter still sparkling in his eyes. "I can respect that."

As the conversation flowed, I felt a warmth spreading between us, a connection that felt both refreshing and terrifying. It was easy to forget the heat of our previous arguments when faced with the comfort of this shared moment. But underneath the laughter lingered an undeniable tension, a current that hinted at something more than just camaraderie.

"I should probably get going," I finally said, glancing at the time on my phone, reluctant to break the spell of our evening. "I have an early meeting tomorrow."

"Don't let work consume you entirely," he replied, his expression serious now, the glimmer of humor fading. "You deserve to enjoy life outside the office."

"Coming from you, that's rich," I shot back playfully, though the sentiment struck a chord. "And what about you? Don't think I didn't notice you diving headfirst into work instead of living a little."

"Touché," he said, a flicker of vulnerability crossing his features before he masked it again. "But it's easier this way."

"Easier or not, I think you should let yourself experience the world outside of those office walls. You never know what you might find," I said, my voice softening. "There's a whole life waiting out there, Lucas."

"Maybe you're right," he replied quietly, the weight of his words hanging between us like a fragile thread. The moment felt pregnant with possibility, and for a heartbeat, I wondered if he might reach out and bridge the space separating us.

Then, as if summoned by my thoughts, the café door swung open, a gust of wind spilling in and carrying with it a burst of laughter. My gaze flickered toward the entrance, and I caught sight of a figure emerging from the shadows—a woman, striking in appearance, with a confident stride that commanded attention. She was tall and poised, exuding an energy that seemed to pull people in.

"Lucas!" she called, her voice bright and cheerful, slicing through the intimate atmosphere we had just built. My heart sank as I watched her approach, a spark of recognition igniting in his eyes. "I didn't expect to find you here! Still buried in work, I see?"

I glanced between them, the warmth I had felt moments ago rapidly evaporating. "Do you know her?" I asked, my voice steady despite the knot tightening in my stomach.

"Just a colleague," he replied too quickly, his expression shifting, masking whatever emotions flickered across his face.

"Colleague? Is that all?" she teased, a playful glint in her eye. "I'm not interrupting anything important, am I?"

"No, just a casual chat," Lucas said, his tone curt, but I could see the way his body tensed, the way his smile didn't quite reach his eyes.

"Good! I wouldn't want to pull you away from your...friend." The emphasis on the last word hung in the air, a taunt that made my skin prickle.

"Is there something you need?" Lucas's voice was sharp, cutting through the tension.

"Oh, don't be like that," she said, waving her hand dismissively. "I just wanted to see if you were joining us for drinks later. Everyone is waiting for you."

"I'm not sure," he replied, casting a sidelong glance at me. I felt exposed, as if a spotlight had suddenly been trained on our moment, illuminating all the unspoken words we had been dancing around.

The woman, undeterred, leaned closer, her presence invasive. "Come on, it'll be fun. We can't let you miss out on a good time." She turned her attention to me, her eyes assessing. "And who's this? Your new project partner?"

"Just wrapping up some ideas," I said, forcing a smile despite the swirling emotions inside. "Nothing too exciting."

Lucas's gaze darted between us, and I could see the inner conflict playing out. "I think I'll pass tonight," he said finally, but the woman's expression shifted, a flicker of disappointment masked by feigned understanding.

"Suit yourself. Just remember, Lucas, life isn't all about work," she shot back, an edge to her tone before she turned to leave, her heels clicking sharply against the floor.

As she exited, I felt the weight of her presence linger, suffocating the air between us. "So, that was interesting," I ventured, trying to lighten the mood, but my heart was racing, caught in the unexpected turmoil.

"Sorry about that," Lucas said, his voice low, almost strained. "She can be...persistent."

"Seems like it," I replied, my stomach twisting with uncertainty. "I didn't realize you had such a close connection with her."

"It's nothing," he insisted, but I could see the shadow of something more behind his eyes, a flicker of doubt that mirrored my own.

The air thickened with unspoken questions, a rift opening between us as my mind raced. Had I been too quick to let my guard down? As I prepared to leave, I couldn't shake the feeling that there was more to Lucas than met the eye, and the sudden appearance of this woman had stirred a storm of complications just beneath the surface.

"Emma," he said, catching my wrist gently as I turned to walk away, the contact igniting a spark of electricity. "Can we talk? I mean really talk?"

I nodded, uncertainty dancing in my chest as I realized the magnitude of the moment. Just as I was about to respond, a loud crash echoed from outside, followed by a series of frantic screams. I turned, heart racing as I scanned the street, my stomach sinking as I saw a chaotic scene unfolding.

A car had skidded into a lamppost, shards of glass scattering across the pavement, and the world suddenly spun into chaos. I glanced back at Lucas, the intensity of his gaze matching the panic that flooded the air, and for a split second, we both knew that everything was about to change.

Chapter 4: Shadows of the Past

The note appeared one dreary Tuesday morning, slipped beneath the clutter of papers on my desk like a whisper of warning. It was plain, unadorned, but the words were stark and alarming. "Stay away from Lucas. He's not what he seems." The handwriting was a scrawl, shaky yet urgent, sending a chill skittering down my spine. I stared at it for a long moment, the dim light of the office casting shadows that danced around the edges of my doubt.

At first, I brushed it off as a prank, a childish attempt to provoke. Lucas had that effect on people, even those who hardly knew him. He was the enigmatic figure lurking in the corner of every crowded room, charming yet exasperating. My thoughts drifted back to the first time I'd met him—the way his laughter seemed to punctuate the air, how his dark hair fell just so, framing a face that could've graced the covers of magazines. He was magnetic, captivating in a way that both thrilled and terrified me.

But as I stared at that note, curiosity gnawed at me, relentless as a dog with a bone. Who could have written it? What could Lucas possibly have done to inspire such fear? It was absurd to entertain the idea that he was a danger, yet there was a persistent voice in my mind, one that urged caution. Every instinct told me to tread lightly, to turn away from the allure of his mysterious depths. Still, I felt rooted to my chair, my fingers curling around the edge of my desk as if anchoring myself against the rising tide of confusion.

Despite the warning, the world beyond my office seemed to shift into sharper focus every time Lucas entered it. I recalled our conversations, the way he had looked at me, as if I were the only person who mattered in that moment. There was a vulnerability to him that he kept expertly hidden behind a façade of confidence. I wanted to believe in the man I had glimpsed—passionate, intelligent, perhaps even misunderstood. I felt drawn to him, not just out of attraction, but from a deep-seated need to unearth the truth behind that facade.

Yet the deeper I dug, the more unsettling discoveries I made. I began to uncover threads of scandal tied to his name, whispers of involvement in dealings that had nearly toppled several companies. There were hushed conversations in the break room, sideways glances from colleagues that made my skin prickle. Each revelation felt like a stone dropped into a still pond, sending ripples of suspicion through my mind.

I had never been one to shy away from difficult truths. My job required a tenacity that had seen me through many trials, but this was different. This was personal. Each piece of information seemed to distort the Lucas I thought I knew. It felt impossible that the man who made me laugh could also be embroiled in such darkness. I was left staring at the tangled web, wondering where he truly stood in it all.

Determined to confront him, I invited Lucas for coffee after work, my heart a riot of anticipation and dread. The café was cozy, filled with the scent of roasted beans and cinnamon, the gentle hum of conversation a soothing backdrop to the storm brewing in my mind. I chose a secluded corner table, my fingers tracing the rim of my cup as I awaited his arrival. The moment he walked in, my breath caught. The warm light enveloped him, casting an almost ethereal glow around his figure.

"Hey," he greeted, a playful smile breaking across his face. "What's with the serious vibe? You look like you're about to interrogate me."

"Funny you should mention that," I replied, trying to keep my tone light, the words feeling like lead in my mouth. "I found something today—an anonymous note. It warned me to stay away from you."

His expression flickered, a shadow passing through those deep, expressive eyes. "Really?" he said, his voice casual, but I could hear the underlying tension. "People have a way of spreading rumors. You shouldn't let them get to you."

"It's more than that," I pressed, unable to shake the unease pooling in my stomach. "I've heard things—about your past, about your work. Why don't you just tell me the truth?"

"Isn't it better to let the past be the past?" he deflected, his charm slipping momentarily to reveal a guarded demeanor. "You have to understand; everyone has skeletons."

"Skeletons are one thing," I countered, leaning in, my heart racing as I navigated the minefield of this conversation. "But if it's affecting your present, shouldn't I know? I can't keep pretending like this doesn't matter."

The tension thickened, palpable and heavy, hanging between us like a dark cloud. Lucas's gaze flickered away, and for a heartbeat, I thought I saw fear in his eyes, a raw honesty that made my pulse quicken. But just as quickly, he masked it behind a veil of indifference. "You're overthinking this. People are drawn to drama, and the truth is often lost in the noise."

I couldn't shake the feeling that he was holding back, keeping a part of himself locked away like a precious secret. "But I want to know you, Lucas. I want to understand," I said softly, the words tumbling out before I could catch them.

He hesitated, and for a moment, I thought he might open up, shatter the walls he'd constructed. But then he smiled, a wistful twist of his lips that seemed more sad than sincere. "Some things are better left buried, don't you think?"

The coffee turned cold between us, an unspoken distance stretching as I wrestled with my instincts. He was both fascinating and frustrating, the pieces of him I was beginning to uncover tantalizing yet tantalizingly out of reach. My heart ached with confusion as I realized that I was inexplicably tethered to him, like a moth to a flame, drawn closer even as I felt the heat threatening to scorch me.

As we left the café, the evening air was thick with unvoiced emotions, swirling around us like the fall leaves caught in a gentle gust. I wanted to trust him, but the shadows of doubt loomed larger, making it hard to discern where his truth ended and the web of lies began. I knew then that I had to tread carefully, even as every fiber of my being yearned to unravel the mysteries that wrapped around him, to embrace the warmth of his presence and the danger it promised.

The following days passed in a surreal haze, a whirlwind of normalcy peppered with the extraordinary. I found myself at work, my hands busy but my mind ensnared in the delicate threads of doubt that had woven themselves around my thoughts. Lucas's laughter still echoed in my ears, each note an intoxicating reminder of the connection we shared, but the shadows loomed larger, more ominous with every passing hour. The office was buzzing with the usual chatter, the hum of printers and the occasional burst of laughter punctuating the air, yet my heart raced with a disquiet that felt distinctly out of place.

One afternoon, as I scrolled through the mundane emails piling up in my inbox, the little voice inside my head nudged me again. The note I'd received still felt like a bruise—an unwanted reminder of a truth I wasn't ready to confront. It had become an itch I couldn't scratch, pushing me to search for more, to uncover the reality behind Lucas's enigmatic smile. I found myself retracing steps in my mind, replaying our conversations, the way his gaze would flicker when I got too close to a subject he didn't want to discuss.

I decided to take a leap into the unknown, a reckless step that could either reveal his truth or shatter the delicate veneer of our budding friendship. The following weekend, I headed to the library, a labyrinth of knowledge that had always felt like a sanctuary.

Sunlight streamed through the tall windows, dust motes dancing in the warm rays, creating a serene atmosphere that belied the turmoil brewing inside me. I buried myself in research, pouring over news articles and business reports, seeking the elusive threads that might link Lucas to the scandals swirling around him.

Hours melted away as I scoured the archives, the musty smell of old books wrapping around me like a comforting blanket. I uncovered stories of companies brought to their knees by fraud, scandal, and betrayal. Each headline sent a shiver down my spine, each name whispered a warning. There was a familiar one among them—his father's company, once a titan in the industry, had crumbled under the weight of financial mismanagement and deceit. It took everything I had to swallow the knot forming in my throat as I realized Lucas's name was often mentioned in hushed tones, shadowed by the cloud of his family's failures.

"Is this your idea of a weekend getaway?" A teasing voice broke through my thoughts, and I glanced up to see Claire, my ever-energetic coworker, perched on the edge of the table, her head tilted with curiosity. "What's so riveting? I didn't know you were a fan of dusty tomes and scandalous corporate histories."

I tried to laugh it off, but it came out half-hearted, lacking the enthusiasm I usually had for banter. "Just... doing some research. You know, trying to get ahead."

Her brows knitted in suspicion, eyes sparkling with mischief. "Uh-huh. More like trying to dig up dirt on someone." She leaned closer, conspiratorial. "Spill. Who's the target?"

I hesitated, my instincts screaming to guard my thoughts, but Claire had a knack for peeling away my layers. "It's Lucas. I got this anonymous note warning me about him. So, I thought I'd look into it."

"Lucas?" she echoed, feigning shock. "Why would anyone warn you about that dreamy man? He's like a walking romance novel cover. You know, brooding yet charming."

"Exactly," I replied, a wry smile tugging at my lips despite the weight of uncertainty that still pressed down on me. "That's what makes this all so confusing. He's... well, he seems genuine. But now I'm questioning everything."

"Welcome to the world of attractive men," Claire quipped, rolling her eyes dramatically. "It's basically a requirement that they come with baggage. But let me ask you this—what do you really know about him?"

Her question hung in the air like an unsaid incantation, forcing me to confront the reality of our interactions. I thought about his laugh, the way he made me feel seen, how he could light up a room just by walking into it. But then, the shadows crept back in—his evasiveness, the layers of mystery that encased him like armor.

"I don't know enough," I admitted, frustration spilling over. "Every time I try to dig deeper, he changes the subject. It's like he's hiding something."

Claire's eyes gleamed with understanding. "Or maybe he's protecting you from whatever darkness he's carrying. People don't just open up about their pasts, especially if it's messy."

"I wish I knew what he was protecting me from," I sighed, running a hand through my hair. "This whole situation is a tangled mess, and I feel like I'm standing at a precipice, ready to fall."

"Then it's time to take control," she declared, the spark of mischief lighting her eyes. "Why not confront him? Call him out on the note. You deserve to know what's real, and if he's worth your time, he'll respect your need for clarity."

Her words resonated within me, igniting a flicker of resolve. I knew what I had to do. Later that evening, I sent Lucas a message, my fingers trembling as I typed. "Can we talk? There's something I need to discuss."

His response came swiftly, a simple "Sure, when?" I felt a mix of anticipation and dread flutter in my chest, the weight of what I was about to uncover pressing heavily on my shoulders.

As I approached our meeting place—a quaint café nestled at the edge of the town, filled with the aroma of freshly baked pastries and rich coffee—I steeled myself. The warm ambiance enveloped me, but beneath the comfort lay an undercurrent of anxiety. Would this conversation lead to understanding, or would it unravel everything we'd built?

Lucas arrived shortly after, his presence like a dark wave washing over me. He offered that trademark smile, a charming façade that momentarily masked the tension brewing between us. "Hey there, what's up?"

I took a breath, the weight of my decision settling in. "I got a note at work. It warned me to stay away from you."

His smile faltered, surprise flickering in his eyes before they hardened, a storm brewing beneath the surface. "Who sent it?"

"I don't know. But it got me curious, and I started looking into your past," I confessed, the words spilling out before I could second-guess myself. "There are rumors, Lucas. About your family, the company..."

His expression shifted, something darker crossing his features. "And what did you find?"

"Nothing concrete. Just shadows and whispers. But it's enough to make me question everything."

"Everything?" His voice held an edge, a mixture of frustration and concern. "Or just me?"

I felt the air thicken, every heartbeat echoing with uncertainty. "I don't want to doubt you. But I can't ignore what's out there, either."

"People love to spread rumors, especially about my family. They thrive on drama and scandal," he replied, his voice low, almost pleading. "You don't know the whole story."

"Then tell me," I urged, the intensity of the moment coiling tighter between us. "I want to understand."

He hesitated, the shadows creeping back into his gaze. "It's complicated. But what matters is how I feel about you. I don't want to drag you into my past."

"Then let me decide if I want to be in it," I countered, pushing against the walls he was trying to build. "You owe me that much."

The challenge hung in the air, a tentative truce forming in the space between us. Lucas's eyes bore into mine, searching for something, maybe even finding it. I could feel the tension shift, the electricity of unspoken words crackling like a live wire.

For a moment, time stood still, and I sensed that whatever path we chose from here would change everything.

As Lucas's gaze bore into mine, the air between us crackled with an intensity I had never felt before. I could see the gears turning in his mind, a tumult of emotions shifting behind those dark, expressive eyes. His vulnerability flickered at the edges, but it was smothered beneath layers of guardedness. I felt a pulse of adrenaline racing through me, urging me to push forward, to delve into the heart of the enigma that was Lucas.

"I'm not just some rumor," he said quietly, his voice low, each word carefully measured. "I'm trying to move on, to build something real. But the past has a way of clawing back, doesn't it?"

"Then help me understand it," I insisted, leaning closer, my heart hammering in my chest. "I don't want to lose you before I even know you."

His expression darkened, and a shadow passed over his face. "It's not that simple. There are people who would love to see me fail. They thrive on my family's mistakes."

"I'm not them," I replied, desperation creeping into my voice. "I'm here because I want to know you, not your family's ghosts."

A flicker of something—fear, perhaps—crossed his features, and I felt a pang of empathy. Lucas was wrestling with his past, and I was determined not to let it come between us. But I knew if I wanted to peel back the layers, I had to tread carefully.

"I can't change what happened before," he said finally, his voice barely above a whisper. "But I can show you who I am now."

"Then show me," I urged, my heart racing with the promise of discovery. "Show me your truth."

Lucas exhaled slowly, the tension in his shoulders easing just a fraction. "I'll try. But you have to promise not to judge too quickly. There are things you won't want to hear."

"I can handle it," I replied, determined.

We settled into a rhythm of conversation, the initial awkwardness gradually dissolving into a shared vulnerability. He recounted the tale of his family's rise and fall—the lavish parties that masked the fractures, the whispers behind closed doors, and the crushing weight of expectations that had suffocated him for years. Each word fell from his lips like a confession, raw and honest, leaving me captivated and horrified all at once.

"I was so focused on proving I could be different, on escaping the shadow of my father's legacy," he said, his voice thick with emotion. "But every time I thought I was free, it pulled me back in."

I felt a surge of compassion for him, my heart breaking at the thought of the burdens he had carried alone. "But you're not your family's mistakes," I insisted. "You're your own person. You have a choice."

"Do I?" he countered, his eyes searching mine for something—reassurance, maybe, or the confirmation that I wouldn't turn away. "I've made choices that haunt me. The things I've done... they aren't easily forgotten."

"You've changed," I said, leaning in further. "You're here now, with me. That matters."

His gaze softened, and I felt a warmth blossom between us, a flicker of hope amidst the darkness that had clouded our conversation. Just as I thought we were on the cusp of something beautiful, a shadow crossed his face again.

"I wish I could believe that," he murmured, breaking our connection, the retreating warmth leaving a chill in its wake. "But there are still people watching. Waiting for me to slip."

"Then let me help you," I urged, my determination firm. "You don't have to face this alone. Whatever it is, we can tackle it together."

"I can't put you in danger," he replied, a fierce protectiveness flashing in his eyes.

"Lucas," I said, my voice steady, "I've already been dragged into this mess. You can't keep me at arm's length. I care about you."

His eyes narrowed, a mix of conflict and longing swirling within them. The moment felt charged, as if the very air around us was heavy with unspoken truths. I held my breath, waiting for him to respond, to finally let down the walls he had built so carefully.

But just as his lips parted, the door swung open with a sudden crash, and a gust of wind rushed in, scattering papers across the café like startled birds. A figure appeared, silhouetted against the light, a face I recognized only too well.

"Lucas!" The voice was sharp, laced with urgency. It was Mia, his childhood friend, a woman with a presence that demanded attention. Her eyes flitted between us, assessing the situation, her expression unreadable. "We need to talk—now."

The atmosphere shifted dramatically, tension snapping like a taut wire. Lucas's face tightened, the easy camaraderie we'd shared moments before evaporating into a cloud of unease.

"What's wrong?" he asked, his tone clipped, all traces of vulnerability vanishing in an instant.

"We don't have time for this," Mia replied, her voice low but insistent, a sense of urgency evident in her posture. "It's about your father. We're running out of options, and he's not backing down."

My heart raced, the shift in the room palpable as I took in Lucas's reaction. His bravado crumbled, leaving behind the boy I had begun to understand. In its place stood a man grappling with the weight of family and legacy, the looming shadow of his past once more closing in around him.

"Wait," I interjected, the pieces of the puzzle shifting in my mind. "What do you mean? What's happening?"

Mia turned to me, her gaze piercing. "It's not just about Lucas anymore. There are forces at play that could endanger you too."

Lucas's jaw clenched, the tension in the air thickening as he stepped closer to Mia, a protective instinct flashing in his eyes. "What do you know?"

"I wish I didn't have to be the one to tell you," she replied, her voice softer now, laced with concern. "But we're running out of time, and it's not just your past that's coming back to haunt you. It's about to get worse."

The weight of her words hung between us, heavy with implications I couldn't yet grasp. As Lucas glanced back at me, his expression tumultuous, I felt the ground beneath my feet begin to shift. This was no longer just about me uncovering his secrets; it was about a looming threat that had the power to pull us both under.

And as the shadows of the past began to close in, a singular thought pierced through the chaos: I was in deeper than I'd ever intended, and there was no turning back.

Chapter 5: Under the Surface

The night air wraps around us like a comforting blanket as we walk through the dimly lit streets, the soft glow of the streetlights casting warm pools of light onto the pavement. The distant sounds of the city fade into a gentle hum, allowing the quiet of the evening to settle between us. I glance sideways at Lucas, catching him in a moment of contemplation, his brow furrowed as if he's sifting through a particularly complex problem. In those fleeting seconds, the intensity of our professional relationship feels almost tangible, like a live wire thrumming with unexpressed emotions.

"Do you always walk home alone?" Lucas asks, breaking the silence. His voice is low, almost conspiratorial, as if sharing a secret meant just for me. I shake my head, trying to brush off the weight of the moment.

"Not always," I reply, my heart racing unexpectedly at the thought of admitting how often I avoid going home alone. It's a simple truth, yet it feels laden with implications. "I usually take the subway or catch a ride with someone."

"Smart move," he nods, and I can't help but notice the way his gaze lingers on me, assessing, as if he's committed to ensuring my safety. "This city can be... unpredictable."

The way he says it, his voice heavy with an unspoken understanding, sends a shiver down my spine. I picture the darkened alleyways and the stories I've heard of late-night misadventures. But here with Lucas, the danger feels diminished, almost laughable, in the face of the warmth radiating from his presence. It's a strange mix of comfort and tension that draws me closer to him, even as the city seems to conspire to keep us apart.

As we turn onto a quieter street, lined with trees whose leaves rustle softly in the evening breeze, he begins to share snippets of his childhood—tales of growing up in a small town, where the stars seemed brighter and the nights were filled with the sounds of crickets. His voice is rich with nostalgia, painting a picture of a life so different from the hustle and bustle of our current surroundings.

"I used to climb trees in my backyard," he recalls, a wistful smile breaking through his otherwise serious demeanor. "I had this old oak that I claimed as my own. I'd sit in its branches for hours, just watching the world go by."

The image of a young Lucas, carefree and adventurous, tugs at my heart. I picture him, small and scrappy, scaling the heights of that oak, oblivious to the weight of the world that would eventually settle on his shoulders. It's disarming, this glimpse into his past, and I find myself yearning to know more.

"What else did you do?" I ask, genuinely curious. "Did you have a favorite spot, like a secret place?"

He chuckles softly, the sound rich and warm. "I did. There was this creek just beyond the town limits, where we'd go to fish and swim. It felt like our own little paradise. My friends and I would build rafts out of fallen branches and pretend we were explorers."

I can't help but smile, imagining him laughing with friends, the sunlight glinting off the water as they splashed around without a care. "You sound like you had a lot of fun," I say, envious of those uncomplicated days.

He nods, but a shadow crosses his face, an undercurrent of sadness weaving through the memories. "It was great until it wasn't," he murmurs, the words heavy with unspoken loss. "Things changed when my dad got sick. The town felt smaller, the sky dimmer."

Suddenly, the lighthearted banter that typically punctuates our interactions feels inadequate. I want to reach out, to offer comfort, but I hesitate, unsure of the boundaries between us. Instead, I opt for honesty. "I know what that's like," I admit. "I lost my mom when I was younger. It was like the ground fell out from under me. Everything changed."

His eyes soften as he meets my gaze, and in that moment, the distance between us shrinks. "I'm sorry," he says sincerely, and I sense the weight of his empathy. "It's hard to grow up too fast."

"Yeah, it is," I reply, the honesty of our conversation making me feel vulnerable yet oddly liberated. "But we keep moving forward, right? We have to."

Lucas smiles, a flicker of admiration igniting in his expression. "Exactly. It's all we can do. Sometimes, I think the past shapes us, but it doesn't define us." He pauses, the weight of his words lingering in the air like the scent of rain on pavement. "We have the power to rewrite our stories."

A silence settles between us, comfortable and profound, as we continue to walk side by side. I can feel the energy between us shifting, as if the very air crackles with potential. We are two souls navigating the complexities of life, both of us weighed down by our histories yet somehow buoyed by our shared resilience. It feels like a beginning, and I can't help but wonder where this newfound connection might lead.

As we approach my building, I hesitate at the entrance, reluctant to break the spell we've woven during our walk. Lucas looks down at me, his eyes dark and intense, and for a heartbeat, the world around us fades away. The tension that has simmered beneath the surface surges, threatening to overflow into something more profound. It's in the way he leans slightly closer, the warmth of his body radiating towards me, making my heart race with anticipation.

But then, just as quickly, the moment shifts. He steps back, clearing his throat, the tension dissipating into a mix of nervousness and relief. "Well, here we are," he says, a hint of awkwardness creeping into his tone. "Safe and sound."

I smile, my heart still thumping in my chest. "Thanks for walking me home, Lucas. I really enjoyed it."

"Me too," he replies, his expression softening again, a quiet intensity lingering in the air between us. It feels like the door to something new has cracked open, inviting us to step through, yet we stand at the threshold, both acutely aware of the vast potential that lies ahead.

The next few days at work are a whirlwind, charged with the electric tension that lingers in the air whenever Lucas and I share a space. Meetings feel more like a delicate dance, each interaction layered with meaning, each word carefully chosen. I catch him stealing glances, his eyes flickering to mine before darting away, as if afraid to linger too long on the spark that ignites between us. Every brush of our hands or shared smile sends my heart racing, a reminder that beneath our professional facades lies a burgeoning connection that neither of us knows how to navigate.

The office, with its sleek glass walls and sterile lighting, feels strangely suffocating as I sit at my desk, pouring over a presentation that suddenly seems insipid compared to the chaos of my emotions. My thoughts drift back to our late-night walk, the way the streetlights danced in Lucas's eyes, illuminating the warmth and depth that lay just beneath the surface. It's a memory I can't shake, the sweetness of his laughter mingling with the melancholy of his past, wrapping around me like a comforting shawl.

By Friday, the tension has reached a boiling point. Lucas is on the other side of the conference table, looking devastatingly handsome in a navy blazer that complements the sharp lines of his jaw. He leans back slightly, arms crossed, his posture relaxed, yet his eyes betray a storm of thoughts swirling just beneath the surface. I try to focus on the presentation, but every time I glance at him, my heart skips a beat.

"Are we boring you, Lucas?" I quip, my voice light but laced with challenge, daring him to reveal the turmoil brewing beneath his composed exterior.

"Not at all," he shoots back, a playful glint in his eye. "I was just contemplating the sheer excitement of quarterly projections." The sarcasm drips from his words, and the room erupts in laughter, easing the mounting tension that had clung to us like a second skin.

Our colleagues continue with the presentation, oblivious to the charged atmosphere between us. I can feel Lucas's gaze still on me, heavy and insistent, and I struggle to maintain my composure. How is it possible that a single look can unravel my thoughts so completely?

Later that day, as we gather our things to leave, Lucas moves closer, his voice dropping to a conspiratorial whisper. "Do you want to grab a drink? I think we both need it after today."

The invitation hangs in the air, thick with possibility. My heart does a little flip as I weigh my options. On one hand, I should be responsible and go home. But on the other, the thought of sharing more of these moments with him is almost intoxicating. "Sure, why not?" I say, attempting to sound casual, but my heart is thumping so loudly I'm sure he can hear it.

The bar we choose is a cozy little place tucked away from the bustling streets, adorned with dark wood and low-hanging lights that cast a warm glow over the patrons. The atmosphere is relaxed, and as we settle into a booth in the back, I can feel the stress of the week melt away. Lucas orders us a couple of craft beers, and I can't help but admire the way he commands the space around him. It's an effortless charisma that draws people in, and I find myself wanting to know more about the man behind the charm.

"So, what's your poison?" he asks, leaning back against the booth, his casual demeanor disarming.

"Surprisingly, it's not beer," I say, smirking. "I'm more of a whiskey girl."

He raises an eyebrow, impressed. "Whiskey, huh? I should've known you'd have an adventurous side."

"Adventurous?" I scoff playfully. "I like to think of it as having good taste."

He laughs, the sound deep and genuine, and I can't help but feel a flutter of satisfaction at having sparked such a reaction. We dive into light-hearted banter, sharing stories about our work, our lives, and everything in between. The conversation flows effortlessly, revealing snippets of our personalities—his playful sarcasm matching my quick wit, creating a rhythm that feels natural.

"Do you ever miss the small-town life?" I ask, curious to delve deeper into the memories he shared during our walk.

Lucas takes a thoughtful sip of his drink, his expression shifting as he contemplates. "Sometimes. There was a certain simplicity to it, you know? But I love the energy of the city. It feels alive."

"Alive?" I echo, raising an eyebrow. "I think it's chaotic. You never know when a pigeon might decide to take aim at you."

"True, but that's part of its charm. Plus, where else would you get to meet characters like me?" He grins, and I roll my eyes, laughing.

"You have a point," I admit, feeling the tension shift, softening into something more playful. "But for the record, I prefer my characters less feathery."

As the evening progresses, I find myself captivated by his stories, each one revealing another layer of his complexity. He speaks of ambition, dreams of climbing the corporate ladder, and the sacrifices he's made along the way. Yet there's an undercurrent of something deeper, a yearning for connection that mirrors my own desires.

Then, just as I'm about to open up about my own struggles, the conversation takes an unexpected turn. Lucas leans in closer, the intensity in his eyes causing my breath to hitch. "You know, I've really enjoyed getting to know you these past few weeks," he says, his tone sincere. "It feels different—like we're not just colleagues anymore."

The air thickens with unspoken possibilities, and my heart races as I search his face for any hint of where this might lead. "I feel it too," I admit, the vulnerability of the moment wrapping around us like a cocoon. "But it's a bit... complicated."

"Complicated is good," he replies, a challenge glimmering in his eyes. "It means there's something worth fighting for."

My heart swells at his words, hope and fear warring within me. Just as I open my mouth to respond, the sound of laughter erupts from a nearby table, snapping us back to reality. I feel the moment slip through my fingers like grains of sand, the weight of unspoken emotions hanging heavily between us.

Lucas and I exchange a look, the spark of connection still alive but now tinged with uncertainty. We both know that this could change everything, and yet, as we sit in the warm glow of the bar, I can't shake the feeling that maybe, just maybe, we're on the brink of something beautiful and terrifying.

The evening stretches on like a soft blanket, wrapping around us in the bar as we continue our conversation, the world outside fading into insignificance. With each word exchanged, the connection between Lucas and me deepens, weaving a tapestry of shared experiences and unspoken hopes. As he speaks, the dim light catches the angles of his face, highlighting the shadows of thought that cross his features, making him look almost regal in this intimate setting.

"So, what about you? What was your childhood like?" Lucas asks, his voice a mix of genuine curiosity and something softer, almost coaxing. I can sense the shift in the air, as if he is opening a door and inviting me in.

I hesitate, the words stuck in my throat for a moment. It feels oddly vulnerable to peel back the layers of my past, but the sincerity in his gaze encourages me. "It was... chaotic, to say the least," I finally say, a laugh escaping me that feels half-hearted. "My parents worked nonstop to keep things afloat. It felt like a race against time—everyday life just pulling us in different directions."

"Sounds exhausting," he replies, his expression softening. "Did you have any reprieve? Hobbies? Friends?"

"Not really. I threw myself into my studies, hoping to escape for a few hours," I admit, a bittersweet smile tugging at my lips. "Books were my best friends. They took me places I could only dream of."

"Ah, a fellow bookworm," he teases, the corners of his mouth lifting in that trademark smirk. "So, did you ever dream of being an author? Writing your own escape stories?"

"Maybe," I say, my cheeks warming slightly. "I think I was too busy being practical to entertain such fantasies. But who knows? Perhaps one day I'll surprise myself."

Lucas leans in closer, his demeanor shifting as the playful banter begins to fade, replaced by a more serious undertone. "You should. You have a way with words. I can see the creativity in how you express yourself, even in reports." He pauses, studying me intently. "Life is too short not to follow those dreams, you know?"

The sincerity in his words resonates deeply, stirring something inside me that's been dormant for far too long. Just then, our server approaches, interrupting the moment with a fresh round of drinks. As she sets the glasses down, I take a moment to collect my thoughts. The air between Lucas and me is charged, and I know the next step is crucial.

After she leaves, I take a deep breath. "Maybe I will write that book," I say, testing the waters, gauging his reaction. "But it would probably be a messy romance filled with all the chaos of life."

"Messy romance sounds good to me," he grins, his eyes twinkling with mischief. "It's relatable. And I could use some tips on navigating the chaos."

"Is that a challenge?" I ask, my heart racing at the playful spark igniting between us. "Because I'm up for it."

"Let's do it," he replies, his expression suddenly serious. "You can teach me about love and I'll teach you about how to survive in a boardroom. We'll make quite the team."

The suggestion lingers between us, fraught with potential, and I can't help but imagine the possibilities that lie ahead. Just then, the ambient noise of the bar fades, and the atmosphere shifts, as though the universe itself is holding its breath, waiting for our next move.

But before I can respond, my phone buzzes on the table, slicing through the moment like a knife. I glance down at the screen, my stomach twisting. It's a message from my sister, the kind of message that makes your heart drop. I quickly read the words, my breath catching in my throat. "I need you to come home. Now."

Lucas notices my sudden change in demeanor, concern etched across his features. "What's wrong?" he asks, his voice low, full of worry.

"It's my sister. Something's happened," I reply, my heart racing as I scramble to gather my things. "I have to go."

He rises to his feet immediately, his presence both comforting and grounding. "I'll drive you. Where do you need to go?"

As we rush out of the bar and into the cool night air, the reality of the situation crashes over me like a wave. My sister's tone had been urgent, too urgent for just a casual call. The streets blur past us as Lucas speeds through the city, and my mind races with worry. What could have happened? I had left her just hours ago, everything felt so normal then.

"What did she say?" Lucas glances at me, his eyes intense, trying to glean any information from my silence.

"She didn't say much," I respond, feeling my heart pound in my chest. "Just that I needed to get home."

"What could be so important?"

I shrug, my mind spinning. "I don't know. I just wish I had stayed home instead of going out."

Lucas's grip on the wheel tightens, and I can feel the tension radiating from him as he navigates through the traffic. "We'll get there, and you'll find out. Just breathe."

The words hang in the air, both a comfort and a reminder of the uncertainty that looms over us. I try to calm myself, but the closer we get, the more my anxiety builds.

When we finally pull up in front of my apartment building, the sight of it brings a rush of dread. The familiar space now feels alien, ominous. I leap out of the car, adrenaline coursing through my veins as I sprint toward the entrance.

"Wait!" Lucas calls after me, his footsteps echoing behind me. But I can't stop; I need to know what's going on.

I race up the stairs, my heart pounding in my ears, and burst through the door to my apartment. The scene that greets me is one I never expected. My sister is sitting on the couch, her eyes red-rimmed, a look of panic etched across her face. But next to her is someone I had never anticipated seeing—someone who shouldn't be here, not now, not ever.

"Why are you here?" I gasp, my voice shaking, as my world tilts on its axis. The unexpected twist slams into me, and the realization hits like a punch to the gut. Everything I thought I knew is about to unravel.

Chapter 6: Secrets in the Dark

In the dim glow of the office lights, the familiar scent of fresh coffee mixed with the faint tang of printer ink surrounded me, creating an oddly comforting cocoon. The hum of the overhead lights and the rhythmic clicking of keyboards were the soundtrack to my evenings with Lucas, a strange symphony that played as we navigated the uncharted waters of our growing connection. Each late-night work session had become a ritual of sorts, punctuated by laughter and shared glances that held more than the typical office camaraderie. Yet beneath the laughter lingered an undercurrent of something more—a tension that both excited and unnerved me.

It was inevitable that our closeness would raise eyebrows. The office buzzed with speculation, hushed whispers trailing behind us like ghostly echoes. I could feel the weight of their gazes whenever Lucas and I entered the break room or shared a quick moment at the copier. Their assumptions pricked at the edges of my mind, a constant reminder that our bond had morphed into something that could be construed as scandalous. Lucas, ever the suave charmer, put on a brave face, but I could see the subtle shifts in his demeanor—the way he pulled away just enough to maintain a façade of professionalism, even as he sought me out for late-night collaborations that blurred the lines of our relationship.

It was during one of these evenings that the air shifted, turning heavy with unspoken words. We had been poring over spreadsheets, but I sensed a storm brewing beneath Lucas's calm surface. The glow from his laptop cast a soft light across his features, revealing a flicker of something dark in his eyes. I set my pen down, the faint sound echoing in the quiet room, and looked at him, my heart quickening at the thought of what he might say.

"Can I ask you something?" he began, his voice low and measured, as if weighing each word like precious stones.

"Sure, you can ask me anything," I replied, trying to keep my tone light despite the seriousness etched on his face.

He hesitated, fingers running through his hair in that all-too-familiar gesture that signaled his discomfort. "It's about my past," he said finally, and the gravity of his words settled between us. "There's someone... a rival from years ago. He's resurfaced."

I leaned forward, concern knitting my brows. "What do you mean? Is he here, in the city?"

Lucas glanced at the door, the shadows creeping in as the last vestiges of daylight faded. "I don't know. But I've seen him. At least, I think I have." He looked away, his gaze distant, lost in memories I desperately wanted to pull him from. "He has a grudge against me. A real vendetta."

The revelation hung in the air, and I felt a chill sweep through me. "What did you do to him?" I asked, my curiosity battling with my instinct to protect him.

"It was a long time ago. He was a colleague, someone I thought was a friend," Lucas replied, his voice tight. "We competed for a position at another firm. I got it; he didn't. But it wasn't just about the job. He lost everything—his reputation, his standing. I didn't think he'd take it this far."

I could see the fear threading through his words, unspooling like a delicate ribbon. It shook me to my core. This was no longer just about office gossip or misplaced affections; there was something sinister lurking in the shadows of Lucas's life, a threat I couldn't ignore. "Have you talked to anyone about this? The police, maybe?"

Lucas's expression hardened, and he shook his head. "No, I don't want to make it a big deal. If he's really watching me, drawing attention will only make things worse. I've managed to avoid him so far, and I'd like to keep it that way."

"Lucas, you can't handle this alone. If he's dangerous—"

"Which is exactly why I can't involve you," he interjected, his tone sharper than I expected. "I don't want you getting mixed up in my problems. This is my mess to deal with."

His defensiveness stung, and for a moment, I felt the walls close in around me. "You think I'm going to just walk away because it gets tough? I care about you, and that means I'm in this whether you like it or not." The words escaped me before I could rein them in, my heart racing with the truth of my declaration.

Lucas paused, the tension crackling like electricity between us. His expression softened, but there was a wariness in his eyes that didn't vanish. "I don't want you to get hurt," he said quietly, his voice almost a whisper.

I crossed my arms, the protective instinct surging within me. "You think I'm scared? This is about more than just you now. If there's a threat out there, I need to know about it."

He sighed, the weight of his past pressing down on him. "I appreciate your concern, but I need you to trust me. I can handle this."

But could he? The uncertainty gnawed at me, an insistent whisper that told me I couldn't just sit back and watch as he faced whatever danger loomed on the horizon. I couldn't let him slip further into that dark space where secrets festered, where shadows lengthened and wrapped around him like a vice.

As the evening wore on and the office emptied, I felt an uneasy resolve settle in my chest. I would not let this end here. The moment Lucas stepped out of the door, I knew that I couldn't remain a passive observer in his life. I had to dig deeper, uncover whatever truths lay buried in his past, no matter how dark they might be. After all, love meant standing together, even when the world conspired to keep us apart.

The night wore on, a velvet expanse broken only by the flickering screens of our laptops. The rhythmic tapping of keys was a comforting backdrop, yet the weight of unspoken words lingered heavily between us. I could feel the tension in the air, thick enough to cut with a knife, and I wanted nothing more than to reach across the divide that Lucas had unintentionally created. His guarded demeanor was new, a sharp contrast to the easy banter that had characterized our late nights before. It felt as if he were trying to build walls, and I was left grappling with the feeling that something sinister was lurking just beyond them.

"Why don't you let me help?" I asked, my voice softer than I intended, almost a whisper in the quiet of the room. "You don't have to go through this alone, you know."

Lucas paused, the fingers hovering over his keyboard, and I caught a fleeting glimpse of vulnerability—his eyes clouded with uncertainty. "I appreciate that, really, but this isn't something you want to get tangled up in. It's complicated." His words came out like a plea, but the determination in his gaze suggested a man resolved to bear his burdens in solitude.

"Complicated is my middle name," I shot back, a playful grin spreading across my face to lighten the mood. "Look, I'm all for emotional independence, but this is a bit much, don't you think? I'm already tangled up in office gossip, so why not add a sprinkle of intrigue?"

He chuckled, the tension easing slightly, though the shadow of worry remained. "Intrigue is one way to put it. You've no idea what you're asking for. This isn't just office drama—it's personal."

"Tell me about it then. It might help," I pressed, leaning forward, the earnestness in my tone stripping away the playful facade. The flicker of fear in his eyes only deepened my resolve. "I can't help if you don't let me in."

Lucas let out a long sigh, the kind that seemed to carry the weight of uncounted sleepless nights. "Alright," he said finally, the reluctant agreement hanging in the air like the first crack of thunder before a storm. "But promise me you won't get involved beyond this conversation."

"Cross my heart and hope to die," I declared, throwing in a playful salute that made him smile, albeit weakly.

He rubbed the back of his neck, a gesture I recognized as a sign of his discomfort. "It's about Thomas Grey. He was—well, he still is—a colleague from a firm I used to work at. When we were vying for the same promotion, things got out of hand. He lost, and I guess it spiraled from there."

"Spiraled how?" I asked, my curiosity piqued.

"Let's just say he has a reputation for being vindictive. It's not just a few unkind words; he's capable of more. He's made threats before, and the last I heard, he was involved in some shady business."

"Shady business? You mean like wearing sunglasses indoors or more like selling art forgeries?" I joked, but Lucas's expression remained serious.

"More like criminal charges," he replied, his voice low. "He's not just a rival; he's dangerous. And now he's here, and I can't shake the feeling that he's been watching me."

The gravity of his words settled heavily in my chest. "What do you mean, watching? Like a creep lurking in the shadows?"

"More like a ghost that won't let go," he said, his voice laced with a mixture of frustration and fear. "I've caught glimpses of him around town. Once at a café I frequent, another time near my apartment. It's unsettling."

A chill raced down my spine, and I leaned closer, the urgency of the moment igniting something fierce within me. "What if he's planning something? You need to protect yourself—"

"Which is why I've been trying to keep you out of it," Lucas interrupted, his voice firmer now. "I don't want you to become collateral damage in this. You deserve to be safe, not entangled in my past."

"But it's already too late for that," I countered, my heart racing. "You're my friend, Lucas, and I can't just sit back while you're dealing with something like this. You need to have someone watching your back."

He looked at me, his expression a mixture of gratitude and exasperation. "You have a stubborn streak, you know that?"

"Stubbornness is a virtue," I replied, meeting his gaze with a defiance that I hoped conveyed my sincerity. "You're not alone in this, and I'm not going to pretend everything is fine while you're out there being hunted by your past."

Lucas let out a breath, his shoulders relaxing just a fraction as he considered my words. "You really want to help?"

"Of course, I do. Just point me in the right direction," I said, determination surging through me. "I've dealt with my fair share of dramatic ex-boyfriends and petty office politics. This? This is nothing."

"Let's not kid ourselves; it's definitely something," he countered with a teasing smirk, a flicker of admiration lighting his eyes.

The air crackled between us, a blend of tension and unspoken feelings that had been building for weeks. I could sense the shift, a recognition of the deeper connection that anchored us, the understanding that we were inextricably linked by more than just office camaraderie. It was a thrilling, terrifying realization, and in that moment, I decided that I would do everything in my power to keep him safe.

Just as we were beginning to formulate a plan, the sudden jangle of Lucas's phone startled us both. He glanced down at the screen, and his expression changed instantly—an amalgam of concern and irritation flaring to life. "It's my boss," he muttered, swiping to answer the call.

"Hey, I'm—" he started, but the voice on the other end cut him off, the words rapid and urgent.

I could only catch snippets of the conversation, but the growing tension in his posture told me all I needed to know. "No, I can't... Yes, I understand," he said, his brow furrowing. "I'll be right there."

As he hung up, I could see the storm brewing behind his eyes. "What's wrong?" I asked, instinctively reaching for his hand.

"It's Thomas," he said, the words falling from his lips like a death knell. "He's been spotted near the office."

My heart raced as panic gripped me. "What do we do?"

Lucas took a deep breath, steadying himself. "We need to be careful. I can't let him see you. You need to go home—"

"Not a chance," I interrupted, a fire igniting in my belly. "I'm not leaving you to face this alone. What if he tries to make a move?"

"Then we'll deal with it together," he conceded, a spark of determination igniting in his eyes. "But promise me, no heroics. We play this smart."

"Smart and stubborn, remember?" I shot back, a grin breaking through the tension. "Now, what's our plan?"

As we huddled together, the office bathed in shadows and anticipation, I felt a sense of purpose wash over me. Lucas was more than a colleague; he was someone I cared deeply about, and whatever secrets lurked in the dark would not keep me from standing by his side.

The atmosphere in the office had shifted, each moment heavy with the promise of confrontation. As Lucas and I exchanged whispered plans, my heart thudded in rhythm with the clock ticking away the precious minutes. Outside the window, the city hummed with life, oblivious to the storm brewing within the walls of our workplace. I could feel the charge in the air, a palpable tension that wrapped around us like a thick fog. The urgency of our situation pushed aside the light banter that usually filled our conversations, and instead, an electric silence enveloped us.

"Okay, here's what we'll do," Lucas said, running a hand through his tousled hair, the hint of desperation in his voice. "I'll go to the office entrance and take a look around. You stay here and keep an eye on the back exit. If you see anything, anything at all, call me. Understand?"

"Absolutely," I replied, a fierce resolve igniting within me. "But are you sure you want to go out there alone? What if he's waiting for you?"

"I can't let fear dictate my actions. Besides," he added with a half-smile that barely reached his eyes, "I'm not as easy to intimidate as you might think."

His attempt at levity did little to calm my nerves. "You keep telling yourself that, but I'd prefer you come back in one piece," I shot back, crossing my arms defiantly. "I'm not going to let you become a statistic, Lucas."

"Stubborn as ever," he replied, his tone teasing yet filled with an underlying current of gratitude. "It's one of the things I like about you."

"Flattery will get you everywhere," I quipped, the tension easing just slightly as I gestured toward the door. "Now go. I'll keep the home fires burning—well, metaphorically speaking. Let's just hope we don't need a fire extinguisher by the end of this."

Lucas's laughter rang out, a beautiful sound that temporarily dispelled the darkness creeping at the edges of our minds. He paused at the door, casting me one last glance, his expression serious once more. "Promise me you'll stay alert."

"Promise," I said, watching as he slipped into the shadowed corridor, leaving me behind to wrestle with my racing thoughts.

I paced the small confines of the break room, the fluorescent lights casting a sterile glow over the mundane decor. The clock ticked ominously, each second stretching longer than the last. I leaned against the cool surface of the counter, peering out of the window, my heart in my throat as I strained to see beyond the glass. The street below was alive with pedestrians, unaware of the chaos brewing just above them. I caught sight of Lucas emerging into the dim light outside, the figure of a man moving swiftly past him. My breath caught in my throat as my instincts screamed that something was off.

It wasn't just a feeling; it was a visceral reaction. I could see Lucas scanning the area, his body taut with concentration. And then, in the periphery of my vision, I spotted him—Thomas Grey. He was lurking in the shadows of a nearby alley, his stance rigid, an aura of menace surrounding him like a dark cloud. I grabbed my phone, heart racing as I pressed the screen.

"Lucas, get out of there!" I whispered urgently, my voice trembling with fear.

"Why? What do you see?" His voice crackled over the line, laced with confusion and determination.

"Thomas is right behind you! He's—"

Before I could finish my warning, a sudden commotion erupted outside, followed by the unmistakable sound of shattering glass. My heart plummeted as I glimpsed a flicker of movement. The figure of Thomas was no longer hidden in the shadows; he had emerged, his eyes glinting with malicious intent.

"Lucas!" I screamed, desperation flooding my voice. "He's coming for you!"

I bolted toward the door, adrenaline surging through me as I swung it open. My instincts took over, propelling me into the chaos of the night. I sprinted down the corridor, praying that I would reach him in time. The air was charged with tension, the night darker than I remembered as I raced toward the entrance.

Outside, the scene was surreal. The streetlights flickered, casting eerie shadows that danced in time with my racing heart. Lucas was backing away from Thomas, his expression a mix of anger and fear. The rivalry between them was palpable, the air thick with unspoken threats. I ducked behind a parked car, my breath shallow as I tried to comprehend the gravity of the situation.

"Why are you here, Thomas?" Lucas demanded, his voice steady despite the danger. "What do you want?"

"I want what's mine," Thomas spat, stepping closer, the menace radiating from him palpable. "You think you can just take everything from me and walk away unscathed? This isn't over."

"Don't come any closer!" Lucas warned, raising his hands in a defensive posture. "You need to leave. This is my life now."

"Your life?" Thomas laughed, a cold, cruel sound that echoed in the empty street. "You have no idea what you're up against. You've been playing with fire, and I'm here to make sure you get burned."

I could feel the tension snapping like a taut wire, the impending confrontation sending shockwaves through me. "Lucas!" I called out, stepping forward instinctively, desperate to intervene.

But as soon as my voice cut through the air, all hell broke loose. Thomas lunged, and Lucas instinctively dodged to the side, their bodies colliding in a struggle for dominance. Panic surged within me, an icy grip wrapping around my heart as I watched the two men grapple.

"Get back!" Lucas shouted, shoving Thomas away with a force that surprised even him.

I rushed forward, unable to stand by any longer. "Stop it! Both of you!" My voice rang out, desperate and authoritative, cutting through the chaos like a beacon.

Lucas turned briefly to me, confusion flashing across his features, but before he could respond, Thomas seized the moment. "You should have stayed out of this, sweetheart," he sneered, his eyes glinting with malice as he turned his attention to me. "You've just made a mistake."

Time seemed to freeze as I registered his intent, a dark realization dawning upon me. In a swift motion, Thomas reached for something concealed beneath his jacket. The moonlight glinted off the metal, a sharp flash that sent my heart racing in terror.

"Run!" Lucas shouted, his voice strained with urgency.

But before I could process his command, a loud bang shattered the night, the sound echoing around us like a gunshot. A blinding pain lanced through my shoulder, knocking me back. My world tilted, the ground rushing up to meet me as darkness threatened to envelop my vision.

In that fleeting moment, as the chaos erupted around me, I realized with chilling clarity that the shadows of our past had come crashing into our present. And just like that, everything I knew was on the precipice of being irrevocably changed.

Chapter 7: Caught in the Crossfire

The dawn broke like a sliver of glass, sharp and cruel, filtering through the curtains and bathing my room in an uneasy light. I lay still for a moment, cocooned in the remnants of sleep, when something caught my eye—an envelope, stark against the wooden floorboards. The moment I saw it, a knot tightened in my stomach. With trepidation, I pushed back the covers and slipped out of bed, my feet cool against the floor as I approached the door.

As I bent down to pick it up, the world outside seemed to grow eerily quiet, the usual morning sounds dulled as if the universe itself held its breath. My hands trembled slightly as I opened the envelope, the paper crisp and foreign. Inside, a single sheet bore a warning scrawled in jagged, hurried handwriting: Stay away from Lucas. He's dangerous, and they will use you against him.

The words hit me like a slap, sharp and unforgiving. My heart raced as the message settled in—an icy certainty that pricked at the back of my mind. The implications tangled with my emotions, igniting a firestorm of fear and anger within me. How could someone know about Lucas? Who were these shadowy figures lurking in the background of his life? I knew I needed answers, and not just for my sake but for his as well. I had to confront him, to demand clarity amid the chaos that had enveloped us.

I dressed quickly, barely noticing the clothes I pulled on—jeans, a worn T-shirt, and my favorite leather jacket, the one that felt like armor against the outside world. Each piece seemed to ground me, preparing me for the confrontation that awaited. The air outside was brisk, charged with an energy that mirrored my own turbulent thoughts. I stepped into the day, the sunlight filtering through the trees lining the street, and yet the warmth felt distant, overshadowed by the chill of the warning that still clung to me.

The school buzzed with its usual rhythm, students rushing to classes, laughter echoing through the hallways. But I felt like a ghost moving through it all, invisible and detached. When I finally spotted Lucas at our usual meeting spot—the worn bench near the cafeteria—I hesitated, uncertainty creeping in. He looked up, his expression shifting from casual amusement to immediate concern as our eyes met. The playfulness that often danced in his gaze had dulled, replaced by a shadow of anxiety that set my nerves on edge.

"Hey," he greeted, his voice low and tentative, as if he sensed the storm brewing within me.

"Hey," I managed to reply, though my voice felt small in comparison to the urgency bubbling inside. I took a deep breath, grounding myself, and slid onto the bench beside him. "We need to talk."

He nodded slowly, the tension palpable between us. "What's wrong?"

I pulled the envelope from my pocket, my hands shaking slightly as I handed it to him. "I found this this morning," I said, watching his face closely as he unfolded the paper. His eyes widened as he read the warning, the color draining from his cheeks.

"Where did you get this?" he demanded, looking up at me, panic flickering in his expression.

"It was just left at my doorstep," I replied, the gravity of the situation weighing heavily in the air. "What's going on, Lucas? Who are these people?"

He exhaled slowly, running a hand through his tousled hair, the frustration evident in his movements. "I didn't want you to find out this way. I—I thought I could keep you safe." His voice trembled slightly, and I felt a pang of empathy amidst my confusion.

"Safe from what?" I pressed, my voice sharp. "I want to know the truth."

He hesitated, weighing his words. "I have a past, a complicated one. There are people—powerful people—who don't take kindly to what I did. They'll use anyone to get to me. I can't let them hurt you."

"Then let me help," I insisted, anger bubbling to the surface. "I'm not afraid of your past, Lucas. I'm afraid of losing you."

His gaze softened, and for a fleeting moment, the walls he'd built around himself seemed to waver. "You don't understand what you're asking. These are dangerous people. You're putting yourself in the crossfire."

"I refuse to back down," I shot back, my determination unwavering. "I care about you too much to just walk away because it's easier. You're not the only one who's scared. I'm terrified, but running from this won't make it go away."

Lucas's expression shifted, a mixture of admiration and frustration clouding his features. "I can't stand the thought of you getting hurt because of me. You deserve a normal life, not this mess."

"But I don't want normal," I countered, my voice steady now. "I want you. Whatever this is, we can face it together. Don't shut me out."

Silence stretched between us, heavy and fraught with unsaid words. I could see the conflict in his eyes—the pull of his past warring with the feelings he had for me. Just when I thought I might break through, he shook his head, frustration etched in every line of his face. "You don't know what you're asking. I've made enemies. I'm not sure how far they'll go to get what they want."

A rush of heat surged through me, a mix of anger and fear colliding in my chest. "Then tell me what to expect. I deserve to know the danger I'm walking into."

He looked away, his jaw tightening, and I could see the battle within him. I reached out, my fingers brushing against his, and in that moment, the world outside faded. "Please, Lucas. I won't let you face this alone."

He turned back to me, his eyes searching mine, as if looking for a glimmer of hope amid the chaos. For a moment, time stood still, the noise of the bustling school falling away, and it was just the two of us—caught in the storm, yet standing firm.

"I'll tell you everything," he finally said, his voice low but resolute. "But you have to promise me one thing."

"Anything," I replied, my heart pounding in my chest.

"Promise me you'll be careful. Promise me you won't take unnecessary risks."

"I promise," I vowed, a fierce determination igniting within me. "But you have to promise me too—no more secrets."

As the unspoken tension hung in the air, a sense of resolve settled over me. We were caught in the crossfire, but I wouldn't let fear dictate my choices. I chose to stand by him, to unravel the threads of his past, no matter how dangerous it may be. Together, we would face whatever darkness lay ahead, and I would fight to keep the light between us alive.

The air crackled with a tension that felt almost tangible, a charged silence hanging between us after Lucas reluctantly agreed to share the burden of his past. I watched as he wrestled with his thoughts, his brow furrowed and his gaze averted. The weight of unspoken truths hung in the air, pressing down on my chest like an unyielding weight.

"You have to understand," he began, his voice low and hesitant, "there are things I've done, choices I've made that put everyone I care about at risk. These people, they won't stop until they get what they want. And right now, that's you."

"Me?" I echoed, disbelief threading through my words. "What could they possibly want with me? I'm just... me."

Lucas met my eyes, a storm of emotions swirling within his. "That's exactly the problem. You're just you, and that makes you vulnerable. They'll target anyone connected to me, hoping to manipulate me into doing their bidding."

"Sounds like a cliché villain monologue," I quipped, attempting to lighten the heavy atmosphere. "You should have added a sinister laugh for dramatic effect."

He cracked a small smile, the tension easing just a fraction. "You're right. I should work on my delivery."

But as the smile faded, the seriousness of the situation returned, dragging us both down into the depths of uncertainty. "What do they want?" I pressed, my voice steady but my heart racing.

Lucas took a deep breath, the weight of his past pressing heavily on him. "Power, control—whatever they can leverage. I got involved with a group that operates in the shadows. At first, I thought it was about making a difference, but it quickly turned into a game I wasn't prepared to play."

"You were trying to help people?" I asked, surprise lacing my tone.

"Help people," he repeated, shaking his head in disbelief. "Or so I thought. I was young, naïve. I didn't realize how far they would go to protect their interests. I tried to get out, but they don't let go that easily."

My heart ached for him. This wasn't just some reckless kid caught in a bad decision; this was a person who had found himself in a web of consequences he hadn't asked for. "So what now?" I whispered, leaning in closer. "How do we fight against that?"

Lucas looked away, his jaw tightening. "You shouldn't have to fight anything. I should be the one protecting you."

"Good luck with that," I shot back, the sharpness of my words cutting through the tension. "I'm not going to sit on the sidelines while you take all the risks. I'm in this with you, whether you like it or not."

He regarded me with a mix of admiration and frustration, the conflict evident in his features. "You're infuriating, you know that?"

"I've been told," I replied, unable to suppress a smirk. "But I'm also not going to let you push me away. So what's the plan, hero?"

Lucas shifted on the bench, a wry smile creeping onto his lips as he weighed his options. "There's a meeting tonight. A safe house where some of my old contacts gather. If we can figure out what's happening, we might be able to plan a way out of this mess. But I can't have you there. It's too dangerous."

"And you think I'll just let you go alone?" I challenged, crossing my arms defiantly. "I'll just hide in a corner and do my nails while you fight off the bad guys?"

He chuckled softly, but the seriousness quickly returned to his eyes. "No, you're not going to hide. You'll probably be the one throwing punches while I'm left trying to keep you safe. But you really can't come. It's not just about me; it's about you. They wouldn't hesitate to use you against me."

I leaned closer, my voice dropping to a whisper. "You said they target people connected to you. If I'm not there, won't that just make me an easier target? I'd rather face them with you than be some helpless pawn waiting for you to come back."

He studied my face, searching for any sign that I might relent. But all he found was a fierce determination reflected in my gaze. "You're stubborn."

"Stubbornness is my best quality," I quipped back, trying to keep the mood light despite the seriousness of our conversation.

"More like your only quality," he teased, the corners of his mouth lifting slightly. But beneath the playful banter lay a deep-rooted concern that I could feel even from across the bench.

"Look," I said, my voice firm, "I know you're trying to protect me. But I can't just stand by while you go off to face whatever danger awaits. We're in this together. You have to trust me."

Lucas's expression softened, the fight slowly ebbing away. "Fine. But you have to promise me that if things go south, you'll listen to me and get out of there, no questions asked."

"I can agree to that," I said, my heart pounding with a mixture of excitement and fear.

As we discussed the details of the meeting, the sun dipped lower in the sky, casting long shadows across the school grounds. The world around us buzzed with life, but it felt as though we were wrapped in our own cocoon, suspended in time. There was an unspoken bond forming, solidifying as we shared our thoughts, fears, and plans, each revelation drawing us closer together.

After school, as I prepared for the evening ahead, I felt a nervous energy pulsing through me. I dressed carefully, selecting a fitted black shirt that hugged my form without being too revealing and a pair of dark jeans that lent me a sense of purpose. I opted for boots—practical, but also a reminder that I was stepping into a realm of uncertainty.

When the time finally came, I found Lucas waiting for me by his car, a sleek black sedan that seemed to belong in a spy film rather than a high school parking lot. His expression was serious, the earlier lightness replaced by a focused determination. "You ready for this?" he asked, his eyes searching mine for any hint of doubt.

I nodded, feeling the weight of the moment settle over me. "As ready as I'll ever be."

The drive to the safe house was filled with an uneasy silence, the only sounds coming from the engine and the faint rustle of leaves outside. I watched the landscape flash by, my mind racing with thoughts of what awaited us. With each turn, I could feel the anticipation tightening in my chest, a mixture of fear and exhilaration swirling within.

When we arrived, the safe house stood modestly among the trees, a nondescript building that blended into its surroundings.

Lucas parked the car and we stepped out, the air cool and crisp. He turned to me, his expression unreadable. "Whatever happens in there, just remember why we're doing this."

"Together," I reminded him, reaching for his hand.

With a quick squeeze, we crossed the threshold into the unknown, the door creaking ominously as it swung open. The scent of old wood and damp earth enveloped us, and I steeled myself for whatever lay ahead, resolute in my commitment to stand by Lucas's side, no matter the darkness that threatened to engulf us.

The atmosphere inside the safe house was thick with unspoken tension, a palpable weight that pressed against my chest as Lucas led the way. The dim light cast long shadows across the walls, creating a sense of claustrophobia despite the spaciousness of the room. Dust motes danced in the air, illuminated by the lone bulb hanging overhead. I could hear my heartbeat echoing in my ears, a frantic rhythm underscoring the gravity of our mission.

Lucas paused, scanning the room as if he were memorizing every detail. I caught sight of a few scattered chairs, a rickety table, and the remnants of someone's hastily abandoned belongings—an old jacket draped over a chair, a half-empty cup of coffee forgotten on the table. There was a disheveled air to the place, as if it had seen too many frantic meetings and too many secrets whispered within its walls.

"Stay close," he murmured, pulling me slightly to his side as we stepped further into the room. The quiet intensity of his voice sent a shiver down my spine, mixing with the anticipation that swirled around us.

"Should we be worried about being ambushed?" I asked, trying to lighten the mood, though my voice trembled slightly.

"Only if you keep cracking jokes like that," he replied, shooting me a sideways glance that almost broke through his serious demeanor. "Let's just focus."

I took a deep breath, forcing myself to settle into the seriousness of the situation. This wasn't some ordinary rendezvous; we were stepping into the unknown, diving into the depths of Lucas's troubled past and whatever enemies lurked just outside. "Right. Focus. Got it," I replied, my resolve firming up.

Suddenly, the door swung open with a creak that echoed through the silence, and a tall figure stepped inside. His presence was commanding, with sharp features and an air of authority that immediately drew my attention. Lucas tensed beside me, the shift in his posture making it clear that this man was someone significant—someone tied deeply into the fabric of his past.

"Lucas," the man greeted, his voice a low rumble that carried an edge of authority. "I see you brought company." His gaze flicked to me, assessing, as if weighing the worth of my presence.

"Ryan, this is—" Lucas started, but Ryan cut him off, his eyes narrowing as if he already knew more than Lucas had shared.

"I know who she is," Ryan said, his tone sharper now. "And I don't like it."

"Great, we're off to a lovely start," I chimed in, attempting to inject a bit of humor into the tension, but it fell flat as Ryan's gaze hardened further.

"Lucas, you can't drag her into this. She's a liability," Ryan warned, his voice unyielding.

"Hey, I'm right here!" I interjected, crossing my arms defiantly. "I can speak for myself, thank you very much."

Lucas turned to me, concern etched across his face. "This isn't a game. You don't understand the risks involved."

"I may not understand everything, but I know enough to know I'm not leaving you to deal with this alone," I shot back, feeling the fire of determination ignite within me. "You think I'm just going to sit at home and wait for danger to knock on my door?"

Ryan ran a hand through his hair, frustration simmering just below the surface. "You have no idea what we're up against. This isn't just a couple of angry guys in suits. This is serious."

"Exactly," I replied, matching his intensity. "So why should I be on the sidelines? You need all the help you can get, and I refuse to let you face this without me."

Lucas stepped between us, a quiet authority emanating from him as he focused on Ryan. "I brought her because she deserves to know. We're in this together, and we need her to understand what we're dealing with."

The air thickened with tension as Ryan scrutinized Lucas, the weight of their history heavy in the room. Finally, he sighed, the fight seemingly draining out of him. "Fine. But if anything happens to her—"

"Nothing is going to happen," Lucas interrupted, his voice resolute. "We need to focus on the task at hand."

"Task?" I repeated, raising an eyebrow. "What task? Should I be taking notes on your dangerous adventures? Because if so, I'll need a notebook."

Ryan shot me an incredulous look, but Lucas suppressed a smile, a hint of amusement creeping into his expression. "We're trying to piece together information about the group that's after me. They're not just powerful—they're connected. We need to find out what they want and how to stop them."

"By breaking into their headquarters?" I suggested, the idea forming half-jokingly in my mind.

Lucas shook his head, his expression turning serious again. "No. We need to gather intel first. Find out who's involved, what their endgame is. We can't rush in blind."

"Smart thinking," Ryan conceded, though his eyes still bore the weight of concern. "We've got some contacts who might be able to help us."

Lucas turned to me, his gaze softening. "Just remember to keep your head down and let me handle the more dangerous stuff. I can't lose you to this."

I opened my mouth to protest, but the weight of his words settled in my chest. The gravity of our situation wasn't lost on me, and for the first time, doubt crept in. "Okay," I said slowly, "but you have to promise that you won't keep me in the dark. I want to be part of this."

"Deal," Lucas replied, though his eyes darkened slightly as if he still didn't entirely trust the situation. "But if anything goes sideways—"

"I know, I know," I interrupted, waving my hand dismissively. "Run like the wind. I got it."

With a nod, Ryan moved to a nearby table cluttered with papers and maps, his brow furrowed in concentration. "We need to figure out who's calling the shots. They're not just going to sit back and let us gather information without trying to stop us first."

"Then we'll move quickly," Lucas said, stepping closer to Ryan. "What do we have?"

As they dove into a discussion, I took a step back, scanning the room. The shadows seemed to deepen, a sense of foreboding washing over me. Suddenly, the door creaked open again, and a chill swept through the room, sending a shiver down my spine.

A woman stepped inside, her demeanor calm but her eyes sharp. "You shouldn't be here, Lucas," she said, her voice smooth yet laced with an underlying threat. "This isn't a safe place for you—or her."

My stomach dropped. The air shifted, and I could feel the tension reweaving itself into something darker, more dangerous. Ryan turned sharply, his expression shifting to one of immediate concern. "What do you mean?"

The woman's gaze flicked to me, assessing. "You're already in too deep. If they find out you're here, they'll come after you both."

"What are you talking about?" I asked, my heart racing as the situation spiraled. "Who are you?"

"Just someone who knows how this game is played," she replied, her lips curling into a slight smile that didn't reach her eyes. "And it's a game you don't want to lose."

Before I could process her words, the sound of heavy footsteps echoed from outside, each step reverberating like a drumbeat of impending doom. My pulse quickened as the door rattled, and I exchanged a panicked glance with Lucas.

"What did you do?" Ryan demanded, stepping protectively in front of me.

"I didn't do anything," she replied, her calm facade beginning to crack as the footsteps grew louder. "But they're here now."

The door burst open, and figures shrouded in darkness flooded the room, their intentions unclear but their presence undeniable. I felt a surge of adrenaline as the reality of our situation crashed down on me. We were no longer just caught in a web of secrets; we were in the crosshairs of something far more dangerous, and the stakes were higher than I ever imagined.

As the figures advanced, a chilling realization hit me. There was no escape, and the game was only just beginning.

Chapter 8: The Line Between Love and Hate

Our heated exchange had left the air thick with an energy I couldn't ignore. Lucas had stormed away, but not before I had witnessed the crack in his facade, the way his fists clenched in frustration, revealing a vulnerability that pulled at my heartstrings. I stood there, still fuming, yet strangely electrified, feeling the tension wrap around us like a cocoon. It was infuriating and intoxicating all at once.

Days passed since that argument, each one dragging its feet as I tried to piece together what had happened between us. Lucas returned to his usual cool demeanor, the mask firmly in place, and I found myself navigating a landscape filled with sharp thorns and hidden pitfalls. Each time our gazes collided, it felt like a collision of worlds, a fraying rope threatening to snap, and my stomach tightened with a mix of anxiety and anticipation. I couldn't decipher if I was drawn to him or repulsed by the uncertainty hanging in the air like a fog that refused to lift.

It was on a particularly rainy afternoon, the kind that made the world outside my window look like a watercolor painting left to bleed into itself, that I decided I couldn't stand this charade any longer. I needed to confront him, to break through the wall he had erected between us. My heart raced as I made my way to his favorite spot in the library—a hidden nook where sunlight streamed in through a tall, narrow window, illuminating the dust motes dancing in the air like tiny fairies.

I found him hunched over a book, brow furrowed, the very picture of concentration. But the moment I stepped into the light, his head snapped up, eyes widening as they met mine. The tension was palpable, a taut string pulled tight, threatening to snap if either of us made the wrong move. "What do you want, Emily?" he asked, the edge in his voice slicing through the quiet.

"I want to talk," I replied, attempting to keep my voice steady, even as my heart thundered in my chest. "About what happened the other day."

He shifted uncomfortably in his seat, the avoidance palpable. "There's nothing to talk about," he insisted, but even I could hear the tremor of uncertainty beneath his bravado.

"Really? Because it felt like there was a lot to say. You can't just pretend it didn't happen, Lucas." I stepped closer, the space between us shrinking, hoping my proximity would coax him into dropping his defenses. "We're not in some bad teen drama. We have real feelings here—"

"Feelings? That's rich coming from you," he interrupted, his tone biting, but I caught the flicker of something else behind his steely facade. "You're the one who pushed me away first."

"Pushed you away? Are you kidding me?" I exclaimed, frustration boiling over. "You're the one who builds walls like you're trying to create a fortress! I thought we were friends, and then you act like I'm a stranger."

His expression softened momentarily, the corner of his mouth twitching as if he was fighting back a smile. "Well, you do have a knack for making things complicated."

"Me? Complicated?" I said, forcing a laugh that felt foreign on my lips. "Look who's talking! I'm not the one who flips between being a jerk and being...whatever that was." I gestured wildly, my hands moving through the air like I was trying to grab the intangible connection we had shared.

"Maybe it's just easier to be a jerk," he muttered, looking down at his book, a stark contrast to the turbulent sea of emotions swirling between us. "It keeps people at a distance."

"But that's not what you want, is it?" I challenged, stepping into his space, feeling the warmth radiating from him, intoxicating and familiar. "You're afraid, Lucas. Afraid of what this is—of what we are. And I get it. I do. But if you keep pushing me away, you'll never find out."

His gaze flickered up to mine, and for a moment, the world around us faded. The rain continued to patter against the windows, a rhythmic backdrop to the charged silence between us. I could see the battle waging in his eyes, the fight between what he wanted and what he thought he should do.

"Maybe you're right," he said finally, the resignation in his voice sending a shiver down my spine. "But it's not that simple, Emily. There's a line—"

"Between love and hate?" I interrupted, feeling a spark of defiance ignite within me. "Maybe it's just a line we've drawn ourselves. One we can choose to cross."

The moment hung heavy, the air charged with possibility. Lucas was so close I could see the flecks of gold in his brown eyes, and the reality of our situation crashed over me. I wanted him. I wanted all of him—flaws and all—and it terrified me.

He reached out, brushing his fingers against my arm, a fleeting touch that sent electric currents racing through my skin. "What if it blows up in our faces?" he asked, a mixture of fear and hope etched across his features.

"Then we'll figure it out together," I whispered, my breath mingling with the warmth radiating from him. "I'm tired of pretending. Let's just be honest."

As he leaned closer, I felt the weight of the world fall away, replaced by the intoxicating pull of his presence. It was in that moment I realized that love and hate weren't so far apart; they were simply two sides of the same coin, waiting for someone brave enough to flip it over.

I stood in the cafeteria the following day, watching Lucas across the bustling room as if he were a character in a film I couldn't turn off. He sat at a table with his friends, laughter spilling out of him like sunshine breaking through storm clouds. The familiar ache of longing twisted in my chest as I recalled the moment we shared—the brush of his fingers against my arm, the way his eyes softened when he thought I wasn't looking. Yet here he was, a mask of indifference plastered over the warmth I had briefly glimpsed.

"Earth to Emily," Jess said, waving a hand in front of my face, pulling me from my reverie. "You're staring again. If you keep this up, you'll start a fire with that gaze."

"Shut up," I muttered, fighting a blush that crept up my cheeks. "I'm not staring. I'm... observing."

"Sure, let's go with that." She rolled her eyes playfully. "Just don't let him see you ogling. You might have to stop wearing those heart-shaped glasses."

A laugh escaped my lips, even though my heart sank at her teasing. "Not everyone wears heart-shaped glasses, Jess."

"True, but I think you're mistaking the look in his eyes for a romance novel," she countered, a knowing smile dancing on her lips. "That kind of tension? It belongs in stories, not high school."

I wanted to argue, to defend the simmering connection I felt whenever I was near Lucas, but the uncertainty lingered. Perhaps Jess was right. Maybe this was a fantastical tale I had woven from threads of hope and delusion. As I took a bite of my sandwich, the taste was bland and unfulfilling, much like the reality I faced.

When lunch ended, I rushed to my next class, determined to ignore the electric undercurrent that connected me to Lucas. But as I entered the room, I found him sitting in the front, the desk between us a chasm that felt insurmountable. It was as if the universe conspired against us, urging us to embrace the chaos of our emotions while simultaneously pushing us apart.

Throughout the lesson, I could feel his gaze on me, a gentle pressure that made my skin tingle. Every time I met his eyes, they were shields, cold and unreadable, but there was something lurking beneath—something I desperately wanted to unearth. After class, I slipped out into the hallway, and he followed, a shadow behind me.

"Emily," he called, his voice low and tentative.

I turned to face him, my heart racing. "What do you want, Lucas? To pretend yesterday didn't happen?"

"No, I—" He paused, running a hand through his hair, a gesture of frustration that only deepened the line of tension between us. "I don't know how to deal with this. I'm not good at the whole feelings thing."

"Neither am I," I admitted, the truth tumbling out before I could stop it. "But ignoring them won't make them go away."

"Right, but what if it complicates things?" He stepped closer, and I could smell the faint hint of his cologne mingling with the sharp scent of the classroom. My resolve faltered, swayed by the intensity of his presence. "What if we ruin what we already have?"

"Are you saying we have something?" I shot back, my tone sharper than intended. "Because it seems to me that you're doing a fantastic job of pretending it doesn't exist."

His frustration mirrored my own, and for a moment, we stood there, caught in a web of emotions, neither willing to break the silence that had wrapped itself around us. Then, unexpectedly, Lucas leaned in slightly, lowering his voice as if afraid the walls themselves might hear. "Maybe we should just be friends, then. That way, it won't get messy."

"Friends?" I scoffed, unable to hide the bitterness in my tone. "You mean like how you're friends with all the other girls, keeping them at arm's length? Or friends like the kind who share secrets and trust each other?"

He flinched at my words, and the sight was both satisfying and painful. I realized I was pushing him, testing his boundaries in a way I had never dared before. But with every barb, every challenge, I was equally terrified of what he might reveal.

"Why do you always have to make this so complicated?" he replied, frustration bubbling just beneath the surface. "Can't we just... hang out without the drama?"

"Hang out?" I echoed incredulously. "You think that's possible when we have this tension between us? It's like trying to light a match in a hurricane."

His mouth twisted into a half-smile, and for a moment, the weight of our arguments seemed to lift. "I like the way you think, even if it's completely impractical."

"Impractical?" I shot back, a smile threatening to break through my facade. "This whole situation is downright absurd, Lucas. We're stuck in this endless loop of anger and attraction."

"Then maybe we should try something different." He took a step closer, the distance between us evaporating as he looked deep into my eyes, searching for something. "What if we just... embraced the absurdity?"

My breath hitched at the challenge in his words. "You mean dive headfirst into chaos and see if we sink or swim?"

"Exactly." The confidence in his tone was infectious, igniting a flicker of hope deep within me. "Why not? We're already in too deep. What's a little more chaos?"

Before I could respond, the bell rang, echoing through the hallways and shattering the moment. I blinked, reality crashing back down around us like a wave, the chance of exploration slipping through my fingers like sand.

As we walked in silence toward our next class, a storm brewed inside me—excitement intertwined with trepidation. Could we really navigate this new territory without losing ourselves in the process? The answer felt elusive, but the thrill of uncertainty sparked something within me. The line between love and hate had shifted once more, and I was left wondering how far we would go to discover where it truly led.

With the tension still crackling between us, the days morphed into a peculiar routine. Lucas and I navigated the school halls like dancers performing a complicated tango, our steps choreographed by unspoken words and lingering glances. I found myself hyper-aware of him, analyzing the smallest of movements—a flick of his hair, the way he leaned against the lockers, casually cool yet somehow accessible. Yet, despite our proximity, he remained frustratingly distant, like a star I could see but could never reach.

In the late afternoons, I often sought refuge in my favorite spot at the park—a secluded bench overlooking a pond where the sun dipped low, painting the sky in hues of orange and pink. It was my sanctuary, a place where I could escape the swirl of emotions and contemplate my next move. But even there, I felt his presence looming large. The thought of him infiltrated my mind, uninvited yet welcomed.

One Friday, as I sat wrapped in a cocoon of thoughts, Jess plopped down beside me, a whirlwind of energy as always. "You're looking pensive. Planning to write a novel about unrequited love?" she teased, nudging me playfully.

I chuckled, grateful for her lightness. "More like contemplating the mysteries of teenage angst."

"Oh please, you're overthinking this," she said, a knowing smile on her lips. "It's Lucas. Just talk to him."

"Talk? Is that what you call this silent war we're waging?" I retorted, rolling my eyes. "Every time I think about confronting him, my stomach drops."

"Because you like him," she stated, her gaze piercing through my defenses.

"I—well, I'm not sure," I stammered, caught off guard. "I mean, we have this... thing, but it feels like a minefield."

"A minefield of feelings," she quipped, crossing her arms as she leaned back against the bench. "Isn't that what makes it exciting?"

"Exciting? More like terrifying," I replied, feeling the weight of my own heartache. "What if I end up getting blown to bits?"

"Then at least you'd have a story to tell," Jess said with a shrug, her playful demeanor softening. "But seriously, you need to find out where he stands. If you keep dancing around each other, you might miss the music entirely."

Her words sank in, resonating with the unease that had become my constant companion. I glanced back toward the school, where I could just make out Lucas's figure through the window, laughing with friends. My heart tugged at the sight, a mix of longing and frustration threatening to consume me.

That evening, I decided I needed to confront him once and for all. I texted him, a nervous flutter in my stomach as I typed the words: Can we talk?

The response came back almost immediately: Where?

The park? I sent back, hoping he wouldn't flake out.

A few minutes later, my phone buzzed again: See you in 10.

As I paced back and forth on the familiar path to the pond, my thoughts raced, swirling like leaves caught in a storm. What would I say? How could I lay bare my feelings without losing the fragile connection we had? When Lucas finally arrived, the sight of him made my breath hitch. He looked effortlessly handsome, his casual t-shirt and jeans accentuating the easy confidence he wore like a second skin.

"Hey," he greeted, hands shoved deep into his pockets, eyes scanning the ground as if searching for something elusive.

"Hey," I replied, trying to sound casual but feeling the weight of the moment hanging between us like a dense fog.

We stood in silence for a beat, the sounds of chirping crickets and rustling leaves filling the void. Finally, I blurted out, "I think we need to talk about what's going on between us."

Lucas looked up, surprise flashing in his eyes before they hardened into that familiar guarded expression. "Do we?"

"Yes, we do! This back-and-forth is ridiculous," I said, frustration spilling over. "We can't keep pretending that nothing happened. You're driving me crazy."

A flicker of uncertainty crossed his face, and I seized the moment. "What are you so afraid of? It's like you keep pushing me away even though you don't want to. I saw it in your eyes that day we argued."

He took a step back, creating an invisible barrier that felt as heavy as steel. "It's complicated, Emily. I'm not the guy you think I am."

"Then show me who you are! Stop hiding behind this wall," I urged, my heart racing. "I want to understand, but you keep making it impossible."

His expression shifted, confusion battling with something darker, something raw. "You don't know what you're asking for," he said, his voice low and intense.

"Then tell me," I pleaded, taking a tentative step forward, drawn by an invisible force that surged between us. "Please."

With a deep breath, he looked at me, and for a brief moment, the walls cracked. "What if I told you that I'm not ready for all this? That I'm afraid of messing it up? That I don't even know what I want?"

"Then let's figure it out together!" My voice was a little too loud, a desperate plea against the backdrop of the evening sky. "I'm not expecting you to have all the answers. I just need you to be honest."

The silence stretched, punctuated by the soft rustle of leaves. Lucas's gaze faltered, his thoughts spiraling in a direction I couldn't predict. Just when I thought he might open up, he turned away, looking out over the pond as if it held the answers he was too afraid to face.

"I can't," he finally whispered, a pained expression settling on his features. "It's not that simple."

Before I could respond, a loud crash echoed through the park, jolting both of us from our moment. A group of teenagers on bikes had collided near the entrance, laughter and shouts ringing out in the chaos. It was the kind of noise that pierced the quiet, breaking whatever fragile connection we had built in those tense moments.

Lucas sighed, the moment slipping through our fingers like water. "See? This is why I can't do this," he said, his voice low and filled with frustration. "Too much chaos, too many variables."

"Lucas—" I started, but he shook his head, his expression resolute.

"I need to go," he said, turning away, the distance between us widening. I felt a chill of despair settle in my chest as he walked away, each step dragging me deeper into the void that threatened to swallow me whole.

"Wait!" I called after him, desperation creeping into my tone. He paused but didn't turn back. "You can't just walk away like this. Not after everything!"

"Why not? It's what I'm best at," he replied, his voice barely above a whisper, and just like that, he vanished into the encroaching shadows, leaving me alone at the edge of the pond, uncertainty swirling around me like the leaves caught in the wind.

As night fell, the weight of his absence loomed large, and I felt the world closing in, the lines between love and hate blurring once more, leaving me teetering on the edge of something I couldn't quite define. Just then, my phone buzzed, and I glanced down, my heart racing as I read the message that appeared on the screen:

I'm sorry. Meet me at the old oak tree. It's important.

A shiver of foreboding crept up my spine. What could be so important that he had to see me again? The air felt charged, heavy with the promise of confrontation, and I could only hope that this time, the conversation wouldn't end with him walking away.

Chapter 9: Whispers in the Dark

The notes began innocuously enough, just slips of paper tucked neatly beneath my door or crumpled in the corners of my mailbox. At first, they felt like harmless pranks—naught but whimsical jabs from someone with a penchant for drama. But with each new note, the whimsy evaporated, leaving behind a sense of foreboding that seeped into my bones. The latest one, a simple scrawl that read, "You can't hide from the truth," sent my heart racing and my mind spiraling into chaos. I found myself glancing over my shoulder more often, half-expecting to see someone lurking in the shadows of the corridor.

In the dim light of my room, I sat cross-legged on the floor, surrounded by a fortress of pillows and blankets, trying to drown out the unease with thoughts of Lucas. He was a constant whirlpool of emotions, drawing me in and pushing me away in the same breath. One moment, he was all warm smiles and soft touches, whispering sweet nothings that left my heart racing. The next, he would retreat into himself, his laughter fading like echoes in a cave, leaving behind a chill that clung to the air.

It was maddening. Each encounter felt like stepping into a live wire. He could flicker between tenderness and distance, and I found myself both exhilarated and terrified, unable to predict what version of him I would get from one moment to the next. Today, he had met me in the library, that sacred space filled with the scent of aged books and polished wood. The way he leaned against the bookshelf, arms crossed and eyes sparkling, made my stomach flutter. But then, the moment I dared to reach for his hand, he pulled away, a cloud passing over his features, leaving me feeling as though I were in the eye of a storm.

"Lucas," I had ventured cautiously, the name tumbling from my lips like a prayer, "what's going on with you?" The question hung in the air between us, charged and electric. He sighed, running a hand through his dark hair, the motion both familiar and foreign. The flicker of something—fear? Regret?—crossed his face, but it vanished before I could decipher it.

"Nothing, really," he had replied, his smile stiff, eyes darting away as if seeking refuge from whatever battle raged within him. "Just... tired, I guess."

Tired. The word reverberated in my mind, heavy and insistent. It was a convenient cover for a deeper turmoil that I could feel but couldn't touch. I had wanted to shake him, to demand he reveal the secrets he seemed so desperate to bury. But something held me back—a fear that if I pressed too hard, he might shatter like fragile glass. Instead, I had swallowed my frustration, nodding along as if I understood, though every fiber of my being screamed that I didn't.

As I sat there in my fortress of solitude, the notes fluttering ominously at the back of my mind, I found myself weighing my options. I could confront Lucas again, pushing him to share whatever shadow loomed over him, but what if it drove him further away? Or I could retreat into the false security of silence, pretending that nothing was amiss. But that choice felt like surrender, and surrender wasn't something I could stomach.

The latest note lay crumpled beside me, a taunting reminder that someone knew too much. "They're watching," it had read, the words scrawled in a jagged hand that set my teeth on edge. I shivered, the very air in my room feeling suddenly thick and suffocating. Who was watching? And why did it feel as if the very walls were closing in on me, trapping me in a web of secrets I didn't understand?

With a burst of determination, I stood up, shaking off the creeping dread that threatened to drag me under. I needed answers—not just for myself but for Lucas too. I had to confront whatever was lurking in the shadows, whether it be the author of those notes or the secrets that hung over Lucas like a dark cloud.

Maybe if I could pull him back into the light, we could face this darkness together.

The night air was brisk as I stepped outside, the stars flickering like distant beacons overhead. Each step toward Lucas's house felt heavy with purpose. The path was familiar, a route I had walked countless times, yet tonight it felt fraught with tension, as if the ground beneath me were alive, crackling with unspoken warnings. My heart pounded in time with the rhythm of my thoughts, all of which spiraled around the same question: What was Lucas hiding?

I approached his door, hesitating for just a moment as the weight of the unknown pressed down on me. I could feel the cool wood beneath my fingertips, grounding me as I knocked softly. The sound echoed in the stillness, and for a moment, I feared he might not answer. But then, the door creaked open, revealing Lucas with that familiar half-smile that both ignited my heart and sent a jolt of anxiety through me.

"Hey," he said, his voice a soothing balm, yet I could see the flicker of uncertainty behind his eyes.

"Can I come in?" The words were out before I could second-guess myself. I needed to talk, to peel back the layers of confusion that wrapped around us both like a shroud.

"Sure," he replied, stepping aside to let me in. As I crossed the threshold, the warmth of his home enveloped me, a stark contrast to the chill I had felt outside. But the warmth was deceptive; the tension hung thick in the air, as if the walls themselves were holding their breath, waiting for the storm to break.

The door closed behind me with a quiet finality, and I found myself enveloped in the comforting chaos of Lucas's room. It was a sanctuary of disarray, with clothes strewn about like the aftermath of an artistic explosion and music notes taped to the walls, their ink faded but the sentiments still vibrant. A part of me always felt at home here, yet tonight, the familiar surroundings only amplified the tension prickling at my skin.

"Make yourself comfortable," Lucas said, his voice carrying a lilt of nervousness that contrasted with the usual ease between us. He flopped onto his bed, running a hand through his hair, the tension in his posture evident. I perched on the edge of a nearby chair, heart racing as I gathered my thoughts. The space between us felt charged, pulsing with unspoken words and half-formed confessions.

"Look, we need to talk," I began, my voice steady despite the turmoil swirling inside me. I studied his face, searching for any sign of the boy who had once laughed freely, the one who had pulled me into a world of reckless adventure. The boy who had kissed me with an intensity that made the universe shrink down to just us.

"Yeah, I figured you might want to," he replied, his tone casual, but his eyes betrayed him—flickering away from mine, a subtle dance of avoidance. It infuriated me. "But maybe we could just... not?" He shifted, creating a space between us that felt palpable, like an invisible wall had risen overnight.

I could feel my heart thumping hard against my ribcage. "Not talking about it won't make it go away, Lucas. I'm worried about you. You've been distant, and these notes... they're getting worse."

He leaned back, folding his arms behind his head as if bracing for a storm. "You worry too much. It's probably just some dumb prank."

"Some dumb prank?" I echoed incredulously. "They're not just notes, Lucas! They're threats. Someone knows things about me—about you—things that no one should know." My voice escalated, fueled by the frustration bubbling just beneath the surface. "I can't just pretend everything is fine when it's clearly not."

A shadow flitted across his face, one that felt all too familiar, like a phantom of a past hurt. "It's better if you don't get involved," he murmured, the words tumbling out like leaves falling from a tree in autumn. "I don't want you to get hurt."

"Then help me understand!" I shot back, unable to mask the desperation seeping into my words. "I can't stand here watching you push me away while I'm getting these notes. I don't want to be left in the dark, Lucas."

He hesitated, the tension in the air palpable, thick as fog. "You don't know what you're asking," he finally said, his voice low, almost a whisper. "You don't know what it means to be in the dark."

The weight of his words hung between us, and for a moment, I considered letting it go, retreating to the safety of silence. But I couldn't. Not anymore. "Try me," I urged, heart racing as I leaned forward, inching closer to the precipice of his guarded world. "I'm not afraid of the dark, Lucas. Not if you're there with me."

He met my gaze then, and for the briefest moment, the walls around him seemed to waver, exposing a glimmer of something raw and genuine. "It's not just my darkness you'd be facing," he said, and I could hear the tremor in his voice, the struggle embedded within.

"Then let me decide for myself," I insisted, the strength in my voice surprising even me. "Let me choose to be part of this. You're not the only one who gets to decide what's dangerous."

"Fine," he snapped, finally sitting up straight, the fight igniting in his eyes. "But don't say I didn't warn you. You have no idea what you might uncover."

My breath hitched, excitement intertwining with dread. "I don't care. I want to know."

He took a deep breath, as if preparing to plunge into icy water. "Okay, but if we're doing this, there's no turning back."

I nodded, resolute. "I wouldn't want it any other way."

The air thickened with anticipation as Lucas stood, running a hand through his hair again—a habit that revealed his agitation. He moved to his desk, rifling through scattered papers and abandoned guitar picks until he finally retrieved a small, weathered notebook.

The cover was faded, and I could see the corners had been creased from frequent use.

"This is my family journal," he said, placing it on the table between us. "It has everything—the good, the bad, and the really bad." His eyes darkened, a storm brewing behind them. "Our family has secrets, things that have haunted us for generations."

I leaned closer, my fingers itching to touch the book, to unravel the mystery that lay within its pages. "Secrets?"

"Yeah, you could say that," he replied, his tone clipped. "It's why I've been... different. I don't want you dragged into it. I don't want you to see the things I've seen, the pain that comes with knowing."

"Knowing what?" My voice was barely above a whisper, the anticipation thrumming through me like a heartbeat.

Lucas took a deep breath, his vulnerability laid bare. "My family is... complicated. There's darkness in our past, things that affect how we are now. The notes, they're connected to that darkness." He paused, searching my face for understanding. "And I've tried to keep you out of it, to protect you."

A chill ran down my spine. "What kind of darkness?"

He shifted uncomfortably, the weight of unspoken truths pressing heavily between us. "The kind that comes with knowing that some battles aren't meant to be fought."

I could feel the resolve tightening around me like a cocoon. "We fight them together. Whatever it is, I'm not afraid, Lucas. Not with you."

He looked at me, a myriad of emotions flickering across his face—fear, relief, anger, and something deeper, a yearning that caught my breath in my throat. "You don't understand," he said, but I could see the barrier he had so carefully constructed beginning to crack.

"Then let me," I insisted, my heart racing with a mix of fear and exhilaration. "Let me understand."

And just like that, the air shifted, crackling with the weight of possibilities, the uncharted territory of our entwined fates unfolding before us like the pages of a long-lost book, waiting for its story to be written.

As I watched Lucas, the weight of the notebook settled heavily between us, like an uninvited guest that demanded attention. He hesitated, fingers brushing the cover as if he were reconsidering whether to unveil the truths nestled inside. I leaned forward, heart racing, eager for him to take the leap and share the stories that would tether us together, even as they threatened to pull us apart.

"Look, whatever it is, it can't be worse than what I'm already facing," I said, my voice steady but laced with urgency. "We're in this together, remember?"

He swallowed hard, his gaze flicking from the notebook to my face, and I could see the internal battle waging behind those deep-set eyes. "I'm not sure you really mean that," he replied, his voice a mix of challenge and concern. "You think you want to know, but the truth could change everything. It could change us."

"Change can be good," I countered, a spark of defiance igniting within me. "Maybe knowing the truth will help us face whatever's out there, instead of running from it. You can't keep hiding behind your walls forever."

With a resigned sigh, Lucas opened the notebook, revealing pages filled with spidery handwriting and smudged ink. "Fine. But promise me you won't freak out."

"Freak out?" I echoed incredulously, leaning closer to catch the first glimpse of the secrets that had weighed so heavily on him. "You clearly underestimate my ability to handle drama."

A ghost of a smile flitted across his lips, but it faded almost immediately, leaving a serious line etched between his brows. He flipped through the pages, tracing a finger over passages as if summoning the strength to share them. "It's not just family drama, you know. It's... complicated."

"Complicated is my middle name." I grinned, trying to lighten the mood, but his expression didn't waver.

He finally settled on a page, the words blurring together as my eyes scanned the delicate script. "The Rowen family has been marked by a curse for generations," he began, his voice low and steady. "It's not just some legend; it's real. Every member has something within them that manifests in dangerous ways. My great-grandfather was the first to—" He hesitated, searching for the right words. "He didn't just make mistakes. He made choices that altered our lives forever. And the notes... they're part of that legacy."

I felt the gravity of his confession settle in my stomach, heavy and unsettling. "What kind of choices?"

Lucas shifted, his posture taut, as if bracing for impact. "The kind that attracted dark attention. You have to understand, the Rowens have always been... special. There are forces that want to use that for their own ends."

I sat back, absorbing his words, the reality crashing over me like cold water. "So, the notes... they're threats?"

"More than that," he replied, the shadows creeping back into his eyes. "They're warnings. Someone knows about our family, about the curse, and they're coming for us."

A chill swept through me, ice settling in my veins. "What do they want? You said it's a curse. How can someone use that against you?"

"It's not just the curse they're after; it's the power it can unlock. If they manage to break it, they could control the Rowens, and everything we are would be at their disposal." Lucas's voice was taut, each word a thread of tension winding tighter around us.

I felt my heart thump painfully in my chest. "And you think I'm in danger because of this?"

"Not just you," he said, locking his gaze onto mine, a storm brewing within. "Anyone close to me. Anyone who gets too close to the truth."

"Then we have to figure this out," I said, a determination surging through me. "We can't let them win. We need to find a way to break this curse or whatever holds you and your family captive."

"Don't you see? It's not that simple," he said, running a hand through his hair again, frustration spilling over. "The more you dig, the more danger you're putting yourself in. You can't fight a shadow if you don't even know where it lurks."

"But I'm already in this," I insisted, my voice unwavering. "We're already in this. I won't just sit back and let someone intimidate me or threaten you. We'll find a way. Together."

His eyes softened, a flicker of appreciation shining through the tumult. "You really are stubborn, you know that?"

"Stubbornness is one of my finer qualities." I smirked, trying to lift the heaviness that hung in the air. But the moment hung in the balance, tension thick enough to slice with a knife.

We stood there for a moment, two souls anchored in an unsettling truth, our fates intertwined more tightly than I'd ever anticipated.

But then, from somewhere deep within the house, a sharp sound pierced the silence—like glass shattering, followed by the unmistakable thud of something heavy hitting the floor. Lucas and I exchanged alarmed glances, the gravity of our earlier conversation fading in an instant.

"What was that?" I whispered, adrenaline coursing through my veins.

"I—I don't know," he stammered, eyes wide as he moved to the door, every instinct screaming at me to follow. "Stay here."

"Like that's going to happen," I shot back, hurrying after him, my heart racing at the prospect of whatever awaited us beyond the door.

As we crept down the hall, the ominous silence amplified every creak of the floorboards beneath our feet, tension coiling tighter with each step. The once-familiar corridors now felt alien, cloaked in shadows that seemed to pulse with unseen threats.

Lucas paused outside the living room door, hand poised on the handle. "Are you ready for this?" he murmured, and the seriousness of his tone sent a shiver through me.

I nodded, fear and excitement mingling into a potent cocktail of anticipation. "Whatever it is, we'll face it together."

With a deep breath, he flung open the door, revealing a scene that jolted the air from my lungs. The room was in disarray, furniture toppled, and the shattered remnants of a glass frame littered the floor. But what caught my eye was a figure standing in the middle of it all—cloaked in darkness, a silhouette that seemed both familiar and terrifyingly foreign.

"Lucas," the figure drawled, voice smooth like silk but edged with something sinister, "you've been a hard boy to track down."

In that moment, I understood that whatever was happening was far more than just a family curse. We were standing at the precipice of a deeper darkness, and it had finally come to claim its due.

Chapter 10: A Taste of Betrayal

The office event buzzed with the kind of energy that thrummed in my veins, an intoxicating blend of laughter, clinking glasses, and the seductive scent of gourmet hors d'oeuvres wafting through the air. I had dressed carefully, choosing a deep emerald dress that hugged my curves in all the right places, hoping to feel both confident and comfortable among the sea of colleagues. Underneath the glittering chandeliers that hung like delicate stars from the high ceilings, everyone seemed lost in their own worlds, caught up in the unspoken hierarchy of ambition and charm that thrived within our corporate walls.

But as I sipped on my second glass of sparkling water, my eyes drifted to a corner of the room where Lucas stood, his back turned to me. He was engaged in a hushed conversation with a man whose presence was like a dark cloud against the bright backdrop of the event. There was something inherently wrong about him—his clothes were ill-fitting, a little too worn and rugged for this upscale gathering. The man's expression was fierce, with a deep furrow carved into his brow and a jaw that could probably slice through glass if given half the chance. I strained to catch snippets of their dialogue, but the distance and the ambient chatter swallowed their words, leaving only the palpable tension hanging between them.

My heart thumped in my chest, each beat echoing a mix of anxiety and curiosity. Lucas had always been the picture of composure, his charismatic smile drawing people in like moths to a flame. But now, his posture was rigid, arms crossed protectively over his chest, his body language signaling an unease I had never witnessed before. What were they discussing that warranted such secrecy? It felt intrusive to observe, yet I couldn't tear my gaze away.

As if sensing my scrutiny, Lucas's head snapped around, our eyes locking for a fleeting moment. His expression shifted from surprise to something darker, a look that could cut glass—a warning etched across his features. The conversation came to a grinding halt, and the other man took a step back, his eyes narrowing at me with a hint of menace before he turned and melted into the crowd like a shadow at dusk.

I fought the instinct to rush over and demand answers. Instead, I waited, heart racing, as Lucas approached me, his brow furrowed in a way that made my stomach twist. There was a part of me that wanted to shout, to unleash my torrent of questions, but the tense atmosphere hung heavy in the air, stifling my words.

"Hey, everything okay?" I ventured, trying to sound nonchalant, as if I hadn't just witnessed something that felt so monumental.

"Fine," he snapped, the edge in his voice like a serrated knife. "What do you want?"

"I just thought you might want to talk about..." I gestured vaguely toward where the man had stood, but he cut me off.

"Drop it, Emily." The steeliness of his gaze sent a shiver down my spine. "It's none of your business."

My heart sank, his words slicing through the facade of warmth I'd been trying to create between us. "It feels like my business when you're talking to someone like that. Who was he?"

He stepped back, putting distance between us, the air between us thickening with unspoken words. "It's complicated," he muttered, refusing to meet my eyes.

"Everything with you is complicated," I shot back, frustration bubbling to the surface. "What is this, Lucas? A game where I'm not invited to play?"

"Just leave it," he hissed, turning on his heel and storming away. I felt the words die on my lips, swallowed by a sense of helplessness that churned in my gut.

That night, as I lay in bed staring at the ceiling, thoughts spiraled like a tornado. What had he meant by "complicated"? What choices could he have made that weighed so heavily on him? The unanswered questions clung to me like shadows, relentless and inescapable.

Around midnight, the sound of knocking jolted me from my restless slumber. Groggy and disoriented, I stumbled to the door, a mix of dread and anticipation thrumming in my veins. I opened it to find Lucas swaying slightly, his eyes glazed, an all-too-familiar hint of alcohol on his breath.

"What are you doing here?" I asked, half-stunned. He stumbled inside, not bothering to answer, and my heart raced with concern.

He collapsed onto my couch, running a hand through his hair, his usually impeccable appearance now disheveled, revealing a vulnerability I had never seen before. "I messed up," he mumbled, voice low and gravelly. "God, I can't even... I don't know where to start."

"Start with the truth," I urged gently, my heart softening at the sight of him—so raw and unguarded.

"I can't," he groaned, leaning back against the cushions. "There are things I've done—decisions that I can't just undo. I thought I could keep it together, but it's all falling apart."

My instincts kicked in, a fierce desire to reach out and comfort him, to peel back the layers of his anguish. "You can tell me anything, Lucas. I promise."

He looked at me then, his eyes shimmering with unshed emotions. "You don't know what you're asking for," he whispered. The words hung in the air like a challenge, daring me to step closer to a precipice I wasn't sure I could handle.

Before I could respond, he abruptly stood, the moment shattered like glass. "I shouldn't have come here," he muttered, the weight of his burdens evident in his voice. "I'm sorry."

"Wait, don't just leave!" I called out, desperation creeping into my voice. But before I could reach for him, he slipped out of my apartment, leaving me in the suffocating silence, questions swirling like smoke in the wake of his departure. I was left alone, the taste of betrayal lingering bitterly on my tongue, each unanswered question echoing in the stillness.

Morning light filtered through the thin curtains of my apartment, casting a muted glow across the living room. I sat curled up on the couch, clutching a steaming mug of coffee that offered little comfort against the turmoil swirling in my mind. The echoes of last night's confrontation played on repeat, like a scratched record that refused to let me escape its relentless grip. Lucas's face lingered in my thoughts—the mix of vulnerability and anger still so raw and haunting.

The muted hum of the city outside did little to drown out the chatter in my head. I was torn between the urge to reach out to him and the instinct to keep my distance, the last remnants of his drunken confession still echoing in my ears. It was maddening, trying to reconcile the magnetic man I knew with the one who had just walked away, leaving a fissure of confusion in his wake.

As I took another sip of coffee, my phone buzzed to life on the table, its screen lighting up with a text from Jess. "Brunch? I need to talk about you and Mr. Mysterious." I couldn't help but smile at her audacity. Jess had a knack for diving headfirst into my life with all the subtlety of a freight train.

I typed back, "Sure, I'll be there in half an hour," and quickly threw on some clothes—a soft sweater that wrapped around me like a warm hug and jeans that hugged just enough in all the right places. The chill of the morning air nipped at my skin, but I welcomed it; it felt grounding against the storm of thoughts still whirling in my mind.

The café was bustling when I arrived, a mix of cheerful chatter and the rich aroma of freshly brewed coffee filling the air. I spotted Jess at a corner table, her hair cascading in loose waves, already animatedly waving at me. She was as radiant as ever, her energy contagious, and I felt a flicker of my mood lift as I approached.

"Finally! I was about to send a search party." She grinned, motioning for me to sit. "So, spill the tea. What happened with Lucas last night? You looked like you'd seen a ghost."

I took a deep breath, the weight of my thoughts threatening to spill out all at once. "It's complicated, Jess. I mean, we had this moment, and then he just left. It's like he wants to talk but is terrified of what that might mean."

Jess raised an eyebrow, leaning in closer as if the details would somehow grant her access to the mysteries of the universe. "So, you're saying he's a hot mess? Classic. And you're a sucker for those, aren't you?"

"Hey!" I laughed, my cheeks warming at the truth in her words. "I'm not saying I'm drawn to chaos. It just... it felt like there was something he wanted to say. Something important. And then he bolted."

"Men are like that. All cryptic and brooding," she said, taking a sip of her mimosa. "You need to confront him. Grab him by the collar and shake some sense into him. Otherwise, you'll just drive yourself crazy."

"I don't want to be that person," I replied, a twinge of guilt curling in my stomach. "What if he's dealing with something serious? I don't want to push him away."

"Or you could just sit back and watch him self-destruct," Jess countered, her tone shifting to something more serious. "You deserve better than a half-hearted conversation. You deserve the full package."

I pondered her words as our brunch order arrived—avocado toast for me and a towering stack of pancakes for her. The flavors burst on my tongue, grounding me as I mulled over my dilemma.

Maybe I was just a coward, afraid to risk the fragile connection we had built.

As we chatted, Jess's attention suddenly shifted, her gaze locking onto something behind me. "Oh great, here comes the storm," she muttered, and I turned to see what had caught her eye.

Lucas stood at the entrance, his demeanor markedly different from the night before. Gone was the vulnerable man who had stumbled into my life, replaced by a crisp, polished version that blended seamlessly into the bustling crowd. The sunlight outlined his figure, sharpening the angles of his jaw, but there was a tightness to his expression that didn't sit right. He scanned the room, eyes landing on me, and the moment stretched uncomfortably, a silence where chaos should have reigned.

"Wow, look at that," Jess whispered, her voice a playful tease. "He's here for you. This should be good."

I shot her a glare, feeling exposed under Lucas's piercing gaze. He approached our table, his smile tight but genuine. "Mind if I join you?" he asked, a casualness that felt forced, as though he were trying to mask the turmoil roiling beneath the surface.

"Sure," I replied, trying to keep my tone light despite the tension in the air. Jess raised an eyebrow at me, clearly amused.

Lucas slid into the seat next to me, his presence both comforting and unnerving. "I didn't expect to see you here," he said, glancing at Jess, who had barely stifled a grin.

"I could say the same," I replied, my heart racing as I took a sip of my coffee, looking for some semblance of courage in the warm liquid. "What brings you out? Coffee and brunch? Or just stalking me?"

He chuckled softly, but it didn't reach his eyes. "A bit of both, I suppose."

Jess, ever the bold one, leaned in. "So, what's the deal with you two? Are we doing this, or should I start planning an intervention?"

"Jess!" I hissed, mortified. Lucas's eyebrows shot up, surprise mingling with amusement.

"I like her," he said, a hint of a smile breaking through his tension. "Very direct."

"Yeah, you'd say that," I muttered, shooting Jess a warning glare.

Before Lucas could respond, Jess deftly changed the topic, her sharp wit cutting through the palpable awkwardness. "So, Lucas, what's your secret? How do you manage to look both charming and slightly menacing at the same time?"

He grinned, a genuine spark igniting in his eyes. "It's a talent. My mother always said I had a knack for keeping people on their toes."

"Is that what we're calling it?" I interjected, feeling emboldened by the banter. "Keeping people on their toes sounds suspiciously like 'I'm too enigmatic for my own good.'"

His laughter danced through the air, warming the space between us. "Maybe you're right. Or maybe I'm just waiting for the right moment to pounce."

"On me?" I shot back, feigning innocence. "How very predatory."

Lucas leaned closer, the playful spark in his eyes intensifying. "Only if you're the prey worth catching."

Just as I was about to retort, my phone buzzed insistently on the table. The moment shattered as I glanced down, my heart dropping when I saw the caller ID flash across the screen. My stomach knotted with anxiety as I accepted the call, the world around me fading into a distant hum.

"Hello?" I answered, my voice unsteady.

"Emily, it's Ryan," came his voice, urgency threading through the line. "You need to come home. Now."

I felt the air shift, an unseen weight pressing down on me. "What's wrong?"

"Just hurry," he said, the tension palpable even through the phone.

I shot a look at Lucas and Jess, who both seemed to sense the change in my demeanor. "I— I have to go," I said, my heart racing as I stood up, already pushing through the crowd, urgency propelling me forward.

"Wait! What's going on?" Lucas called after me, his voice laced with concern. But I didn't stop. Whatever had just shifted in my life, I could feel the pull of something darker creeping in, and I couldn't shake the feeling that it had something to do with him.

The streets felt different as I navigated my way home, the usual hum of city life now replaced by a cacophony of racing thoughts. Each step was heavy, burdened by the weight of Ryan's urgent call. I could almost feel the ground shift beneath me, as if the very city I loved was conspiring against me, twisting into something dark and unknown. My mind flitted back to Lucas, his enigmatic smile, and the way his laughter had seemed to thaw the icy grip of my anxiety just moments before everything changed.

The moment I stepped through my apartment door, the comforting familiarity of my space washed over me. Yet, the air felt charged, thick with an unnameable tension. I dropped my bag by the door, the sound echoing through the silence. Ryan was already pacing the small living room, his brow furrowed, worry etched across his face like an unreadable book cover.

"Emily," he began, his voice low and strained, "you need to know what I found out."

I braced myself, my heart pounding in anticipation. "What is it? Is it about Lucas?"

He hesitated, running a hand through his tousled hair. "It's bigger than that. I was digging into some things... and I found a connection—between Lucas and that guy you saw him with."

A chill swept through me, creeping up my spine. "What do you mean? What connection?"

Ryan stopped pacing, locking eyes with me, a mixture of concern and urgency swirling in his gaze. "The man's name is Samir Kade. He's not just some random guy; he's involved in some pretty shady business. I found reports linking him to illegal deals, blackmail—he's bad news, Emily."

"Why was Lucas talking to him?" The question hung in the air, heavy and suffocating.

"I don't know, but it can't be good." Ryan's voice lowered further, almost a whisper. "You need to stay away from him. This could be dangerous."

"I can't just walk away from him," I shot back, frustration flaring. "I care about him, Ryan. I saw something in him—a side that made me think he was better than this."

"People aren't always what they seem," he replied, his tone firm. "You have to protect yourself first. I don't want you getting mixed up in whatever this is."

I shook my head, my thoughts spiraling. "And if he's in trouble? What if he needs me?"

Ryan took a step closer, his eyes pleading. "Then you help him by staying safe. You don't know what you're dealing with."

The words hung in the air like an unwelcome fog, the reality of my situation crashing down on me. I felt trapped, caught between my feelings for Lucas and the ominous threat looming over us. "I have to talk to him. I need to know what's going on."

"Emily—" Ryan started, but I cut him off, determination flooding my veins.

"Just tell me where I can find him," I insisted, the gravity of the situation igniting a fire within me.

"Look, I don't think that's a good idea. If he's involved with Kade, confronting him could put you both in danger," Ryan warned.

Ignoring his hesitation, I grabbed my phone and sent a quick message to Lucas, my fingers trembling as I typed. "We need to talk. It's important." I hit send, my heart racing as I awaited his response.

Ryan exhaled, watching me with a mix of admiration and worry. "You really think he'll open up after last night?"

"I have to try." I brushed past him, not willing to second-guess my instincts. Lucas might be a riddle wrapped in a mystery, but he was still the one I wanted to trust.

An hour passed like molasses, every minute stretching unbearably long. Just as I began to doubt my decision, my phone buzzed with an incoming call. Lucas's name lit up the screen, and I answered without a moment's hesitation.

"Hey," his voice came through, low and somewhat guarded.

"Lucas, I need to see you. It's urgent," I urged, anxiety threading through my words.

"Can it wait? I'm... busy." There was a heaviness in his tone, a hesitation that made my heart sink.

"No, it can't," I pressed, my resolve hardening. "You were talking to someone last night, and now I'm hearing things about you that I don't like. I can't just sit here wondering."

A long pause stretched between us, filled with unspoken words and unresolved feelings. "Emily, I really can't talk about this right now," he finally said, his voice strained.

"Why not?" I demanded, frustration bubbling to the surface. "If you care about me at all, you owe me that much."

His silence spoke volumes, and I could hear the gears turning in his mind, weighing options I couldn't fathom.

"I'll come to you," he finally said, resignation lacing his tone. "But you need to understand, this isn't just about us anymore. There are things I can't explain."

"Then explain what you can," I urged, desperation creeping in. "I need to know you're safe."

"Just give me a little time." The line went dead, leaving me standing in the middle of my living room, heart racing.

Minutes later, I grabbed my jacket and headed out, determination propelling me forward. The streets felt electric, alive with possibility, but underneath the surface, a current of unease thrummed, hinting at the storm brewing ahead.

As I approached the bar where we'd agreed to meet, my pulse quickened. It was a dive—a place where shadows mingled with the smoky air, and secrets were traded over cheap drinks. I spotted Lucas sitting in a dimly lit corner, his back to the wall, an air of tension clinging to him like a second skin.

"Hey," I said, sliding into the seat across from him. The ambiance shifted as he turned to face me, and for a moment, it felt like we were suspended in time, the chaos of the world around us fading into the background.

"Thanks for coming," he said, but there was a distance in his eyes, a wariness that sent a chill down my spine.

"I couldn't wait any longer. What's going on with you? That man you were talking to—"

"Samir Kade," he interrupted, his voice low. "I don't want you to get involved with him or anyone connected to him."

"Why? What does he want with you?"

Lucas hesitated, the flicker of vulnerability in his eyes threatening to break the carefully constructed walls he had built around himself. "He's not someone you want to know. Let's just say, our connection isn't one I'm proud of."

"What does that mean?" I pressed, leaning in closer.

He ran a hand through his hair, frustration seeping through the cracks of his facade. "It means I made some choices I can't take back. Kade is dangerous, and being associated with him could put you at risk."

My heart sank as the weight of his words crashed over me. "And what about us? Do you even care how this affects me?"

"Of course, I care," he snapped, the sharpness in his voice a veil over the turmoil within him. "But sometimes, caring means staying away."

Before I could respond, the bar door swung open, a gust of wind bringing a sense of foreboding with it. My gaze flicked to the entrance, where a figure stood silhouetted against the light, their posture rigid, scanning the room like a predator hunting for prey.

"Lucas," I whispered, my heart racing as the figure stepped into the bar, revealing a familiar face—Samir Kade.

"Stay close," Lucas murmured, his tone shifting to one of urgency as he reached for my hand. "We need to get out of here, now."

My pulse thundered in my ears, fear gripping me as I processed the implications of Kade's presence. Just as we turned to leave, Kade's voice cut through the din of the bar, smooth and menacing. "Leaving so soon? I was hoping we could have a little chat."

Panic surged through me, and I glanced at Lucas, who was already tensing, ready to protect me from whatever chaos Kade intended to unleash. My mind raced, the reality of the moment crashing in around us. In that instant, I realized we were standing on the edge of a precipice, and there was no turning back.

Chapter 11: Unearthing the Past

The air was thick with the scent of rain-soaked earth as I stepped into Lucas's hometown, a place where every cracked sidewalk and peeling paint whispered stories long forgotten. The sleepy streets stretched out before me like an old quilt, patchworked with memories—some warm, others frayed at the edges. I parked my car in front of a diner that looked like it hadn't changed since the fifties, its neon sign flickering stubbornly against the overcast sky. The bell above the door jingled, and I was enveloped by the aroma of coffee and freshly baked pies. It was comforting, yet the heaviness in my chest reminded me why I was here.

"Can I get you something?" The waitress, an older woman with kind eyes and a hairnet that had seen better days, approached my booth.

"Just coffee, please." I offered a smile, grateful for the normalcy amid my quest for the truth. As I stirred in sugar, I glanced around the diner, taking in the scattered patrons who seemed lost in their own worlds. My heart raced; this was the heart of the town, the place where Lucas had grown up. I needed to talk to someone who could help me understand him.

After a few sips, I summoned my courage and asked the waitress if she knew Lucas. She paused, her hands on the counter, a shadow flickering across her face. "Lucas? The Rowen boy?"

I nodded, urging her to continue.

"He was a good kid," she said slowly, her eyes drifting towards the window, as if peering into a time long past. "But that family... they've had their share of troubles. It's not just him, you know? It's the whole clan."

Intrigued, I leaned closer, my heart pounding with the thrill of discovery. "What do you mean?"

"His father—never was the same after the accident." She hesitated, then added, "That boy had to grow up fast. The family went through hell after that." Her voice lowered, conspiratorial. "There were whispers... scandals. It's a small town, and news travels fast."

"Accident?" I pressed, wanting to pry open the door of his past.

"Car crash. It took his mother," she replied softly, a hint of sadness in her eyes. "The Rowens never quite recovered. People talk about curses, but I think it's just life throwing stones at them."

I thanked her and slipped out of the diner, the weight of her words anchoring me as I wandered the streets. A small park lay nearby, the kind where children would laugh and play, but today it was empty, save for a few squirrels darting through the grass. I found a bench beneath a large oak tree, its branches like skeletal fingers reaching for the sky. Here, I could collect my thoughts and unravel the threads of Lucas's history.

The deeper I dug, the more tangled the story became. Lucas had always seemed so composed, an enigma wrapped in a tailored suit. Yet, each piece I uncovered revealed a fragile boy who had learned to hide his wounds beneath a veneer of strength. I recalled the fleeting moments when his walls would crack—his laughter that never quite reached his eyes, the way he flinched at sudden sounds, as if anticipating something dreadful.

Determined, I sought out the local library, hoping to unearth more about the Rowen family. The building smelled of old books and dust, a musty aroma that felt like a time capsule. I approached the librarian, a middle-aged woman with thick glasses perched precariously on her nose.

"I'm looking for information on the Rowen family," I began, my voice steady despite my racing heart. "Especially Lucas Rowen."

Her brows knitted together in thought. "The Rowens... yes, they're quite a subject around here." She led me to a section of local history, her fingers trailing along the spines of well-worn books. "There are records of their family scandals, if you're interested in that sort of thing."

My pulse quickened as I flipped through the brittle pages of a historical account. There were mentions of wealth lost, accusations of wrongdoing, and lingering grudges that had shaped the town's perception of the Rowens. As I absorbed the details, I felt the specter of Lucas's legacy weigh heavily on my shoulders.

"Did they ever find out who was responsible for the crash?" I asked, a nagging question rising to the surface.

The librarian paused, her lips thinning. "Some say it was an accident, but others believe it was more sinister. The Rowens have always attracted trouble. It's a town full of secrets, my dear."

Her cryptic words hung in the air, making my skin prickle with unease. I thanked her and stepped back out into the gray light, each breath mingling with the scent of impending rain. I was no longer just a curious bystander; I had entered a web of intrigue that wrapped tightly around Lucas and his family.

Back at the park, I sat on the bench again, the cool breeze tousling my hair. The more I learned, the more I wanted to reach out to Lucas, to let him know that he was not alone in his struggles. Yet, the fear of his past consuming him was palpable. Would he allow me in, or was the chasm between us too wide?

As I lost myself in thought, a figure caught my eye. An older man shuffled down the path, his eyes distant, as if he were carrying the weight of decades. He paused in front of me, glancing at the ground, then at me, recognition flickering in his gaze.

"Are you from the Rowens?" he asked, his voice gravelly, edged with curiosity.

I shook my head, swallowing hard. "No, but I'm trying to learn about them. About Lucas."

His expression softened, and he sat down beside me. "The Rowens are good folks, but they've had their share of sorrow. You be careful—some truths are best left buried."

I nodded, feeling the gravity of his words. But I was determined to unearth the past, to understand the man I was falling for, no matter the shadows it cast.

"Do you know what really happened?" I pressed, hopeful for clarity amid the murky waters of secrets.

His gaze drifted back to the ground. "What I know is a story of love and loss, just like any other," he murmured, lost in thought. "But their love, it turned into a curse that haunts them still."

With that, he rose and ambled away, leaving me in a whirlpool of emotion. I was entwined in Lucas's history now, each revelation a thread binding me closer to the heart of the mystery. The path before me was fraught with danger, but the promise of understanding burned bright. I would not let Lucas fight his demons alone, not when I had the strength to stand beside him.

The next morning, the clouds hung low, heavy with the promise of rain, and I felt the weight of my purpose as I meandered through the streets of Lucas's hometown. The town was a patchwork of history, each building a chapter in a story that seemed to blend seamlessly into the others. I passed the local grocery store, its windows adorned with faded posters advertising sales on milk and bread, and imagined a young Lucas running through the aisles, his laughter ringing out like a bell, before the shadows had taken root in his life.

My first stop was the town's historical society, an unassuming brick building that seemed to lean against the earth for support. Inside, the walls were lined with sepia-toned photographs and yellowing newspaper clippings, each one a glimpse into a time when the Rowens were woven into the fabric of this community. I approached the receptionist, a woman with a name tag that read "Marge," whose bright smile belied the decades etched into her face.

"Good morning! How can I help you?" Her enthusiasm was infectious.

"I'm looking for information on the Rowen family," I replied, my voice steady despite the anxious flutter in my stomach. "Specifically, Lucas Rowen."

Marge's smile faltered slightly, as if she'd stepped on a hidden nail. "The Rowens have quite the reputation around here. What are you looking for?"

"Anything you can share," I pressed, my heart racing. "I'm trying to understand his past."

She nodded slowly, her gaze drifting as if she were sorting through memories. "Well, Lucas's family has been here for generations. His mother was a beloved figure—always baking cookies for the kids and hosting town events. But after she died..."

The air grew thick with unspoken words, and I leaned in closer, urging her to continue.

"After that, everything changed," she continued, her voice barely above a whisper. "Lucas's father became distant, consumed by grief. They say he was never the same after the accident, and the town's view of the family shifted. Rumors started to swirl, particularly about their wealth. Some thought it was ill-gotten gains, others whispered about hidden secrets."

"Secrets?" I asked, intrigued.

"The kind that fester in small towns," she replied, a knowing glint in her eye. "People here love to talk. Some say Lucas has had to shoulder burdens no boy should have to bear. He grew up fast, and I reckon he's still running from whatever demons haunt him."

My mind raced, piecing together the fragments Marge provided. Lucas was not just a man cloaked in mystery; he was a young man molded by tragedy, battling shadows that extended far beyond what I could see.

"Do you know if Lucas ever talks about his family?" I inquired, hoping for a nugget of insight that would bridge the gap between the man I knew and the boy he once was.

Marge shook her head, a frown creasing her brow. "He keeps to himself. When he comes back to visit, it's like he's a ghost—haunting the familiar places but never truly present. If you want to learn more, you might check the old newspapers. There's bound to be something there."

Thanking her, I made my way to a small reading room filled with dusty volumes and the scent of paper long untouched. As I flipped through the brittle pages of archived newspapers, a sense of urgency surged within me. Each article was a piece of the puzzle—stories of charity events that had dwindled, mentions of Lucas's father in police reports, and rumors that hinted at something darker.

One article caught my eye: "Tragedy Strikes the Rowens: A Family Legacy in Jeopardy." The headline screamed of intrigue and calamity. The article detailed the car accident that had taken Lucas's mother, but it also alluded to a feud with another local family that had left scars on the Rowen name. My heart raced as I absorbed the details, each word painting a more vivid picture of the pain Lucas had endured.

As I poured over the texts, the door creaked open, and a figure stepped inside—an older man, his face lined with the weight of years. He wore a baseball cap and a plaid shirt, exuding a sense of familiarity that instantly made me feel at ease.

"Are you doing some digging into the past?" he asked, his voice warm and gravelly.

I nodded, not wanting to divulge too much just yet. "Just trying to learn more about the Rowens."

He sighed, a sound that carried a mix of nostalgia and sorrow. "They're a good family, despite what folks say. Lucas's mother was like sunshine. She made everyone feel special." His eyes clouded with memories, and I could tell he missed her just as much as Lucas did. "After she died, the whole town changed. People turned on the Rowens. I think they were just looking for someone to blame."

"I've heard about the accident," I said softly, keen to coax more from him. "What really happened?"

His brow furrowed, and he leaned closer, lowering his voice. "They say it was an accident, but there are always whispers. Some think it was more than that—like someone wanted to hurt them." He glanced around as if expecting eavesdroppers. "You should be careful. The Rowens are more than just a family; they're a legacy with roots that run deep. And digging into those roots can uncover things best left buried."

"Like what?" I pressed, the thrill of mystery wrapping around me like a warm embrace.

He hesitated, weighing his words. "People get protective of their stories, especially when they've been wronged. If you care for Lucas, tread lightly. There are things in his past that could hurt him more if they resurface."

His warning hung in the air like a specter, both ominous and compelling. I needed to know more. Lucas was worth the risk, and whatever darkness loomed in his past, I would face it head-on.

Leaving the historical society, I was filled with an electric anticipation. I wasn't just gathering facts; I was unraveling a tapestry of emotions, each thread leading back to Lucas. The rain began to fall, soft at first, then a downpour, but I welcomed it. It washed over me, cleansing the doubts I carried and invigorating my resolve.

Back in my car, the wipers swished rhythmically, their steady cadence matching the pulse of my racing heart. I would reach out to Lucas, and this time, I wouldn't shy away from what I had discovered. The truth, however painful, could be the key to unlocking the door he had sealed so tightly. And as the storm raged outside, I realized that perhaps it was time to embrace the chaos, to step into the storm, and confront the shadows together.

Rain drummed against the windshield, creating a rhythmic backdrop that mirrored the turmoil churning inside me. I had gathered a wealth of information, yet it felt like only the surface of something much more profound. As I drove through the winding roads that led back to the Rowen mansion, the once-comforting familiarity of my own life began to feel distant. The warmth of my world had been eclipsed by shadows that clung to Lucas, shadows I was determined to illuminate.

Pulling into the mansion's gravel driveway, I felt a mixture of trepidation and resolve. The grand structure loomed above me, its windows darkened by the stormy sky, like eyes closed against the world. I stepped out, the rain soaking through my clothes almost instantly, but I welcomed the chill as a reminder of my purpose. I needed to confront Lucas, to share what I had learned, and to let him know he was not alone in facing his demons.

As I entered the mansion, the familiar scent of polished wood and aged books greeted me, but today it felt suffocating, as if the walls themselves held their breath. I moved through the halls, my footsteps echoing in the stillness until I reached the library. It was my favorite room—full of secrets and stories, just like Lucas.

He sat there, a lone figure bathed in the soft glow of a reading lamp, a book resting closed on his lap. The moment our eyes met, I felt an electric pull, a connection that transcended words. But before I could speak, he held up a finger, silencing me.

"Before you say anything, let me guess," he said, a wry smile playing on his lips, though the spark in his eyes was dulled by the weight of unspoken burdens. "You've been digging into my family history again, haven't you?"

"You could say that," I replied, my heart pounding as I took a seat across from him. "And I found some things—things you might want to know."

He leaned forward, a flicker of interest crossing his features. "Go on."

With each word I shared, I watched as a myriad of emotions flickered across his face—surprise, pain, and something akin to relief. "So, they really think there's more to the accident?" he asked, his voice a mixture of disbelief and longing. "That it wasn't just a tragic mishap?"

"People talk, especially in a small town," I explained. "But it sounds like your family was dealing with more than just loss. There were feuds and whispers of betrayal."

Lucas's expression hardened. "My family isn't the only one with secrets. The whole town has them." He ran a hand through his hair, revealing the cracks in his usually composed facade. "You shouldn't have to shoulder my burdens, you know."

"I'm not trying to shoulder them, Lucas. I want to understand you," I said, my voice steady. "You don't have to face this alone."

He sighed, and the weight of his burdens seemed to crush him. "I spent so long pretending I was fine, but every time I come back here, it's like stepping into a trap. The past doesn't just stay buried; it seeps through the cracks."

"I'm here to help you dig it out," I offered, my resolve unwavering. "We can confront it together."

The tension in the room shifted, an unspoken acknowledgment passing between us. The storm outside rumbled, shaking the glass panes, and I couldn't help but feel it mirrored the turmoil brewing within Lucas. Just as I opened my mouth to press further, there was a loud knock on the front door, jolting us both.

"Who could that be?" Lucas muttered, frowning as he stood up.

"I don't know, but I'd rather not find out," I replied, instinctively moving to follow him. My heart raced as he approached the door, a sense of foreboding creeping in.

He opened it, revealing a drenched figure standing on the porch. It was a man in his forties, with sharp features and eyes that glinted like polished stones. He held a small briefcase and wore a look of both urgency and determination. "Lucas Rowen?" he asked, his voice deep and commanding.

"Yes, that's me," Lucas said cautiously, stepping back to allow the man entry. I hung back, my instincts on high alert.

"Good. We need to talk." The man's gaze darted to me, then back to Lucas. "It's about your family."

"What about my family?" Lucas's tone shifted, a defensive edge creeping in.

"I have information regarding your mother's accident—information that changes everything."

The air in the room thickened as the stranger spoke, each word cutting through the tension like a knife. Lucas's expression darkened, and I felt my heart stutter, caught between the weight of his history and the unknown future that loomed.

"Who are you?" Lucas demanded, his posture shifting, a protective instinct igniting within him. "Why should I trust you?"

"My name is Daniel Kline," the man replied, his voice steady despite the storm raging outside. "I was a detective assigned to your mother's case. I've spent years tracking down the truth, and I think I've finally found it."

"Tracking down the truth?" Lucas repeated, incredulity coloring his tone. "What could possibly change what happened that night?"

"More than you can imagine." Daniel stepped closer, his gaze piercing. "But it's not just about your mother. It's about your family's legacy and the shadows that have haunted you all."

As the rain continued to lash against the windows, I felt the gravity of the moment envelop us, an impending storm of revelations ready to be unleashed. The weight of Daniel's words hung heavy in the air, each syllable promising to unravel everything we thought we knew.

"Lucas, wait—" I started, but the urgency in Lucas's eyes cut me off.

"Tell me everything," he demanded, his voice a mix of anger and desperation.

And just like that, the room shifted, a quiet resolve settling in, as if we had stepped into a new reality—one where the past was not only alive but ready to confront us head-on. The storm raged on outside, but inside the mansion, a different kind of tempest brewed, one that threatened to expose all the dark secrets we had fought so hard to uncover.

Then, as Daniel began to speak, the power flickered, plunging us into darkness, a sinister foreshadowing of the chaos that was about to unfold.

Chapter 12: A Moment of Weakness

The engine sputtered and wheezed one last time before succumbing to silence, leaving me stranded in an expanse of nothingness. The pavement stretched endlessly before me, flanked by tall grass that swayed in the evening breeze like waves caught in an unseen tide. I glanced at my phone, but the screen displayed only the dreaded "No Signal" message, a stark reminder that I was utterly alone in this desolate stretch of road. The sun was dipping below the horizon, casting a golden hue over the landscape that belied the sense of dread gnawing at my insides.

I stepped out of the car, hoping for a miracle—a passing car, a friendly face, anything to pull me from this unsettling solitude. But as I surveyed the empty road, a chill ran down my spine. It wasn't just the encroaching night; there was something else lurking in the periphery of my awareness. I scanned the surroundings, my heart hammering in my chest, when a figure emerged from the shadows. He stepped forward, his features sharp and defined, illuminated by the waning light.

My breath hitched as recognition hit me like a punch to the gut. This man was not a stranger; I had seen him before—his face was woven into the fabric of Lucas's stories, a ghostly presence that hovered in the edges of our conversations. He had been an apparition in Lucas's past, a figure shrouded in whispers and warnings, and here he stood, flesh and blood, his eyes a piercing gray that seemed to dissect my very soul.

"Why are you here?" he demanded, his voice low and gravelly, sending tremors through the stillness of the evening. The way he spoke was both accusatory and protective, a strange mix that set my nerves on edge.

"Who are you?" I asked, my voice steadier than I felt.

"I'm someone who knows Lucas better than he knows himself," he replied, his expression hardening. "And I know the danger you're putting yourself in. Leave him alone."

The air grew thick with tension, and the last rays of sunlight flickered like a candle on the verge of snuffing out. My pulse raced as I felt the weight of his words. It was an ultimatum wrapped in a warning, and I couldn't help but feel a rush of anger swell inside me. Who did he think he was, telling me to abandon the one person I was determined to understand? "You don't know me," I shot back, my voice rising defiantly. "You don't get to dictate my choices."

He took a step closer, and I caught a hint of something in his expression—a flicker of concern hidden behind his bravado. "You think you're being noble? This isn't a game. There are things about Lucas that can't be revealed, things that could put you in harm's way."

"What do you mean?" My stomach twisted at his words, a knot of anxiety tightening within me. I couldn't shake the feeling that I was teetering on the brink of something monumental—something that had been building since the moment I set foot in Lucas's world.

"You're curious. I get that. But curiosity has a price, and you're not ready to pay it," he said, his tone darkening as the shadows of the encroaching night deepened around us. The road behind me seemed to whisper in agreement, an unsettling echo of the warnings reverberating in my mind.

Before I could respond, the tension shattered like glass when I pulled out my phone, my fingers shaking as I dialed Lucas's number. It rang only once before I heard his voice, a mix of relief and anger evident in his tone. "Where are you? Are you okay?"

"I—" I hesitated, glancing back at the man who still loomed in the shadows, his eyes boring into me like daggers. "I'm on the road, my car broke down, and—"

"Stay put. I'm coming," he interrupted, the authority in his voice soothing yet alarming. I couldn't explain it, but I felt the weight of his presence even over the phone, his protective instincts igniting a flicker of hope amid the darkness.

As the call ended, the man took another step forward, his gaze intent. "You think he's going to save you? You're a fool if you believe that. You don't know what you're getting into." His words cut through the air, leaving a chill that seeped into my bones.

I couldn't let fear dictate my actions. "Maybe I don't know everything," I countered, refusing to back down. "But I'm not afraid to find out."

"Bravery isn't always a virtue, girl," he sneered, and just as the tension reached a boiling point, I saw headlights piercing through the darkening sky. Lucas's car, a sleek black silhouette against the fading light, came barreling down the road, his furious expression visible even from a distance. My heart soared at the sight, a lifeline thrown into the fray.

The man before me turned, a mix of frustration and resignation etched into his features. "You really think you can protect her?" he muttered under his breath as Lucas skidded to a halt beside me, his car's engine humming ominously in the stillness.

Without a word, Lucas opened the door and pulled me inside, the warmth of his presence flooding over me like a protective blanket. I glanced back, but the man was already retreating into the shadows, a specter swallowed by the night.

"Are you okay?" Lucas demanded, his voice low and tense, the concern in his eyes making my heart ache.

"I'm fine," I said, though my voice wavered. "Just some weird guy giving me the third degree."

He gripped the steering wheel, knuckles white with tension. "You shouldn't have called me. I told you to stay away from this."

"Too late for that," I replied, my defiance pushing back against his anger. "I need to understand what's happening."

"Understanding doesn't always bring safety," he warned, his gaze fierce as he pulled away from the roadside. The scenery blurred past, and I felt the weight of the conversation settle like a storm cloud between us.

"I can handle it," I insisted, even as doubts trickled in, doubt mingling with a determination that refused to wane. There was a darkness lingering in the edges of our lives, and I wasn't about to turn away. Not now.

The car's interior was a cocoon of warmth, a stark contrast to the chill that clung to my skin as we sped away from the abandoned road. Lucas's jaw was set, his profile taut with frustration. He kept his eyes trained on the road ahead, the streetlights casting fleeting shadows across his face, illuminating the tension that had settled like a thick fog. The engine purred reassuringly beneath us, but I could feel the storm brewing in the silence, an unspoken weight pressing down on both of us.

"What did he say to you?" Lucas finally broke the stillness, his voice low but laced with an edge that made me hesitate. The worry etched into his features was unmistakable, as if the very air between us crackled with unasked questions.

"He warned me about you," I replied, the words spilling out before I could think better of them. "Said I should leave you alone, that there are things I don't understand."

His grip tightened on the wheel, knuckles white against the dark leather. "And did you listen?" There was an intensity in his gaze that sent a thrill of unease racing through me, a reminder that I was stepping into a world that was as alluring as it was dangerous.

"I didn't call you to be saved, Lucas," I shot back, surprising myself with the heat in my tone. "I called because I need to know the truth, and if that guy thinks he can intimidate me into backing off, he's got another thing coming."

Lucas glanced at me, a flicker of admiration breaking through the storm clouds of his frustration. "You're stubborn, you know that?"

"Maybe," I allowed, a smirk playing at the corners of my lips. "But I think you might like that about me."

A brief smile danced across his face, but it vanished as quickly as it appeared, replaced by the weight of his thoughts. "This isn't just about us anymore. That man—he's connected to my past in ways I can't explain. You're playing a dangerous game."

"Dangerous? Try exhilarating." I leaned back in my seat, crossing my arms defiantly. "I refuse to be a pawn in someone else's story. If I'm going to be part of this—whatever it is—I deserve to know everything."

"Do you even hear yourself?" Lucas shot back, his voice rising. "You think it's a game, but it's not. There are people who will go to great lengths to keep these secrets buried. This isn't just about curiosity; it's about survival."

His words hung in the air, thickening the tension. A part of me wanted to recoil at the thought of real danger, but another part—perhaps the rebellious streak that had propelled me to this moment—thrust me forward. "Then tell me," I demanded, my voice steady. "Tell me what I'm up against. If you care about me at all, you'll let me in."

He took a deep breath, and for a fleeting moment, I saw a flicker of vulnerability beneath his stoic facade. "It's not that simple. I want to protect you, not drag you into this mess."

"Too late for that," I replied, my heart racing as I watched the emotions flicker across his face—fear, anger, and something softer, something like longing. "You already dragged me in when you let me see a glimpse of your world."

A silence settled between us, pregnant with possibility and uncertainty. I could sense the internal struggle waging within him, a battle between his instinct to shield me from harm and his desire to let me in. Finally, he exhaled sharply, turning to face me fully.

"There are secrets that could destroy us both, and I can't let you get hurt because of my past."

"Tell me about your past," I urged, leaning closer. "Let me help you carry it. If you want to protect me, you have to start by trusting me."

He hesitated, eyes darting back to the road, where streetlights flickered like distant stars. I could see the gears turning in his mind, weighing the risks against the potential of letting me in. With a resigned sigh, he slowed the car, pulling off onto the side of the road where darkness enveloped us like a shroud.

"Fine," he said, his voice barely above a whisper. "But you have to promise that if things get too dangerous, you'll walk away."

"I promise," I replied, my heart pounding as he shared the fragments of his life—the shadows that lingered behind his every smile, the burdens he had carried in silence. "I'm listening."

"The man you saw—his name is Cole. He's part of a group that has been watching me for years, ever since..." His voice trailed off, and the silence stretched, pregnant with the weight of unspoken words.

"Ever since what?" I pressed gently, sensing the vulnerability in his tone.

"Ever since my family got involved in something they shouldn't have," he said finally. "Something dangerous. There were... consequences, and Cole has been trying to clean up the mess ever since."

I furrowed my brow, trying to piece together the puzzle. "What kind of mess?"

"The kind that leaves scars. My family had connections to people who dealt in darker trades—smuggling, information brokering—things that put us on the radar of people who don't take kindly to loose ends. Cole was part of a faction that tried to keep the fallout from hitting us, but it didn't always work."

His gaze was distant, lost in the echoes of his memories. "I thought I had escaped that life when I left home. But it's always been there, lurking just beneath the surface. And now, it seems like it's creeping back into my life, into yours."

The gravity of his words sank in, and I felt a mixture of dread and resolve. "So Cole thinks I'm a threat because I'm close to you?"

"Exactly," Lucas said, his voice tight. "He believes that anyone who gets too close might unearth old secrets or become a target."

"Is that why you pushed me away? Because you thought I couldn't handle it?" My heart thumped loudly in my chest, a cacophony of emotions swirling within me.

"I didn't want to see you get hurt. I thought it would be easier if you stayed away," he confessed, the frustration ebbing from his tone.

"And look where that got us," I said, a hint of a smile breaking through the tension. "You still ended up here with me, spilling your secrets on a deserted road."

He let out a low chuckle, the sound wrapping around us like a warm embrace. "Yeah, I suppose I did."

In that moment, something shifted between us, the air thickening with an unspoken understanding. I had seen beneath the layers he wore like armor, glimpsed the boy he had been before the world turned him into the man he was now. My heart ached for the burden he carried and, for the first time, I felt the weight of our shared journey settle comfortably on my shoulders.

"You don't have to do this alone, you know," I said softly, reaching out to touch his arm, feeling the tension in his muscles relax just a fraction. "I'm here, no matter how dark it gets."

His gaze softened, and I could see the flicker of hope mingling with uncertainty. "I want you here. But I also want you safe."

"I'll take my chances," I declared, a grin breaking across my face. "What's life without a little risk?"

Lucas shook his head, a half-smile tugging at his lips, but I could tell he wasn't convinced. The road ahead was shrouded in shadows, and though we were still enveloped in darkness, I felt a spark of light beginning to illuminate the path.

The silence in the car stretched out, thickening with unsaid words and heavy emotions. As we drove further from the deserted road, the lights of town flickered like distant stars, each one reminding me of the growing storm swirling between us. Lucas's expression was a mix of concern and frustration, and I could feel the tension radiating from him like heat from the asphalt.

"Look, I didn't ask for your life story, but I appreciate the effort," I said, attempting to lighten the mood, though my heart wasn't fully in it. "Besides, I thought secrets were supposed to be intriguing. You've practically turned this into a dark, brooding romance."

He shot me a sideways glance, a hint of amusement breaking through the clouds of his irritation. "You think this is funny? I'm trying to keep you out of danger, and you're turning it into some kind of twisted plot twist."

"Twisted plot twist? Oh, please! That's my specialty. Besides, if danger's involved, you know I'm in. It's not like I have a penchant for knitting or baking." I couldn't help but grin, hoping to coax a smile from him.

Lucas sighed, his shoulders relaxing slightly as he refocused on the road. "You really have a knack for making everything sound trivial, don't you?"

"I prefer to think of it as a coping mechanism. Lighten the mood before we drive off a cliff," I replied, crossing my arms as a shiver ran through me, not entirely from the chill in the air.

The streetlights faded, and we found ourselves on the outskirts of town, surrounded by tall trees that stood like sentinels in the dark.

The landscape felt different here—more foreboding. The shadows felt alive, shifting and whispering secrets that made my heart race. I turned to Lucas, wanting to probe deeper, to pull the layers back, but something in his demeanor warned me against pushing too hard.

"Why did you really leave home?" I asked instead, my voice softer now, almost vulnerable.

He hesitated, a muscle ticking in his jaw. "I thought I could escape the past. I wanted to create a life that wasn't dictated by my family's mistakes."

"By running away?" I challenged gently, sensing the pain hidden beneath his bravado.

"By making my own choices," he countered, his voice sharpening. "I didn't want to be a prisoner of their legacy."

The weight of his words hung in the air, heavy with unfulfilled dreams and fractured hopes. I could see the boy he had once been, burdened by expectations and a family's dark legacy, trying to carve out a piece of the world for himself. It was both heartbreaking and empowering. "But you're still tied to it, aren't you? This Cole guy, the past that's chasing you down."

"Every day," he admitted, his voice barely a whisper. "I can't run forever, and I won't let anyone else get hurt because of it."

Before I could respond, the car suddenly lurched to a stop, the headlights illuminating a figure standing in the middle of the road. My heart dropped as I recognized him—the same man who had confronted me earlier. This time, his expression was cold and calculating, the shadows deepening around him like a cloak.

"What are you doing here?" Lucas growled, his body tense, ready to spring into action.

"I came to warn you," the man replied, his voice dripping with contempt. "You're meddling in things you don't understand. She needs to leave—now."

I pushed open the door, adrenaline flooding my veins. "What do you want from me? Is it Lucas you're after, or is this about something else?"

"Both," he said simply, his gaze flickering from Lucas to me, sizing us up like a predator assessing its prey. "You're a liability. And if you keep digging, you'll regret it."

The air crackled with tension, and I could feel Lucas's fury simmering beside me. "Get out of the way," he demanded, his voice low and menacing. "I won't let you intimidate her."

The man smirked, his eyes glinting with a dark amusement. "You think you can protect her? You're just one more mistake in a long line of them. Your family's mess is about to catch up with you."

"Leave my family out of this," Lucas retorted, anger lacing his words like a whip.

"Too late for that," the man said, stepping closer, his silhouette imposing against the pale glow of the headlights. "Your past has a way of resurfacing. And when it does, it won't just be you who suffers. She'll be caught in the crossfire."

I exchanged a glance with Lucas, my heart racing. The stakes were higher than I had anticipated, and the weight of his past felt like a noose tightening around us. "What does that mean?" I asked, my voice trembling slightly despite my best efforts to remain composed.

"It means you should leave while you still can," he replied, his tone chilling. "There are forces at play that you can't begin to comprehend."

Lucas's hand clenched into a fist beside me, his anger palpable. "I'm not going to let you scare her into submission. I'll protect her, even if it kills me."

"Oh, it will," the man shot back, his voice low and taunting. "That's the point."

In an instant, he lunged forward, and instinct took over. I grabbed Lucas's arm, pulling him back just as the man reached us.

But as I did, the world around us exploded into chaos. The headlights flickered ominously, plunging us into darkness for a split second before illuminating the scene again. The man was no longer just a shadow but a tangible threat, his presence looming like a storm cloud ready to unleash hell.

"Get in!" Lucas shouted, shoving me back into the car as he threw the vehicle into reverse, tires screeching against the pavement. The man lunged at the open door, his fingers grazing the edge as we tore away, the thrum of my heartbeat echoing in my ears.

"We can't let him follow!" I gasped, panic creeping into my voice.

"I know," Lucas replied, his jaw set with determination. He swerved the car onto a narrow side road, the trees whipping past us like phantoms. I could see the man in the rearview mirror, his figure shrinking into the distance, but a sickening feeling settled in my stomach—this wasn't over.

The adrenaline coursed through my veins, mingling with an unshakeable sense of foreboding. As we sped away, I couldn't shake the feeling that we had crossed a line, one from which there would be no return. "What do we do now?" I asked, my voice trembling.

Lucas's expression hardened as he focused on the road ahead. "We figure out what he knows, and we prepare for whatever comes next. Because I promise you, this isn't the end."

Just then, a loud crash echoed behind us, followed by a blinding flash of light. I spun around in my seat, my breath catching as I realized that the man had somehow caught up, the remnants of a vehicle slamming into a tree, flames erupting behind him like a signal flare.

"Oh my God," I breathed, staring wide-eyed at the chaos unfolding. But before I could process what was happening, the world around us plunged into darkness, and a deafening silence engulfed everything.

As Lucas gripped the wheel tighter, the weight of uncertainty loomed heavy in the air, and I couldn't shake the feeling that we were hurtling toward a reckoning—one that might change everything we thought we knew. The darkness enveloped us, and just when I thought I could breathe again, the car suddenly jolted, a loud bang echoing through the night, and I felt the wheels lose grip beneath us.

"What's happening?" I gasped, my heart racing as we skidded off the road and into the unknown, spiraling into a void that threatened to swallow us whole.

Chapter 13: Boundaries Broken

The air was thick with tension, a palpable charge that hummed between us, making every breath feel heavy and electric. Lucas stood across the room, his jaw clenched tight enough that I feared he might shatter something—perhaps the unspoken trust we'd built over the past few months. Shadows danced on the walls, cast by the flickering candlelight, illuminating the storm raging in his blue eyes. My heart raced, caught between the desire to retreat and the undeniable urge to confront the truth that lay festering just beneath the surface.

"How could you?" His voice was a low growl, each word dripping with the bitterness of betrayal. "You think you can just waltz into my life, poke around in the darkest corners, and expect everything to be fine?"

I stood my ground, though my stomach churned with the weight of his words. "I'm not trying to pry, Lucas. I just want to understand you. I want to help."

"Help?" he spat, incredulous. "You have no idea what you're asking. You think you can fix this? You think you can fix me?"

The accusation stung, sharper than I had anticipated. A lump formed in my throat, threatening to choke off my response. "I never said you were broken. I just—I care about you. I want you to let me in."

"Caring doesn't erase the reality of my life," he shot back, stepping forward, closing the distance between us until I could feel the heat radiating off his body. "You don't know what it's like to live with this constant fear, to know that every time you turn around, you're one wrong move away from losing everything."

The truth of his words hung between us like an unyielding fog, suffocating and all-consuming. I took a deep breath, inhaling the faint scent of his cologne mingled with the bitterness of his frustration. I could see the cracks in his armor, the flicker of vulnerability that he desperately tried to hide. It was both terrifying and thrilling, a glimpse into a part of him that he kept guarded like a treasure in a secret vault.

"Then tell me," I urged, my voice softer, coaxing. "Let me in. I want to know your fears, your burdens. You don't have to carry them alone."

A flicker of surprise crossed his features, but it was quickly replaced by the hard lines of his anger. "You think it's that easy? Just spill my guts to you and everything magically gets better?"

"No," I replied, my heart aching at the thought of his pain. "But I can't help if you don't let me see you. All of you."

For a long moment, silence enveloped us, the weight of our words filling the space with an intensity that was almost tangible. I felt the walls around my heart cracking, a mixture of fear and yearning clawing at me. I didn't know how to reach him, how to bridge the chasm that separated our realities. Yet, I stood there, willing to bear the risk, to plunge into the depths of his darkness if it meant we could find a way back to each other.

His gaze softened, just for an instant, and in that moment, the tension shifted. The air between us crackled with something different—an unspoken promise. It was a dangerous invitation, one that led to the edge of a precipice, where we might either plunge into the abyss or soar into something transcendent.

And then, as if the universe conspired to push us over that edge, the air shimmered with a feverish energy. Lucas stepped closer, and before I could draw another breath, he closed the distance between us completely. His hands found my waist, pulling me in with a desperate intensity that stole my breath and ignited a wild fire within me. The world around us faded, leaving just the two of us suspended in a moment where nothing else mattered.

His lips met mine with an urgency that felt like a storm breaking free, fierce and consuming. The kiss was a collision of raw emotion, a clash of fear and longing that we had both kept buried for far too long. I melted against him, surrendering to the sensation, to the dizzying rush of connection that surged through me. My hands tangled in his hair, pulling him closer, as if I could merge our hearts together and chase away the shadows lurking at the edges of our lives.

But even as our bodies moved in perfect harmony, a nagging whisper echoed in the back of my mind, reminding me that this was just a moment—one fraught with complications and unresolved truths. Our passion was a wildfire, beautiful and destructive, and I could feel the heat threatening to engulf us both. The intimacy we forged in that single breath made the distance between our realities painfully evident.

The next morning, I awoke wrapped in the warmth of his embrace, the sunlight spilling through the window, casting a golden hue across the room. Lucas lay beside me, his expression relaxed in sleep, a stark contrast to the storm that had brewed between us just hours earlier. A rush of affection washed over me, mingling with an unsettling awareness that our night together hadn't erased the weight of his secrets or my own.

As I traced my fingers lightly across his arm, a mix of elation and trepidation bubbled within me. There was an undeniable bond forged in the chaos of our confrontation, yet the specter of his past loomed large, a reminder that our moment of connection was built on a fragile foundation. I didn't know how to navigate the path ahead, didn't know if we could bridge the divide between his fears and my longing to understand. The truth was that love, in all its glorious complexity, was never as simple as we hoped.

The morning light streamed through the thin curtains, illuminating the space in soft hues that felt like a warm embrace. As I lay there, cocooned in the blankets and the lingering warmth of Lucas beside me, a sense of serenity washed over me, tempered only by the weight of reality lurking just beneath the surface. The memories of our passionate night felt like a fever dream, vivid yet tinged with uncertainty. I could feel his breathing, steady and deep, like a soothing rhythm that wrapped around my racing thoughts.

I was still grappling with the intensity of our connection, wondering how one night could shift the foundation of everything we knew. My heart thrummed with the exhilaration of love, yet I could hear the distant echoes of the fight we'd had, the accusations that had been flung like arrows. A part of me cringed at the thought of facing him when he woke, unsure of how to bridge the gap between our intimate moment and the unresolved tension that still hung heavily in the air.

When he finally stirred, his eyes fluttering open, I caught a glimpse of vulnerability that mirrored my own. "Morning," he mumbled, voice thick with sleep. There was a softness in his gaze that sent a thrill coursing through me, a reminder of the fierce boy who had fought for his secrets just hours before.

"Morning," I replied, trying to sound casual, even as my heart raced. "Sleep well?"

He chuckled, a low, rumbling sound that reverberated through my chest. "Well, better than usual. I can't remember the last time I felt this... relaxed."

The word hung in the air, thick with meaning. Relaxed. It felt like a fleeting promise, an oasis amid the chaos. I propped myself up on one elbow, meeting his gaze with a cautious smile. "I suppose we can credit that to my questionable decision-making skills."

Lucas arched an eyebrow, amusement dancing in his eyes. "Questionable is an understatement. You know I could have ended up as an angry panther again if you kept poking around my life."

A playful smile tugged at my lips. "At least then I'd have a good excuse for needing a new wardrobe."

"Ah, yes, the tragedy of losing clothes to a shapeshifting rage," he said, feigning a dramatic sigh. "Truly heartbreaking."

I couldn't help but laugh, the sound filling the space between us with lightness. But beneath the laughter, the truth loomed like a shadow. The momentary reprieve only highlighted the reality of the world we inhabited, where laughter was often chased away by the heavy burdens we carried.

"What are you thinking?" he asked, his tone shifting as he studied my face, the humor fading to concern.

I hesitated, the words dancing on my tongue, caught between my desire to share and the instinct to shield him from more hurt. "I just—"

"Just what?" he pressed, the intensity in his eyes sharpening. "We can't keep pretending that everything is fine. You know that, right?"

"I know," I admitted, the truth spilling out in a rush. "But I also know that we can't just ignore what happened. It changes everything, Lucas. You can't keep me at arm's length and expect me to stay."

He ran a hand through his hair, the gesture both familiar and foreign, as if he were wrestling with thoughts that were too heavy to bear. "I didn't mean to push you away. It's just... I've spent so long guarding my heart, building these walls to protect myself, and now you're here, crashing through them. I don't know how to navigate that."

The sincerity in his voice struck a chord deep within me, and I could feel the connection we'd forged tighten like a lifeline. "You're not alone in this, you know. I'm not here to judge or fix you; I just want to be part of your life. But I can't do that if you keep hiding."

Silence fell between us, thick and loaded with unspoken words. My heart ached for him, a mixture of love and frustration boiling beneath the surface. I could see the turmoil in his eyes, the battle raging between the desire for connection and the fear of vulnerability.

"Maybe I'm just not good at this," he finally said, his voice barely above a whisper. "Being close to someone. Letting them in."

"Then we'll figure it out together," I insisted, feeling the weight of our shared journey. "One step at a time."

With a flicker of hope lighting his features, Lucas nodded, the resolve in his eyes slowly returning. "Okay, but if we're doing this, I need to be honest with you. There's a lot about my life you still don't know. Things that could put you in danger."

I swallowed hard, a mix of apprehension and determination swirling within me. "Then tell me. All of it."

His expression shifted, a battle of emotions playing across his face. I could see the struggle—his instinct to shield me, to protect me from the storm that was his reality, battling against the undeniable pull of our connection. "It's not just my life. It's the whole family. You don't know what you're getting into."

"But I want to know," I pressed, my heart racing with both fear and excitement. "If we're going to make this work, I need to understand. I can't stand in the shadows anymore."

"Alright," he said, the weight of his decision hanging heavily in the air. "But I need you to promise me something. If it gets too dangerous, if you feel like you're in over your head, you have to walk away."

"Promise me the same," I countered, my voice firm. "I won't run from this. I want to be here, even when it's hard."

As our eyes locked, a quiet understanding passed between us, a fragile yet unbreakable bond that shimmered with the potential of what lay ahead. The journey we were embarking on felt daunting, like standing at the edge of an abyss, but together, we would face whatever came our way.

We spent the morning wrapped in conversation, the laughter gradually returning as Lucas opened up about the shadows that loomed over his family. Each revelation was a layer peeled back, exposing the scars that had shaped him into the boy I had come to love. With every story, every truth laid bare, the distance between us shrank, replaced by an intimacy that felt both exhilarating and terrifying.

As the sun climbed higher, casting a golden glow across the room, I felt the warmth seep into my bones, igniting a fierce determination within me. I would stand by him, fight for him, and together we would face whatever darkness threatened to overshadow our light.

The morning stretched languidly around us, golden rays of sunlight filtering through the curtains, illuminating the tangled sheets that bore witness to our restless night. I watched Lucas as he stirred, his expression shifting from slumber to awareness, and I felt an irresistible urge to reach out and trace the lines of his jaw, to memorize the way he looked in this moment of quiet vulnerability. But the memory of our heated exchange loomed like a storm cloud, reminding me that this tranquility was precarious, balanced on the knife's edge of unspoken truths.

"Hey," I said softly, hoping to break the lingering tension that hung in the air like thick fog. "What are you thinking?"

He blinked, his gaze searching mine, perhaps gauging if I was ready for the weight of his reality. "Just... wondering how we got here. It feels surreal."

I chuckled lightly, but the nervousness in my chest churned. "Surreal is one word for it. I mean, who would've thought a heated argument would lead to a passionate night? It's almost cliché."

"Cliché is what happens to other people," he countered, the hint of a smile playing at the corners of his lips. "In our case, it was merely inevitable."

The levity in his tone brought a warmth that spread through me, easing some of the tension that had taken root. But reality crept back in, a shadow lurking just out of reach. "So, about last night... Do we talk about it, or just pretend it never happened?"

Lucas's smile faded, replaced by the familiar look of contemplation that had danced across his features during our earlier conversation. "I think we need to talk about it. It's not just the chemistry; it's the whole situation. There's too much at stake for us to gloss over it."

I nodded, biting my lip as I turned serious. "What do you want to say?"

He took a deep breath, the weight of the world reflected in his eyes. "I want to tell you everything. About my family, the curse, the danger that comes with it." He hesitated, as if grappling with how much to reveal. "But I don't want to scare you away."

"Lucas, I'm not afraid of the truth. I'm afraid of losing you because we didn't have this conversation." My voice wavered slightly, a mix of fear and determination. "You've opened up to me before, but this feels different. More serious."

"Because it is different. I've kept you at a distance for a reason. This isn't just about me anymore. It's about us—what we are now—and I don't want to drag you into something dark and dangerous." His expression hardened, a protective edge creeping back into his demeanor.

"Maybe I'm not as fragile as you think," I challenged gently, my heart racing at the sincerity in my words. "I want to be a part of your life, Lucas. I can't do that if you keep shutting me out."

He ran a hand through his tousled hair, a sign of his internal struggle. "Okay. Then let's do this. But promise me, if it ever becomes too much, you'll tell me. No holding back."

"Promise." I reached out, taking his hand in mine, a gesture meant to bind our intentions with warmth and sincerity. The warmth of his palm enveloped my fingers, grounding me in the moment.

"Where do I start?" he asked, his voice dropping to a whisper as if afraid the walls would eavesdrop.

"Start at the beginning. How did it all happen?"

Lucas inhaled sharply, his eyes clouding with memories that must have been painful to sift through. "My family has always had... peculiar traits. Each generation is cursed with a spirit of the Zodiac. It manifests as an animal—like my panther—and when we're touched or embraced by someone of the opposite sex, we transform. It's a legacy that's both a blessing and a burden."

I leaned closer, intrigued. "So you're telling me you're part cat? That's kind of amazing."

He shot me a sideways glance, a hint of amusement breaking through his somber expression. "Not exactly the kind of amazing I'd choose, but yes. And when I transform, I lose control. There's a primal instinct that takes over, and it's dangerous."

"Dangerous how?" I asked, the earlier lightness fading as I sensed the gravity of his words.

"Each time I shift, I risk exposing my family. If someone discovers our secret, it could mean disaster for us all. My family has been hunted for generations, and I've spent my life trying to protect them."

A shiver ran down my spine as the implications sank in. "And if you lose control while you're with me...?"

His grip tightened around my hand, a silent reassurance. "That's why I pushed you away. I was scared of what might happen if you got too close. I didn't want to hurt you."

"You won't. I promise," I insisted, squeezing his hand back. "But you have to trust me, Lucas. We're in this together now, no matter how complicated it gets."

He looked down, a flicker of vulnerability washing over him. "You don't know what you're asking. There are people who would love to exploit my family's curse. The closer you get, the more danger you invite."

"Then let me help you. Let me help us." My heart raced with a mix of adrenaline and fear, the stakes rising with every word. "Whatever it takes, I'm in."

Lucas's expression shifted, uncertainty mixing with something more profound, more hopeful. "You're serious about this?"

"I am." I took a deep breath, the gravity of the moment pressing against my chest. "We can face it together. But first, we need to get ahead of this. If there are people hunting your family, we need to know who they are and why."

Just as he opened his mouth to respond, the sharp chime of Lucas's phone cut through the tension, vibrating against the nightstand. He shot me an apologetic glance as he reached for it, a shadow of concern crossing his features. "It could be my family."

The phone screen lit up with an incoming call, and Lucas's expression shifted from relaxed to tense in a heartbeat. "It's my cousin, Madeline," he said, answering the call with a practiced calm that masked the unease bubbling just beneath the surface.

"Lucas?" Madeline's voice crackled through the speaker, urgent and strained. "We need you back at the house. It's happening. They're here."

My stomach twisted at her words, the weight of reality crashing down like a tidal wave. Lucas's eyes widened, a flash of fear flickering across his face. "What do you mean? Who's here?"

"They found us," she replied, panic threading through her tone. "We're outnumbered. You need to come now."

The finality in her voice sent chills through my body. I could feel the room shift, the warmth of our connection evaporating into a chill of dread. As Lucas hung up the call, the gravity of the situation settled heavily between us.

"This is it, isn't it?" I breathed, my heart pounding. "They're coming for you."

"I can't let you get involved in this." His voice was firm, a protective instinct rising to the surface. "It's too dangerous."

"But I'm already involved, Lucas!" I shot back, my voice rising with desperation. "You can't just push me away again."

He looked torn, the weight of the impending storm mirrored in his eyes. "I need you to stay here, safe."

"Safe? And let you face this alone?" I shook my head, the determination surging within me. "No. We do this together."

Before he could respond, the sound of heavy footsteps echoed from outside the door, followed by a loud, ominous knock that rattled the frame. My heart raced, panic clawing at my throat.

"Lucas, they're here," I whispered, the reality settling over us like a shroud.

With a determined look, he grabbed my hand, pulling me close. "Whatever happens next, we stick together. No matter what."

I nodded, heart hammering in my chest, knowing that this was the moment everything would change. The door creaked open, shadows spilling into the room, and I braced myself for the chaos that was about to unfold, my heart pounding in rhythm with the impending storm.

Chapter 14: Under Siege

The rain drummed against the window, a steady rhythm that mirrored the anxiety bubbling in my chest. I stood in the dim light of my apartment, the air thick with the scent of dampness and unease. My mind raced back to the afternoon I had discovered the crumpled note tucked beneath the windshield wiper of Lucas's car—a note that had become the catalyst for our descent into this turmoil. Each word was etched into my memory, an ominous reminder of how quickly life could spiral out of control. Stay away from him. You don't know what he's capable of.

That note had felt like a whisper from the shadows, but as the days passed, those whispers transformed into threats that were all too tangible. The vandalized car, with its shattered windows and defaced paint, was a cruel message—one that turned Lucas's protective instincts into a battle with his own frustration. The break-in at my apartment had felt like a violation, a chilling reminder that we were not just under surveillance but under siege. And the package that arrived, wrapped in brown paper and tied with a string, brought with it a fresh wave of fear. Inside, glossy photos of us—smiling, laughing—were interspersed with dark scrawls warning me to back off. My heart sank, a weight that pressed on my lungs, as I struggled to breathe through the encroaching dread.

"Look at this." Lucas's voice cut through my spiraling thoughts, his tone firm yet laced with concern. He stood in the center of my living room, the flickering candlelight casting shadows across his features, revealing the tension etched around his eyes. I turned, clutching the edge of the kitchen counter, feeling the cool granite beneath my fingertips as if it could ground me. He unfolded the crumpled note from the package, the paper trembling slightly in his grip. "This isn't just about us anymore. They want to instill fear."

"Then let's give them something to really fear," I replied, surprising myself with the steel in my voice. I had never been one to confront danger head-on. The thought of self-defense was an abstract concept I had never considered, but here I was, embracing it out of necessity. I could feel Lucas's gaze steadying me, as if he were weighing my resolve against the backdrop of the chaos unfolding around us.

He nodded slowly, a hint of admiration flashing across his features, chased by the shadows of his past. "We'll face this together. But I need you to be committed, to understand that this isn't just training—it's a fight for our safety."

And so began our unorthodox training sessions. Each evening, after the shadows lengthened and the world outside faded into night, Lucas would guide me through the basics. The first time I felt his hands guiding mine as he demonstrated a block, it sent a thrill through me, a mixture of fear and exhilaration. His movements were fluid, a dance that belied the seriousness of our circumstances. I was clumsy at first, stumbling over my own feet as I tried to mirror his precision, but he never laughed. Instead, he encouraged me, his eyes brightening when I finally executed a move correctly.

"You've got it, but remember, it's about instinct. Trust yourself."

I could see the determination etched into his face, the way his brow furrowed in concentration, hinting at deeper scars, both physical and emotional. This wasn't merely self-defense for him—it was a means of coping with a world that had betrayed him, a world where trust was a fragile illusion.

"Why are you so good at this?" I asked one evening, breathless from the exertion, leaning against the wall as he paused to catch his breath. The scent of sweat and determination mingled in the air around us, and I felt a rush of warmth at the thought of the bond we were forging in this unusual way. "Did you really have to fight like this before?"

His expression shifted, shadows dancing across his features as if they were wrestling with his memories. "You could say I've had some experience. The man we're dealing with... he was a friend once. We fought side by side, trusted each other implicitly." His voice cracked, and he turned away, as if to shield himself from the past that threatened to swallow him whole. "But he chose power over loyalty. When you betray someone like that, it changes everything."

The weight of his confession hung between us, thickening the air. The vulnerability in his voice resonated within me, igniting a fierce need to protect not only myself but him as well. I stepped closer, closing the distance between us, my heart racing at the intimacy of the moment. "I'm here, Lucas. Whatever's coming, we'll face it together. I promise."

He looked down, a flicker of something softer passing through his guarded demeanor. "I don't want to drag you into this," he murmured, a plea wrapped in uncertainty.

"I'm already in it," I insisted, my resolve crystallizing. "Besides, what's the point of fighting if you're doing it alone? I may not be strong yet, but I'm willing to learn."

With each session, I grew stronger, both physically and mentally. The training became a refuge, a way to channel our fears into something constructive. Yet, beneath the surface, the threat loomed larger. Lucas's haunted eyes reminded me that we were racing against time, and I couldn't shake the feeling that something worse lay ahead.

As the night wore on, the storm outside intensified, echoing the tumult within my heart. With each clap of thunder, I wondered how long we could hold off the shadows threatening to consume us, and whether we had the strength to fight back. But amid the chaos, there was a flicker of hope—a bond forged in adversity, a partnership that transcended the boundaries of fear.

In the days that followed, our training sessions morphed into something akin to an intricate dance, each movement layered with purpose. As Lucas guided me through techniques, we fell into a rhythm that felt both comforting and fierce. I could see how the physical exertion was cleansing for him, pushing back against the weight of his past. We were two warriors in a world that felt increasingly hostile, grappling with shadows that loomed larger with every passing day.

One evening, as we took a break, sprawled out on the hardwood floor of my living room, I propped my head up on my hand, watching him wipe the sweat from his brow. The light from the streetlamp outside filtered through the curtains, casting stripes of gold and shadow across his face. "You know, for someone who trains in self-defense, you sure are a terrible cook," I teased, trying to lighten the mood that had grown heavier with each threat.

Lucas chuckled, a sound that vibrated with a mix of relief and resignation. "Cooking was never a priority when survival was the only thing on the menu." His tone was playful, but there was an underlying truth that weighed heavily in the air. I couldn't help but admire the way he navigated his vulnerabilities, how he could laugh at himself even in the face of danger.

"Maybe I should teach you how to boil water," I suggested, pretending to consider it seriously. "I hear it's a fundamental life skill."

"Boiling water is overrated," he replied, rolling onto his back and gazing up at the ceiling. "I prefer the culinary arts of takeout."

"Ah, the lost art of takeout," I mused, leaning back to join him in staring at the ceiling, letting the absurdity of our conversation wash over me like a balm. "Next, you'll tell me that you've never had a homemade lasagna in your life."

"Homemade? Please. The closest I've gotten to that is a frozen meal that probably has a shelf life longer than my career as a fighter."

We shared a laugh, the sound light and bright against the backdrop of our grim reality. But as quickly as the humor flickered to life, the shadows crept back in. The conversations that followed turned more serious, and I could feel the tension tightening around us like an unwelcome embrace.

As the sun dipped below the horizon, transforming the sky into a canvas of deep purples and blues, I felt a shift in the air. The familiar buzz of my phone jolted me from my reverie. I glanced at the screen and felt my stomach drop. Another text from an unknown number, the message ominous and taunting: You think you're safe, but you're not. He will pay.

I looked up at Lucas, whose expression shifted from light-heartedness to concern in an instant. "What is it?" he asked, his voice low, a mix of dread and urgency.

"It's another threat," I whispered, my heart racing. "They're not letting up."

He took the phone from my hand, scanning the message with narrowed eyes. The anger that flashed across his face was palpable, a heat that ignited something fierce within me. "This has to end," he said, determination lacing his voice. "We need to confront him, the one behind all of this."

I felt a rush of adrenaline at the thought. "Confront him? Just like that? You want to storm in like superheroes and demand answers?"

He met my gaze, the intensity of his eyes sending a shiver down my spine. "We can't keep waiting for him to make the next move. This is our lives on the line."

"Okay, but do we even know where to find him?"

He leaned back, running a hand through his hair, a gesture of frustration. "I have a few leads. He's been lying low, but he can't hide forever. We just need to outsmart him."

"Outsmart him, huh? So, we're going with the brains over brawn approach?"

"Exactly," he replied, the corner of his mouth quirking into a half-smile. "We'll be the underdogs. People love a good underdog story."

"Great! But I prefer to keep my underdog status to my cooking skills, thank you very much."

The tension broke for a moment, and laughter filled the room again, a fleeting moment of normalcy amidst the chaos. But as the laughter faded, the reality of our situation loomed heavy, and I felt the weight of the decision pressing down on us.

"Let's meet tonight," Lucas suggested, his voice firming with resolve. "I can gather what I know, and we can make a plan."

I nodded, my heart thudding in my chest. The excitement of action mixed uneasily with the fear of what lay ahead. As we made our way out, the rain had turned to a steady drizzle, the world outside slick and glistening, each streetlamp casting a halo of light that felt both inviting and foreboding.

The café we chose was dimly lit and almost deserted, save for a few scattered patrons engrossed in their own lives. Lucas had ordered coffee before I even arrived, a testament to his preparedness. The warmth of the cup wrapped around my fingers, grounding me as I took a sip, letting the bitter taste settle against the sweetness of the moment.

"Alright, spill it," I said, leaning forward. "What's the plan?"

He leaned in closer, the serious nature of our conversation lending an air of intimacy to our surroundings. "I've been doing some digging. His name is Derek, and he has connections—powerful ones. He was my partner once, but when the opportunity for gain arose, he threw everything away."

I felt the gravity of his words sink in, wrapping around my mind like a thick fog. "You mean he turned on you?"

"Not just on me. On everything we built together." His jaw tightened, the muscle flexing under the strain of repressed emotion. "We had dreams, you know? Plans to make something bigger. But greed changed him."

"And now he wants to take us down."

"Exactly." Lucas's gaze hardened. "But we're not going down without a fight."

As we plotted our course, I couldn't help but admire the fierce determination radiating from him. It was more than just a resolve to protect himself; it was a fierce loyalty to everyone who mattered to him, including me. I felt a surge of something warm and fierce in my chest. We weren't just fighting for survival anymore; we were fighting for each other.

The rain drummed against the windows, a relentless reminder of the storm brewing outside, and I couldn't shake the feeling that we were on the brink of something monumental. The stakes were high, but for the first time since this all began, I felt a flicker of hope sparking in the depths of my being. Together, we would face whatever came next, two warriors against the darkness, ready to reclaim our lives from the shadows that threatened to engulf us.

As we delved deeper into our plans, the café's ambiance shifted, the dim lighting casting long shadows that danced on the walls, mirroring the tension that seemed to thrum in the air around us. Lucas leaned back, crossing his arms, his brow furrowed in concentration. "Derek has a way of making people underestimate him. He plays the long game, waiting for the right moment to strike. We need to outmaneuver him, catch him off guard."

I took a deep breath, the scent of freshly brewed coffee mingling with the distant aroma of pastries. "Okay, so how do we lure him out? It's not like he's going to just walk into a trap."

Lucas's lips twisted into a wry smile, the kind that held both mischief and danger. "Actually, I have an idea. Derek has always had a weakness for the thrill of the hunt. If we can create a scenario that draws him in, we might just catch him off guard."

I raised an eyebrow, intrigued. "Go on. You've piqued my interest."

He leaned in closer, lowering his voice as if sharing a closely guarded secret. "We stage a confrontation, somewhere he wouldn't expect—an abandoned warehouse I know. We make it look like I'm vulnerable, that I've got something he wants."

"Something he wants? What exactly?"

"A few old files he thinks are lost. He won't be able to resist."

It was a bold plan, but I felt a tingle of excitement at the thought of putting ourselves in the line of fire. "And if things go south?"

His gaze locked onto mine, a spark igniting between us. "Then we improvise. We've come this far; we can't back down now."

As the words hung in the air, I felt the gravity of our situation settle around us. We were taking a leap into the unknown, threading a delicate line between bravery and folly. But there was something intoxicating about the risk, a thrill that coursed through my veins as if I had finally stepped into the life I was meant to lead—one filled with danger, loyalty, and a fierce bond with Lucas that felt unbreakable.

With a shared understanding, we made our way back to my apartment, the streets slick and glistening under the streetlights. My heart raced in sync with the rhythm of the rain tapping against the pavement. The air was thick with anticipation, a storm brewing that mirrored the tumult of our plans.

Once inside, we set to work. Lucas rifled through his old documents, pulling out anything he thought might be relevant. I found myself caught between the weight of the mission and the warmth that flooded my heart every time he glanced my way. "You know," I said, trying to lighten the atmosphere as I handed him a stack of papers, "if this whole fighting crime thing doesn't pan out, you might have a future in undercover work. You have that whole 'mysterious stranger' vibe down pat."

He chuckled, a low, rumbling sound that sent a thrill through me. "And you'd be my sidekick? The master of disguise?"

"I can totally pull off a wig," I quipped, flipping my hair over my shoulder dramatically. "I'd even learn how to twirl it like some secret agent."

"Don't let it go to your head, Miss Twirl-It." He shot back, a playful glint in his eyes that grounded me amidst the chaos.

With our banter, the weight of the situation felt a little lighter, but as we prepared, the tension crept back in like an unwelcome guest. Lucas laid out a series of maps, each marked with potential escape routes and hiding spots. As we reviewed our plan, I couldn't shake the feeling that something was off.

The phone rang, breaking the silence that had settled like a thick fog. My heart leaped into my throat as I glanced at the screen. Unknown. I exchanged a wary look with Lucas, who nodded.

"Answer it," he urged, his tone serious.

I swallowed hard, steeling myself as I pressed the button. "Hello?"

A voice crackled on the other end, distorted and low. "You think you're clever, don't you? Setting a trap for Derek?"

My heart dropped, dread pooling in my stomach. "Who is this?"

"Just a friend. Consider this a warning. You're playing a dangerous game."

"Are you working for Derek?"

The laughter that followed was chilling. "Let's just say I know how he operates. You don't want to get caught in his web."

"What do you want?"

"Nothing you can provide. Just... tread carefully. You're in over your head."

The line went dead, leaving a hollow silence that rang in my ears. I looked at Lucas, my breath hitching. "That was... unsettling."

"Unsettling is an understatement." He took a deep breath, the lines of worry etching deeper into his forehead. "We need to move fast. If they know our plans, they could be preparing to counter us."

My stomach twisted as I processed the implications. "So we have a mole? Someone feeding him information?"

"That's what it sounds like," he said, his voice laced with frustration. "We have to be smarter about this. No more slip-ups."

I nodded, feeling the weight of our situation pressing down on us once more. We couldn't afford to let our guard down. As night fell, I felt the shadows deepen, a suffocating blanket that wrapped around us both.

We spent the next few hours fine-tuning our plan, strategizing every possible angle. I could feel the energy buzzing between us, a mix of tension and anticipation. But as we prepared to leave, the world outside felt eerily quiet.

Lucas turned to me, his expression serious. "Are you ready for this?"

I met his gaze, determination igniting within me. "More than ever."

We stepped outside, the air crisp against our skin. The rain had let up, leaving the streets shimmering under the pale glow of the streetlights. We drove toward the warehouse, the headlights cutting through the darkness, illuminating the path ahead.

As we approached the location, a sense of foreboding settled in my chest. "What if Derek isn't alone?" I asked, glancing sideways at Lucas, who was focused on the road.

"He'll have someone with him," he admitted. "But we'll be prepared. We have to trust our instincts."

The warehouse loomed ahead, a hulking structure that seemed to breathe shadows. The moment we parked, a shiver ran down my spine. Lucas turned to me, his eyes fierce and unwavering. "No matter what happens, we stick to the plan."

I nodded, the gravity of our mission settling over us like a cloak. We crept toward the entrance, my heart racing in time with the heavy thud of my footsteps. The atmosphere felt thick, charged with unspoken tension.

As we slipped through the door, the darkness enveloped us, and I could feel the pulse of adrenaline coursing through my veins. The air inside was stale, filled with the scent of rust and decay, a perfect hiding place for secrets.

"Remember," Lucas whispered, his voice low, "stay close."

We moved deeper into the shadows, my breath hitching as every creak of the floorboards seemed to echo like a siren's call. Suddenly, I caught a glimpse of movement at the far end of the warehouse. My heart seized, and I glanced at Lucas, who nodded, signaling me to remain silent.

But before we could react, a figure stepped out from the darkness, his silhouette unmistakable. Derek stood there, a smirk playing on his lips, flanked by two burly men. "I see you've decided to play the hero, Lucas," he taunted, his voice dripping with disdain. "But you've come to the wrong place."

The tension crackled in the air, and I could feel the world tilting beneath me, the stakes higher than ever. The realization that we had walked straight into a trap sank like a stone in my stomach, and with it, the chilling dread that this confrontation was just beginning.

Chapter 15: Trust Tested

The air in the room felt heavier after Lucas's call, like a thundercloud pregnant with rain. He stood there, phone in hand, his expression a mix of confusion and dread. I could almost see the gears turning in his head, twisting thoughts into knots. My heart pounded as the silence stretched between us, thick and oppressive, like the humid air just before a summer storm. He finally looked up, his blue eyes clouded with a shadow I had never seen before. It sent a chill racing down my spine.

"I have to go," he said, his voice low and strained. Each word felt like a punch, dull yet unyielding, in the pit of my stomach. The room suddenly felt like a cage, the walls closing in around me, suffocating me with uncertainty.

"Go? Go where?" I managed to stammer, forcing myself to meet his gaze. The instinct to reach out, to hold him close and anchor myself to the warmth of his presence, was nearly overpowering. But the distance in his eyes told me this wasn't just a casual trip. It was a necessity, a compulsion born from a world I had only just begun to understand.

"I can't talk about it," he replied, the edge of desperation creeping into his voice, the unspoken words hanging heavily in the air between us. It was as if he had slammed a door on everything we had built together in this fragile oasis of trust.

I wanted to argue, to push him for answers, but instead, I swallowed my fears and forced myself to nod. He was a fiercely private person, and I had long ago accepted that some things were meant to remain buried. Yet, the thought of him disappearing into the unknown felt like an anchor dragging me into the depths of the ocean.

"How long?" My voice was barely above a whisper, but the question echoed loudly in my mind. What if he didn't come back? A thousand scenarios played out like a terrible movie in my head—him lost in some distant city, unable to find his way home, or worse, never wanting to return.

"A few days," he said, but the certainty in his voice felt flimsy, like a spider's web trembling in the wind. I caught a glimpse of the raw vulnerability behind his bravado, and it stirred a protectiveness in me that felt foreign yet familiar.

"Promise me you'll be safe," I said, desperation coloring my tone. I wasn't sure if I was asking him to keep himself safe or if I was begging him not to slip away from me.

"Always," he replied, though the tremor in his voice betrayed the strength he was trying to project. He stepped closer, the familiar scent of his cologne wrapping around me like a comforting blanket, but it felt so much less reassuring now, laced with an undercurrent of fear.

With a lingering glance that seemed to etch itself into my memory, he turned and walked away. The sound of the door clicking shut reverberated through me, each second stretching into an eternity, amplifying the silence that enveloped the house like a shroud.

The emptiness that filled the space where Lucas had been was suffocating. I tried to shake it off, forcing myself to move around the house, engaging in menial tasks that had once felt comforting. I organized books on the shelf, wiped down countertops, and sorted through papers that had accumulated like dust in the corners of my mind. Yet, every creak of the floorboards, every whisper of wind against the window felt like a reminder of his absence.

The hours dragged on, each tick of the clock a reminder of his growing distance. I found myself reaching for my phone more often than I cared to admit, half-expecting a message from him, but the screen remained stubbornly blank. The silence in the house became a cruel companion, echoing my insecurities as they crept back, gnawing at my resolve.

I tried to engage in distractions, calling Jess and Melissa, but their voices felt distant, their laughter echoing hollowly in my ears. "You need to get out," Melissa insisted, her cheerful tone clashing with the storm brewing in my heart. "Let's do something fun. You can't just sit there alone."

I knew she meant well, but the thought of leaving the house felt impossible. I wanted to scream at the universe for this feeling of powerlessness, for the unknown that threatened to swallow me whole. Instead, I stayed rooted to my chair, staring out the window as the sky deepened into shades of purple and gray, a reflection of the tumult inside me.

As the sun dipped below the horizon, the shadows lengthened and curled around the corners of the room like a predator waiting to pounce. The reality of our situation seeped into every corner of my mind—Lucas was out there, facing whatever danger had pulled him away, while I was stuck here, helpless and afraid.

I wrapped my arms around my knees, pulling them close to my chest as a sense of dread settled over me. What if he never returned? The thought was a bitter pill to swallow, filling my mouth with the metallic taste of fear. It wasn't just the fear of losing him; it was the fear of facing this reality alone, of walking through the world without the person who had become my anchor, my light in the darkness.

Just then, the sharp trill of my phone broke the silence, slicing through my spiraling thoughts. My heart raced as I lunged for it, praying it was Lucas. Instead, it was a message from Jess. "Come over. We miss you," it read, but I knew it was more than that; it was an attempt to pull me back into the warmth of friendship.

I hesitated, glancing toward the door as if Lucas might walk through it at any moment. But he didn't, and the weight of solitude pressed down on me. I knew I needed to go, to break the chains of anxiety that bound me to this place, if only for a little while. With one last glance at the empty space where he had stood, I grabbed my keys, determined to step into the night and reclaim a piece of myself.

The car ride to Jess's felt surreal, the world outside blurring into a smear of twilight hues—pinks and purples bleeding into deep blues. I was still wrapped in the haze of uncertainty, the words Lucas had left hanging in the air like an unfinished melody. I fumbled with the radio, searching for something to drown out the thoughts that clawed at my mind. When a peppy tune finally burst forth, I couldn't help but chuckle at the stark contrast to my inner turmoil.

How could anyone sing about love when I felt so completely unmoored?

Pulling into Jess's driveway, I parked and sat for a moment, collecting my thoughts like loose change scattered on the floor. I took a deep breath, hoping to draw in a hint of the comfort and familiarity that awaited me inside. Jess was a force of nature—her laugh had a way of brightening even the dimmest days. But beneath that laughter, I sensed something deeper. Her unwavering loyalty had a fierceness that made me believe she could take on the world and win.

I knocked on the door, the sound echoing in the quiet evening. A moment later, it swung open to reveal Jess, her hair tumbling over her shoulders in wild curls, an apron tied around her waist. She was a whirlwind of energy and enthusiasm, even after a long day at work.

"Look who finally decided to join the land of the living!" she exclaimed, pulling me into a bear hug that squeezed the air from my lungs.

"It's not like I was hiding under a rock," I replied, managing a half-hearted smile.

"More like sulking on your couch," she teased, ushering me inside. The warmth of her home enveloped me, a stark contrast to the chill of uncertainty I had left behind. The aroma of freshly baked cookies wafted through the air, a smell that felt like a hug for my soul.

"Is that chocolate chip?" I asked, my stomach rumbling as if it had a mind of its own.

"Duh! I'd never make you suffer through oatmeal raisin. Who even likes those?" Jess rolled her eyes dramatically, leading me to the kitchen.

As we settled at her small dining table, adorned with a festive centerpiece, I tried to shake off the remnants of anxiety that clung to me like a second skin. "So, what's the plan, oh glorious hostess?"

"Well, first, you eat," she insisted, sliding a warm cookie across the table. "Then we talk. You look like you could use a few dozen calories to help with whatever is eating you alive."

I picked up the cookie, taking a bite that felt like biting into a slice of heaven. The chocolate melted in my mouth, and for a moment, it chased away the fear gnawing at my insides. "Lucas had to leave," I finally confessed, the words spilling out before I could stop them.

"Leave? Like, for a trip? Or leave, like, forever?" Jess's brow furrowed as she studied my face.

"Just for a few days," I reassured her, but the tremor in my voice betrayed me. "He got some kind of urgent call, but he won't say who it's from or what it's about."

"That sounds... suspicious." Jess leaned back in her chair, her arms crossed.

"I know," I said, the worry creeping back in. "But I have to trust him, right? I can't just jump to conclusions."

"Trust is a two-way street, my friend. It's like that metaphorical bridge that's only as strong as the two people walking across it." She paused, then added with a sly grin, "But I'm pretty sure you've got some great support beams."

I couldn't help but smile at her attempt to lighten the mood. "You're insufferable, you know that?"

"Absolutely," she replied, her laughter infectious. "Now, let's talk about this plan. You and I are going to have a girls' night—complete with cheesy rom-coms and snacks galore. I've got a whole stash of popcorn waiting to be devoured."

"Cheesy rom-coms, huh? Is that really the cure for my angst?"

"Of course! What's better than watching people stumble through love while you sip wine and eat your weight in snacks?"

I couldn't argue with that logic. The evening unfolded with laughter and banter, each joke and playful jab acting as a balm for my anxieties. Jess had a way of pulling me out of my head, reminding me that the world still spun on its axis, even if my heart felt unsteady.

As the credits rolled on the last movie, I found myself leaning against Jess, both of us giggling at the absurdity of the plot twists. "You know, this is almost better than a therapy session," I mused, feeling lighter than I had in days.

"Almost? I demand full credit for this emotional recovery!" she declared, poking my side.

Just then, her phone buzzed, drawing her attention. She picked it up, her brow knitting in concern as she read the screen. "Uh-oh," she muttered.

"What?" I asked, suddenly wary.

"It's Ryan," she said, her voice dropping. "He's been acting a little off lately."

"Off how?" I pressed, intrigued. Ryan was usually as steady as they came, the calm amidst Jess's chaos.

"He's been distant. I think something's bothering him, but he won't talk to me about it."

Concern flickered in my chest. "Do you think it's about work? Or...?"

"Or something else entirely," Jess finished, her eyes narrowing. "I'm going to call him. Let's see what's up."

As she dialed, a knot of worry twisted in my stomach. The thought of Lucas facing unknown troubles was one thing, but Ryan's moodiness layered an unexpected tension over the evening. I could feel the undercurrents swirling, weaving around us like threads in a tapestry, pulling tighter and tighter.

"Hey, it's me," Jess said, her tone shifting into one of practiced calm. "I was just thinking about you... Yeah, just checking in. Is everything okay?"

I watched her face transform as she listened, her brow furrowing deeper with each passing second. "What do you mean? You didn't show up for our plans?" Her voice grew sharper, and I could feel the weight of her worry. "Ryan, just tell me what's going on."

I held my breath, the atmosphere thickening with each word Jess spoke. I was acutely aware of the power of secrets—how they twisted and turned, leaving uncertainty in their wake.

Finally, Jess ended the call, her expression unreadable. "He said he's busy with something important and couldn't make it tonight."

"But that's not like him," I replied, my heart sinking. "Ryan loves hanging out with you."

"I know. Something's off," she said, her voice low. "And now I can't shake the feeling that whatever it is might tie into what's happening with Lucas."

A chill ran down my spine, as if the shadows lurking at the edges of the room were suddenly closing in. I had wanted to escape my worries, yet here they were, manifesting in new and unexpected ways. The sense of stability I thought I'd found had become a precarious balance, and I realized I might not be the only one teetering on the edge of something unknown.

The phone buzzed on the table, a sound that pulled me from my thoughts and snapped the tension in the room. Jess was still staring at her phone, a deep crease forming between her brows. "You know, I really don't like this vibe we're getting from the universe," she said, finally breaking the silence. "It feels like it's gearing up to throw us a plot twist no one asked for."

"Right? It's like a bad rom-com where the lead actress never gets the guy and instead spends the entire movie in a chaotic whirlwind of misunderstandings." I leaned back in my chair, frustration boiling just beneath the surface. "I mean, what's next? Are we going to find out Ryan's been hiding a secret identity as a cat burglar or something?"

Jess snorted, the tension momentarily lifting. "If he is, that's definitely not the plot twist I want in my life. I'm more of a 'two best friends take on the world' kind of gal." She eyed me carefully, the teasing smile fading slightly. "Seriously, though, it's like everything is unraveling at once. We need to figure this out."

Before I could respond, my phone lit up with an incoming message. My heart leapt into my throat as I recognized the name on the screen. Lucas. The tightness in my chest eased ever so slightly as I opened the text, but the words had me reeling.

I'm sorry, but I can't explain everything now. Just know that I'm okay. I'll reach out when I can.

A thousand questions danced on my tongue, each one more pressing than the last. Why couldn't he just tell me what was happening? What kind of danger was he in? I glanced up at Jess, who was watching me with keen eyes, her earlier humor replaced by genuine concern.

"What did he say?"

"He's okay, I think." I felt the weight of the words, but it was like a fragile balloon tethered to a pin. "But he can't explain. Not yet."

"Great. So we're just sitting here twiddling our thumbs while he goes off to God knows where?" Jess's tone was a mix of frustration and worry. "What if something really bad is happening? What if this is all connected?"

"Then we find out what that connection is," I said, trying to inject confidence into my voice. "He trusts me. He wouldn't just leave without a good reason."

"Trust is a tricky thing," Jess replied, her tone sobering. "It can be a double-edged sword. Just remember that."

Before I could respond, my phone buzzed again, and I almost dropped it in my haste to check. This time, it wasn't Lucas. It was Ryan.

Can we talk? I need your help.

"What's the deal?" I murmured, glancing at Jess. "Ryan wants to talk."

"Maybe he's in trouble, too," she suggested, her eyes narrowing in thought. "Do you think it's about Lucas?"

"Let's find out." I typed back a quick reply, telling him to come over. "This just keeps getting better," I muttered under my breath.

Moments later, the door swung open, and Ryan stepped inside, his usually bright demeanor dimmed. He looked like he hadn't slept in days, his hair tousled and his eyes shadowed. "Hey," he said, a hint of vulnerability in his voice.

"Ryan, are you okay?" Jess immediately asked, concern knitting her brow.

"I don't know," he admitted, running a hand through his hair. "I've been... distracted."

"Distracted how?" I pressed, my heart racing.

"Let's sit," he said, glancing around as if the walls themselves were listening. "I need to explain something."

We settled around the table, the air thick with unspoken words. "I've been digging into some things," Ryan began, his voice low. "Things about Lucas, and the calls he's been getting. I think it's more serious than we realized."

"What do you mean?" Jess leaned forward, her elbows resting on the table.

"There's a lot of rumors swirling about something bigger. Some kind of organization, something dangerous." He took a breath, his gaze darting between us. "And I think Lucas might be caught up in it."

"Caught up in what? What are you talking about?" My voice rose, panic creeping in.

"Look, I can't explain everything right now," he said, his hands shaking slightly. "But there are people looking for him, and it's not just about a simple job or whatever he told you. It goes deeper."

"Why didn't you tell me this sooner?" I demanded, my frustration boiling over.

"I didn't know for sure until now. I thought it was just paranoia at first." Ryan's eyes darkened. "But I've seen things... I've heard things."

"What kind of things?" Jess pushed. "This isn't some sort of conspiracy theory, right?"

"No, it's real. People are missing, and there are whispers about someone trying to take control of the town." His words hung heavy in the air, filling the space with dread.

"What does this have to do with Lucas?" I asked, feeling my heart race again.

"I think he might be a target," Ryan said, his voice trembling. "I'm worried he could be in real danger."

Suddenly, a loud crash outside made us jump, and we all exchanged alarmed glances. Jess moved toward the window, peering out into the dim light. "What was that?"

"I don't know," I said, my heart thudding in my chest. "It sounded like it came from the direction of Lucas's house."

Ryan's eyes widened. "We need to check it out. Now."

"Are you sure that's a good idea?" Jess hesitated, glancing at me.

"We don't have time to debate. If there's something happening, we have to know." I felt a rush of adrenaline as the urgency of the moment propelled me forward.

We rushed out of the house and into the night, the chill of the air biting at our skin. The darkness was thick, wrapping around us like a shroud as we sprinted toward Lucas's place. Every sound, every shadow, felt like a warning.

As we approached the familiar house, my heart sank. The front door stood ajar, swaying slightly in the breeze. I exchanged worried glances with Jess and Ryan, our breaths visible in the night air.

"This can't be good," I whispered, fear clawing at my throat.

"Stay close," Ryan instructed, taking the lead as we stepped cautiously inside. The house was eerily quiet, the usual hum of life replaced by an unsettling stillness.

"Lucas?" I called out, my voice echoing through the empty hall.

Silence answered, stretching out like a taut string ready to snap. I felt Jess clutch my arm, her nails digging into my skin.

"Where is he?" she whispered, panic rising in her voice.

"I don't know," I replied, glancing around. "We need to look for clues."

We moved cautiously through the rooms, searching for any sign of him. The living room was a mess—furniture overturned, books scattered across the floor like fallen leaves. My heart raced as I stepped over a broken picture frame, the glass glinting in the faint light.

Suddenly, I heard a noise from the back of the house—a low thud, followed by a muffled shout. Without thinking, I rushed toward the sound, my pulse racing.

"Lucas!" I shouted, but my voice was swallowed by the darkness.

We pushed through the doorway into the kitchen, the air heavy with tension. And then, my heart dropped into my stomach. There, lying on the floor, was Lucas—his body slumped against the cabinets, his face pale and bruised.

"No!" I gasped, rushing to his side, kneeling down to check for signs of life.

"Lucas!" Jess cried, her voice breaking.

His eyes fluttered open, confusion clouding his gaze as he looked at me. "Emily... you shouldn't have come."

"Like hell I wouldn't," I whispered fiercely, but I could feel the dread creeping back, the terrible realization of what this meant flooding my senses.

As I cradled his head in my lap, I noticed something glinting in the dim light beside him—an object I couldn't quite make out. I reached for it, but before I could grasp it, the front door slammed shut, echoing ominously through the house.

The sound jolted us all, and my heart raced as I turned, dread pooling in my stomach. The silhouette of a figure stood in the doorway, their face obscured by shadows. "I'm afraid you've come at the wrong time," they said, their voice smooth and chilling.

"Get away from him!" I shouted, instinctively positioning myself between Lucas and the stranger.

"Such bravery," the figure replied, stepping into the light, revealing a twisted smile that sent shivers down my spine. "But it won't save you."

I felt Jess and Ryan tense beside me, ready to defend, but the reality of our situation washed over me like cold water. The danger had come to us, and we were standing at the edge of a cliff, teetering toward an abyss that threatened to swallow us whole.

Chapter 16: The Reunion

I felt the first rays of dawn spill into my room, casting a warm glow that seemed to cradle the world in softness. It was a quiet morning, the kind where the chirping of birds and the rustle of leaves whispered promises of new beginnings. Yet, as I lay there, the stillness felt heavy, pregnant with unspoken words and unresolved tension. My heart thrummed with anticipation, each beat echoing the worry that had nested in my chest since Lucas had disappeared into the night weeks ago.

I had imagined countless scenarios about his return—how we might embrace, what words would tumble from his lips, the way our bodies would find comfort in each other's arms. But nothing could have prepared me for the reality that unfolded. When he stepped through the door, it felt like the universe paused, and all I could see was him—worn and weary, his eyes shadowed with a depth of sorrow that hinted at battles fought in silence.

"Lucas," I breathed, almost in disbelief. His name felt foreign on my tongue, yet it was the sweetest sound, a reminder that he was still here. The air between us crackled with unspoken tension, and I took a cautious step forward, my heart racing. He seemed to hesitate, as if the weight of our history held him back, but then he crossed the threshold, pulling me close as if I were his lifeline.

"I can't keep running," he whispered against my hair, the warmth of his breath sending shivers down my spine. His arms wrapped around me, the comfort of his embrace felt like coming home, yet the words he spoke cut deeper than any blade. What did he mean by running? The question loomed over us, heavy and foreboding, but I dared not voice it. I simply sank into his embrace, breathing in the familiar scent of him—wood smoke, fresh air, and something uniquely Lucas.

As dawn broke, the sunlight streamed through the window, illuminating the tiny particles of dust that danced in the air between us, like a million unspoken thoughts floating around. I could feel the gravity of his decision hanging in the air. "Lucas, you're back. You're safe. That's what matters right now," I managed to say, my voice barely above a whisper. I longed to push him for answers, to pry open the secrets he carried like scars across his soul, but there was something sacred about this moment.

He pulled away slightly, enough to look into my eyes. There was an intensity there that made my heart flutter and my stomach twist in knots. It was both terrifying and exhilarating, the promise of truths waiting to be revealed. "I need you to know that... I've seen things, Emily. Things that haunt you. I thought I could outrun them, but they always catch up."

My brow furrowed as confusion washed over me. What could he have faced that would leave him so shattered? I reached up, brushing my fingertips along his jaw, tracing the lines of worry etched in his face. "You don't have to bear it alone. We can face it together."

His gaze flickered, uncertainty swirling within those stormy depths. "I wish it were that simple. There are forces at play that I can't control, and I don't want to drag you into my mess." The conviction in his words stung, but beneath it lay a vulnerability that I found both disarming and alluring.

"You already dragged me in the moment we met, Lucas," I replied, a hint of playful defiance in my tone, though I could feel the seriousness of our conversation wrapping around us like a thick fog. "We're in this together, whether you like it or not. You can't just push me away every time things get complicated."

He sighed, running a hand through his tousled hair, a gesture that revealed just how tired he truly was. "It's not that I don't want you. I'm terrified of what will happen if you see the darkness I carry."

The world outside my window blossomed with life, yet inside, the air felt thick with unspoken fears. "I've faced my own darkness, Lucas. You're not the only one who's fought battles." The truth of my own struggles—the loneliness, the weight of expectations—hung between us, a silent acknowledgment that our lives were woven together with threads of pain and resilience.

Just then, a loud crash from downstairs shattered the moment, echoing through the stillness. My heart lurched as Lucas stiffened, eyes narrowing as he turned towards the sound. "What was that?"

I felt a wave of unease wash over me. "I don't know, but it didn't sound good." The warmth that had enveloped us faded as reality crashed back in, reminding me that danger was never far away.

Lucas stepped back, instinctively moving toward the door. "Stay here," he commanded, his voice firm but laced with an undertone of concern.

"Like hell I will!" I shot back, my heart racing for a different reason now. "I'm not about to sit here while you go off and face whatever that is alone."

He hesitated, eyes searching mine as if weighing the worth of my stubbornness against the risks outside our door. Finally, he relented, a resigned sigh escaping his lips. "Fine. But stay close. I mean it."

With that, we crept down the hallway, the tension between us forgotten as the urgency of the moment took over. The shadows clung to the walls, the flickering light of dawn casting long, eerie shapes that danced in our wake. I could feel the adrenaline coursing through my veins, mixing with the lingering fear of what lay ahead.

The world outside our room was shifting, filled with unseen threats that loomed just beyond the edge of our understanding. Lucas and I moved as one, our hearts beating in tandem as we prepared to confront whatever lay waiting for us, knowing that the reunion we had longed for might just be a prelude to a much darker tale unfolding.

The world outside shifted in shades of gold as the sun climbed higher, the gentle light spilling across the floorboards like a promise. I could still feel the warmth of Lucas's embrace lingering on my skin, a balm against the uncertainty that loomed just beyond our fragile bubble of safety. But the weight of unasked questions hung in the air, thick as the dust motes swirling in the sunlight.

"Lucas, what happened to you?" I finally dared to ask, my voice barely above a whisper, careful not to shatter the delicate moment we'd reclaimed. His eyes flitted to mine, and I could see the turmoil brewing within him, a storm of emotions battling for dominance. "You can't just drop that bomb and expect me to be okay with it."

His lips curled into a faint, self-deprecating smile, the kind that suggested he found humor in the absurdity of it all. "I suppose I've never been great at sharing, have I?" he said, the lightness in his tone at odds with the shadows that clung to him.

"No, you really haven't." I crossed my arms, a playful challenge lighting my gaze. "But you've had time to work on your communication skills while you were off gallivanting through who knows where."

He chuckled softly, and for a moment, it felt like we were back to our easy banter, the playful jabs that colored our days with laughter. But the flicker of light in his eyes was quickly overshadowed by something darker. "It's complicated. I had to deal with some... issues that needed my attention."

"Complicated is just a fancy way of saying you don't want to talk about it," I countered, narrowing my eyes at him. "You're not getting off that easily, Lucas. We can't keep pretending everything is fine while you're clearly battling whatever ghosts haunt you."

He looked away, his gaze fixated on the window, the vibrant morning outside contrasting sharply with the storm within him. "Some things are better left unshared. I don't want to drag you into my mess, Em. You deserve more than that."

"More than that? Lucas, you act like I'm made of sugar. I'm not going to melt away if I hear about your problems. If anything, I want to help." My heart raced as I spoke, the intensity of my feelings surging to the surface. "You can't push me away just because it's easier for you. I'm not some fragile little flower you can protect."

His eyes found mine again, a flicker of admiration mixed with concern. "I know you're strong. But it's not just about you. I can't lose you, not again."

The vulnerability in his voice tugged at my heartstrings, igniting a protective fire within me. "Then let me in, Lucas. Trust me, just as I'm trying to trust you. I'm not going to break. I promise."

He inhaled sharply, his breath hitching as if my words had landed heavily on him. The tension between us felt like a taut string, ready to snap or sing depending on the direction of our emotions.

As if on cue, a loud crash echoed from downstairs, the sound reverberating through the house and snapping us both back to reality. "What now?" I muttered, exasperation flooding my tone.

Lucas immediately turned serious, the playful banter evaporating like morning mist. "Stay close," he instructed, his voice low and commanding.

"I'm right beside you, Lucas," I said, stepping into his shadow, a mixture of fear and determination coursing through me. I couldn't let him face whatever was waiting for us alone, not when I had already come so far to protect him.

We crept down the hallway, each creak of the floorboards echoing like a heartbeat in the silence. As we reached the stairs, I caught a glimpse of the shadows shifting at the bottom, the morning light barely piercing the gloom. My heart raced, anticipation thrumming in my veins.

Lucas paused at the edge of the stairwell, his muscles tense. "Ready?"

"Ready as I'll ever be," I replied, stealing a glance at him. His jaw was set, eyes narrowed in focus, and I couldn't shake the feeling that we were about to step into a confrontation that could change everything.

With a swift nod, he took the lead, and I followed closely, our movements fluid as we descended into the unknown. The sight that met us was nothing I expected—a mess of overturned furniture, books scattered like fallen leaves, and in the center, a figure half-shrouded in shadows.

"Who are you?" Lucas demanded, stepping protectively in front of me, his body a shield against the unknown threat.

The figure turned slowly, and I squinted, trying to make sense of the chaos. As the shadows fell away, revealing a familiar face, I couldn't suppress the gasp that escaped my lips. It was Jess, my best friend, her eyes wide with a mix of panic and excitement.

"Emily! Lucas! Thank goodness you're here!" she exclaimed, rushing toward us, her hands trembling as she gestured wildly to the disaster around her. "You won't believe what's happening!"

"What are you doing here?" I asked, bewildered. "And why did you wreck the place?"

"I didn't mean to! I came to find you—there's something you need to see!" Jess said, glancing back at the mess. "I was looking for clues about what's been going on, and I think I stumbled onto something big!"

Lucas and I exchanged a look, the unspoken question hanging between us. What could possibly be big enough to lead to this chaos?

"Clues about what?" Lucas pressed, his eyes narrowing as he scrutinized Jess's frantic demeanor.

"The disappearances," she said, her voice trembling. "I found some old papers in the library, and they're linked to everything that's been happening. It's worse than we thought."

I felt a chill run down my spine as dread pooled in my stomach. "Worse than we thought? What do you mean?"

Jess took a deep breath, her expression shifting from frantic to determined. "I think someone—or something—is targeting our town. And if we don't figure this out soon, it could come after us next."

Her words hung in the air, a dark cloud looming over our fragile reunion. I glanced at Lucas, his face a mask of concentration as he processed the implications.

"Show us," he said, his voice steady despite the storm brewing around us.

Jess nodded, her resolve solidifying as she led us deeper into the chaos of the room. Each step felt heavy, the weight of our combined fears pressing down as we prepared to face the unknown lurking in the shadows, the danger that threatened to unravel everything we had fought for.

The room was thick with anticipation as Jess led us through the wreckage, her fingers trembling with urgency as she pointed to the scattered papers on the floor. "Look! I found these notes buried under some old books. They're about the disappearances, Emily. There's something sinister going on, and I think it's connected to... something that happened years ago."

I knelt down, my heart racing as I sifted through the disarray. The notes were hastily scribbled, some pages stained with age and others bearing the unmistakable signs of panic—exclamation marks and underlined words that hinted at a growing fear. Lucas crouched beside me, the warmth of his body a constant reminder that I wasn't alone in this chaos.

"Jess, what exactly did you uncover?" Lucas asked, his voice steady despite the tension in the air. "What do these notes say?"

"Here," she said, plucking a page from the pile and holding it up for us to see. "It mentions a local legend about a creature that's said to haunt our town, something that feeds off fear. It's been dormant for decades, but now... it seems to be awakening."

I swallowed hard, the hair on the back of my neck standing on end. "A creature? Like a monster?"

Jess nodded vigorously, her eyes wide with urgency. "Exactly! It's supposed to take the form of someone you know, someone you trust, and lure you in before it strikes."

My thoughts raced, swirling with memories of Lucas's strange absences, the shadows that seemed to cling to him like an unwanted second skin. "But that doesn't make any sense," I argued, my voice laced with disbelief. "We've been living here for years, and nothing has ever happened."

"Maybe that's what it wants you to think," Jess countered, her frustration simmering just beneath the surface. "There have been whispers among the older folks in town, but no one believed them. They brushed it off as old wives' tales. But look around! People are disappearing, and it's not just coincidence."

Lucas's brow furrowed as he studied the notes. "Do any of these mention how to stop it?"

"Not explicitly," Jess admitted, her fingers running anxiously through her hair. "But there's a pattern. Every time someone vanishes, it corresponds with the change of the seasons. It's almost as if the creature is awakening with the earth's cycle."

I glanced at Lucas, his expression unreadable as he absorbed this new information. The weight of the past bore down on him, and I could see the gears turning in his mind. "We need to figure out when the next disappearance is likely to happen," he said finally, a steely determination lacing his tone. "And we need to be ready for it."

Jess nodded, her voice gaining strength. "There's an old map in the library, showing where the last few disappearances occurred. If we can find a pattern, maybe we can predict where it will strike next."

"Then let's go," I said, adrenaline surging through me. "If we can find out when and where it will happen, we can protect ourselves—and the town."

We gathered the scattered notes, tucking them into a folder Jess had salvaged from the floor. With each step toward the library, I felt the excitement building, tempered by a sense of dread. What if we found more than we bargained for?

The library door creaked ominously as we pushed it open, the scent of aged paper and dust wafting toward us like a warning. Books lined the walls, their spines faded and cracked, as if guarding secrets too heavy to bear. I could almost feel the pulse of the building, alive with history and mystery, whispering tales of the past that begged to be uncovered.

Jess led the way, her fingers dancing along the spines of the books as if searching for the right one. "It should be over here, I think." She stopped suddenly, her eyes scanning the shelves until she found what she was looking for. "Yes! This is it!"

She pulled a large, leather-bound book from the shelf, dust cascading like confetti around us. "This map should show the last recorded disappearances," she said, flipping through the brittle pages.

Lucas leaned closer, his breath warm against my ear as he pointed to a sketch of the town and its surrounding areas. "Look! These markers show where the people vanished. They're all clustered around the woods."

I felt a chill creep down my spine as I traced the lines with my finger, noting the close proximity of each incident. "And right here," I said, my finger hovering over a particularly dense cluster of markers. "This is where we found that strange stone circle last summer. It must be important."

"Then that's where we need to go," Lucas stated, his resolve unwavering. "Tonight."

Jess shot him a worried glance. "But what if the creature comes after us?"

"We'll be ready," he replied, a fierce determination in his voice that sent a thrill through me. "This isn't just about us anymore. We have to protect the others."

The weight of his words hung in the air, filling me with a sense of purpose, even as dread clawed at my insides. I had always thought of our town as safe, a haven from the horrors of the world, but now I understood that danger had been lurking in the shadows all along.

"Okay, let's make a plan," I said, taking charge as my heart raced with adrenaline. "We need to gather supplies, flashlights, maybe some kind of weapon—"

"Why not bring a whole arsenal while we're at it?" Jess interjected, her sarcasm a welcome relief in the tension-laden air. "I'm sure that'll really charm whatever's waiting for us out there."

I shot her a mock glare, the tension easing momentarily. "You're right, let's just walk in with our best smiles and hope for the best!"

Lucas chuckled softly, a glimmer of warmth breaking through his worries. "I'll grab some gear. Meet you both at the stone circle at sunset?"

"Sunset," I echoed, my stomach twisting with anticipation. "I'll be there."

As Lucas departed, Jess and I began gathering supplies, our hands moving with purpose yet our minds racing with uncertainty. The sunlight outside began to dim, casting long shadows that danced along the walls, reminiscent of the dangers creeping ever closer.

"Do you think Lucas is okay?" Jess asked suddenly, her voice low as she rifled through the shelves. "He seems... different."

I hesitated, not wanting to voice the fears gnawing at me. "He's been through a lot. I think he just needs to figure it out on his own."

Jess frowned, clearly unconvinced. "Just be careful, okay? We can't afford to lose him again."

"I won't," I promised, though I couldn't shake the unease settling in my gut.

As we finished gathering our supplies, the last rays of sunlight disappeared beyond the horizon, leaving us in twilight. We set out toward the woods, the air thick with anticipation and uncertainty. Each step felt like a countdown, our hearts racing with the knowledge that we were heading straight into the unknown, where shadows held secrets and danger waited with bated breath.

The stone circle loomed ahead, the ancient stones weathered and worn, a testament to time and trials long past. The chill in the air deepened as darkness enveloped us, the silence of the forest stretching infinitely.

And just as we approached, a low growl echoed through the trees, chilling my blood and freezing me in place.

"Did you hear that?" I whispered, terror gripping my heart as the shadows twisted ominously around us.

Jess nodded, her eyes wide, and in that moment, I knew we weren't alone anymore. The forest had awakened, and whatever was lurking in the dark was ready to make its move.

Chapter 17: Breaking Point

The air in Lucas's room felt thick with unspoken words, a palpable tension that wrapped around us like a shroud. I watched him pace the floor, the soft thud of his footsteps barely breaking the silence that hung heavy between us. Shadows danced across his face, accentuating the sharp lines of his jaw, the furrow in his brow deepening with each passing moment. He was a storm cloud, and I was the unsuspecting town beneath, unaware of the tempest brewing.

I had always found solace in the quiet moments we shared, but lately, those moments had become few and far between. Lucas's laughter, once a melody that filled the air, was replaced by a heavy silence that weighed down my heart. I could see the way he clenched his fists, how his jaw tightened whenever the phone buzzed or a car drove by. It was as if the world around him was a ticking clock, counting down to an explosion he desperately tried to avert.

"Lucas," I said softly, breaking the suffocating quiet. The name felt like a lifeline thrown into turbulent waters, but he didn't look at me. Instead, he stopped, staring at the wall as if it held the answers to questions he was too afraid to ask himself. "Please talk to me."

"Not yet," he replied, his voice barely above a whisper. There was an edge to his tone that sent a shiver down my spine. It was a denial wrapped in layers of something darker—fear, perhaps, or shame. I wanted to reach out, to bridge the chasm that had grown between us, but the distance felt insurmountable.

Hours slipped by, the dim light of his desk lamp flickering against the gathering dusk outside. I leaned back against the cool wall, watching as he paced like a caged animal, caught in a labyrinth of his own making. I knew better than to push too hard, to pry open wounds that he wasn't ready to reveal, but my heart ached with a mix of concern and frustration. I needed him to trust me, to let me in.

Finally, when the clock struck midnight and the world outside had succumbed to silence, he stopped. He turned to face me, his expression a tumultuous blend of anguish and determination. "I can't keep this from you anymore," he said, his voice low, trembling like the leaves in a windstorm. "It's... it's about my past."

I straightened, my heart racing as I met his gaze. In those eyes, I saw a tempest brewing—a storm that had long been brewing, threatening to engulf us both. "What happened?" I asked, every fiber of my being attuned to the weight of his confession.

"I'm being blackmailed," he admitted, the words hanging in the air like an unwelcome specter. The revelation hit me like a punch to the gut, leaving me breathless. "It's someone I thought I'd left behind, someone who doesn't care that I've changed. He wants... retribution for something I did."

The room spun as I processed his words. Blackmail? Retribution? My mind raced with a thousand questions, each more frightening than the last. "What do they want?" I asked, my voice barely above a whisper, as if speaking too loudly would summon the shadows lurking just beyond the door.

"A favor. Something dangerous. Something illegal," he replied, his face pale and drawn. "He knows things—things I thought I had buried. I thought I could outrun him, but it seems he's taken a personal interest in making my life a living hell."

Every instinct in me screamed to run, to flee from the impending storm, yet I found myself rooted in place, heart pounding in defiance of my fear. "We can face this together," I said, stepping closer, desperate to close the distance that felt like an abyss. "You're not alone in this."

His expression hardened, the shadows of his past flaring in his eyes. "This isn't something you can just jump into, Emily. It's dangerous. I don't want to put you at risk."

"Too late for that," I shot back, frustration bubbling to the surface. "I'm already in this with you. You don't get to decide what's best for me. I care about you—about us."

For a moment, the air crackled with tension as we faced each other, two opposing forces caught in a whirlwind of emotions. I could see the conflict within him—the desire to shield me from the chaos of his life battling against the undeniable pull of our connection. Then, as if the dam had finally burst, he closed the distance between us, the heat of his body radiating against mine.

"I don't want to lose you," he confessed, voice hoarse with unspoken fears. The vulnerability in his tone pierced through the tension, cutting to the heart of what we had both been avoiding. "You mean too much to me."

I reached up, cupping his face in my hands, grounding him in that moment. "You're not going to lose me. We'll figure this out together. Just tell me what you need."

His eyes searched mine, a mixture of gratitude and despair swirling in their depths. "I need you to promise me that you'll stay safe. No matter what happens. Promise me, Emily."

"I promise," I whispered, my heart racing with an unexpected thrill of danger. We were standing on the edge of something dark and unknown, and yet, somehow, I felt alive—more than I had in a long time. I wouldn't turn away. I couldn't.

In that moment, as the weight of his past loomed over us, a sense of resolve began to grow within me. Whatever storm was brewing on the horizon, we would face it together, hand in hand. I wouldn't let him carry this burden alone; I wouldn't let fear dictate our fate. Together, we would navigate this treacherous path, unraveling the threads of his past while forging a future filled with hope and love, no matter how daunting the journey ahead.

The next few days felt like an eternity, each hour stretching into the next, tainted by an anxiety that coiled in my stomach like a serpent waiting to strike. Lucas was a ghost of his former self, drifting through life in a haze of worry and restless energy. I watched him attempt to engage in our usual routines—sharing coffee in the mornings, studying together in the evenings—but he was always a step removed, as if an invisible barrier separated us. I wanted to reach through that barrier, to pull him back from the edge, but every time I tried, he seemed to retreat further into himself.

"Are you coming to the party this weekend?" Jess asked me one afternoon as we sat outside under the brilliant sun, its warmth contrasting sharply with the chill in my heart. She swirled her lemonade, eyeing me with a mixture of curiosity and concern. "I heard Lucas might be there."

I shrugged, not wanting to admit that the mere thought of seeing him without a hint of the boy I knew sent my pulse racing in the wrong direction. "I don't know. I might just hang back and let him have fun without me."

Jess raised an eyebrow. "Emily, you can't just hide in the shadows forever. If he's going, you should be there. He needs you." Her voice was firm but kind, the way a good friend's should be.

"Does he?" I shot back, the frustration bubbling beneath the surface. "It seems like he's doing just fine pushing me away." My heart ached at the words, but they slipped out before I could stop them.

She opened her mouth to respond, but I cut her off. "I'll think about it, okay? Just... I need some time to figure things out."

As the week dragged on, I felt the weight of my indecision bearing down on me. Lucas was trapped in a cycle of secrets and silence, while I was stuck on the outside, desperate to breach the fortress he had erected around himself. Each time I saw him at school, my heart would leap at the sight of him, only to sink when he turned away, too lost in his thoughts to notice me.

On Friday night, as I stood in front of my mirror, preparing for the party, I felt a sudden wave of determination wash over me. If I was going to help Lucas confront whatever demons haunted him, I needed to stop waiting for him to reach out. I had to show up, not just for him, but for myself. I slipped on a simple but elegant dress, a deep green that reminded me of the forest, then added a pair of heels that made my legs feel long and powerful. I needed to be bold, to remind Lucas of the vibrant life waiting for him just outside his turbulent thoughts.

The party was in full swing when I arrived, laughter and music spilling into the night like a raucous celebration of youth. I scanned the crowd, spotting familiar faces, but my heart raced as I searched for Lucas. He was there, leaning against the wall, his silhouette framed by the twinkling fairy lights strung overhead. But he wasn't alone; Julian Rowen stood beside him, his presence magnetic and confident, drawing attention like a moth to a flame.

I felt an unexpected rush of jealousy at the sight of them together. Julian had a way of commanding a room, his easy smile and flirtatious banter making him the center of attention. He leaned in close to Lucas, a conspiratorial grin on his face, and I felt a knot twist in my stomach. What were they talking about? Did Julian know about the darkness lurking in Lucas's past?

Pushing the thought aside, I wove my way through the throng of bodies, determination guiding my steps. When Lucas finally noticed me, a flicker of surprise lit his eyes, quickly followed by a shadow of something darker—guilt? Fear? It was impossible to tell, but I refused to let his turmoil dim my resolve.

"Hey," I said, forcing a smile as I approached him, trying to radiate warmth despite the chill creeping into my veins. "I came to join the fun."

His gaze softened, but I could see the storm still raging within him. "You didn't have to. I thought you might want to take a break from everything," he replied, his voice low and edged with concern.

"Too late for that," I shot back, crossing my arms defiantly. "You're my best friend, and I'm not about to let you face this alone, whatever it is."

Before he could respond, Julian interjected, his tone playful yet pointed. "Look at you two, all deep and dramatic. What's the secret? Are you planning to run away together or just plot the demise of my social life?" His smile was bright, but I caught the flicker of unease in Lucas's eyes.

"Funny," I said, keeping my voice steady. "But I think we'll save the plotting for another time." I felt Lucas stiffen beside me, and I knew this was the moment to steer the conversation. "Julian, how's your latest adventure? Last I heard, you were charming the socks off some poor unsuspecting tourist in New York."

"Oh, you know me," Julian replied with an exaggerated flair. "I leave a trail of broken hearts and delighted souls wherever I go." He flashed me a grin, one that seemed to hint at hidden depths beneath his playful exterior.

I turned to Lucas, who was watching Julian with an inscrutable expression, and decided to press on. "Let's dance," I suggested, my voice bright with feigned enthusiasm.

"Are you sure?" Lucas asked, his brow furrowing.

"Yes. You can't mope around all night, Lucas. Dance with me." The challenge hung between us, and for a moment, I could see the hint of a smile tugging at his lips, the storm clouds momentarily parting.

With a reluctant nod, he took my hand, and we moved toward the makeshift dance floor. As the music swelled, enveloping us in its infectious energy, I let the rhythm guide me, spinning and twirling, coaxing a reluctant laugh from him. I was determined to pull him from the shadows, to remind him that he was still the boy I had grown to love, even if he was battling a past that threatened to consume him.

As we danced, I felt the tension between us shift, a fragile thread weaving us closer together. Lucas's hand found the small of my back, pulling me into him, and for a brief moment, everything felt right. The world faded away, leaving just the two of us, lost in our own bubble of warmth and connection.

But just as the night seemed to reach its peak, the music shifted, and the atmosphere changed. The party's laughter faded, replaced by a tense hush as a figure stepped into the circle. It was a familiar face, but one I had never expected to see. Ethan, Lucas's older brother, stood at the edge of the crowd, his expression unreadable, tension crackling in the air like static electricity.

In that moment, everything I had built up with Lucas felt precarious, as if we were standing on the edge of a cliff, with the ground crumbling beneath our feet. I could see the recognition in Lucas's eyes, the way the joy faded, replaced by an unsettling mixture of dread and anger. I held my breath, waiting for the storm to break again.

The atmosphere at the party shifted dramatically when Ethan arrived, the very air around him charged with an unspoken energy that drew every eye in the room. He was magnetic, exuding a raw intensity that made the festive lights seem dim in comparison. As he stepped forward, the crowd parted slightly, creating a path that seemed to highlight his presence. Lucas's grip on my waist tightened, his fingers digging into the fabric of my dress as he stood rooted to the spot, a statue of uncertainty caught in a whirlwind of emotions.

"What's he doing here?" Lucas muttered under his breath, his voice low and tight, laced with a simmering anger that was palpable. I turned my head slightly to gauge his reaction, trying to decipher the complex layers of feelings swirling behind his eyes.

"Doesn't he always crash the party?" I replied, forcing a lightness into my tone that I didn't entirely feel. "It's kind of his thing, right?"

The words hung in the air between us, playful yet heavy with the tension that had built up over the past few days.

Ethan's gaze swept the room, finally landing on us. He wore a casual smile that seemed effortless, but beneath that facade, I could sense a storm brewing. "Lucas," he called out, his voice smooth and confident, yet with an underlying sharpness that sliced through the chatter around us. "Long time no see, little brother."

"Don't call me that," Lucas shot back, the words laced with a bite that sent a chill through me. I felt the weight of their history settle like a lead blanket, suffocating the laughter and warmth of the party.

I watched the interaction unfold, caught between the brothers, feeling as if I were holding my breath underwater, waiting for the inevitable moment of eruption. Ethan stepped closer, his expression shifting from playful to something more serious, a glimmer of concern hidden beneath the bravado. "You're still tangled up in that mess, aren't you? It's about time you face it."

Lucas's jaw clenched, and I could see the struggle within him—the desire to protect whatever secrets lay buried in his past battling against the need to confront the truth. "I don't need you to lecture me, Ethan," he replied, each word a carefully measured step back from the brink.

"Then what do you need?" Ethan shot back, frustration evident in his tone. "You think ignoring it will make it go away? That blackmailer won't just vanish into thin air, Lucas. You know that." The tension in the air thickened, the two of them locked in a silent battle that felt far too personal for my presence.

The crowd had begun to thin, the vibrant energy of the party dimming as people sensed the brewing conflict. I took a step closer to Lucas, determined to be his anchor. "Lucas, maybe we should talk about this somewhere quieter," I suggested, my heart racing as I glanced between the brothers. "Just for a moment."

Ethan's gaze flickered to me, an unreadable expression crossing his features. "You're better off without him, you know," he said, his voice unexpectedly soft but laden with warning. "He's not the same person he used to be."

"Neither are you," Lucas countered sharply, and the sting in his words hung in the air, a bitter reminder of their fractured bond. I could see the hurt flicker across Ethan's face, but it was quickly masked by a veneer of cool indifference.

"Maybe you're right, Lucas," Ethan replied, his tone shifting, taking on an edge of calculated calm. "But I don't want you to lose yourself in this. There are things you don't understand—things I thought I could protect you from."

"Protect me?" Lucas laughed, a harsh, bitter sound that echoed in the stillness. "It's too late for that. You should have thought about that before you ran away."

"I didn't run away. I left to save you," Ethan said, his voice rising. "You think this is just about you? That I haven't spent every damn day regretting my decisions?" The words were a fierce gust of wind, scattering the last remnants of the party's light-heartedness.

I stepped forward, my heart racing. "Enough, both of you. Can we not do this here?" I glanced around, feeling the weight of the crowd's gaze, the whispers trailing in our wake. "Lucas, let's get some air."

As I tugged at his arm, he hesitated, his eyes flickering back to Ethan. I saw the indecision writhe within him, the battle of loyalties tearing him apart. "I don't want to leave you with him," Lucas said, his voice strained, his protective instincts flaring.

"Trust me," I urged, locking my gaze with his, hoping to convey the urgency of the moment. "Let's just step outside for a second."

With a reluctant nod, he finally turned away from his brother, following me through the throng of people, the noise fading behind us as we slipped out onto the porch. The cool night air hit me like a wave, invigorating and sharp, a contrast to the suffocating tension inside. I leaned against the railing, trying to steady my racing heart as I glanced back at Lucas.

"Are you okay?" I asked, concern flooding my voice. "You didn't have to face that alone, you know."

He ran a hand through his hair, a gesture of frustration mixed with relief. "I thought I could keep you out of this. I thought I could handle it." The vulnerability in his voice struck me, a reminder of how deeply he was trapped within his own turmoil.

"You don't have to handle it alone," I insisted, stepping closer, grounding him with my presence. "I'm here, and I'm not going anywhere."

Just then, a loud crash echoed from inside the house, followed by a collective gasp from the partygoers. We exchanged worried glances, and before I could voice my concern, Lucas's expression shifted to one of alarm.

"Stay here," he ordered, his voice low and urgent, and before I could respond, he dashed back inside, leaving me alone on the porch. My heart raced as I strained to hear what was happening, the sound of voices rising in a tumult of confusion.

I leaned forward, peering through the doorway, my breath catching in my throat at the sight of chaos unfolding inside. Tables had been overturned, drinks spilled across the floor like colorful rivers of despair. And at the center of it all was Ethan, standing over a figure sprawled on the ground, a look of shock on his face.

"Get back!" Ethan shouted, but his words were drowned out by the rising din. My mind raced as I tried to piece together what was happening. Was someone hurt? Was this the confrontation Lucas had feared?

I stepped into the fray, the instinct to help propelling me forward. The crowd began to part as I moved through, adrenaline pumping through my veins. "What's going on?" I shouted, but no one seemed to hear me.

Just then, Lucas emerged from the crowd, his face pale and eyes wide. "Emily! Get back!" he yelled, panic gripping his words. But it was too late; I was already too close.

In that moment, everything seemed to slow down. A figure lurked in the shadows, their intentions hidden but menacing. I could see Lucas's gaze darting between Ethan and the figure, his expression morphing from fear to determination.

And then, with a swift motion, the figure lunged, and I felt the ground shift beneath me as chaos erupted once more. I stood frozen, caught in the eye of the storm, unsure of what would happen next, fear gripping my heart as I prepared to confront whatever awaited us in the chaos.

Chapter 18: Into the Shadows

The cabin was a rustic relic, nestled in the embrace of towering pines that swayed like silent sentinels against the night sky. Lucas had chosen this place for its isolation, a sanctuary away from the prying eyes of the world. As we arrived, the fading sunlight cast long shadows across the ground, intertwining with the tangled roots of ancient trees. The air was thick with the scent of damp earth and the distant whisper of a bubbling brook. It felt as though we had stepped into a storybook, one woven with secrets and buried truths, where every creak of the cabin and rustle of leaves echoed with the weight of what was to come.

Inside, the cabin was simple yet inviting, with rough-hewn beams overhead and a stone fireplace that crackled softly, its warmth enveloping us like a comforting hug. A faded plaid blanket draped over a weathered sofa beckoned me to settle in, while Lucas busied himself in the small kitchen, rummaging through cabinets for provisions. I watched him, my heart swelling with a mix of admiration and concern. His brow furrowed in concentration, and I could see the tension in his shoulders as he prepared, each movement purposeful yet tinged with an underlying anxiety.

"Do you think he'll come after us here?" I asked, my voice barely above a whisper. The shadows seemed to close in around us, and the thought of Derrick lurking just beyond our refuge sent a shiver down my spine.

Lucas straightened, casting a quick glance towards the window. "I don't know, but we can't take that chance. Derrick's relentless. He won't stop until he gets what he wants." His tone was steady, but I could sense the storm brewing beneath the surface, a tempest of emotions battling for control. "He was once like a brother to me, you know? We grew up together. I thought he'd always have my back."

"Until he didn't," I replied, the words hanging heavily between us. It was a painful truth, one that cut deeper than I imagined. I had witnessed the way Lucas's face contorted with betrayal when he had first spoken of Derrick. There was a rawness to his memories, a vulnerability that left him exposed, and I wished I could shield him from that hurt.

"Yeah," he said, leaning against the counter, arms crossed as if to guard his heart from further injury. "We were inseparable. I trusted him with everything. But power changes people. It can twist the most loyal heart into something dark and unrecognizable."

A silence enveloped us, filled only by the crackling fire and the distant call of an owl. The weight of his words hung in the air like a fog, heavy and suffocating. I wanted to reach out, to pull him from the depths of his memories, but I wasn't sure how to breach that divide. Instead, I offered a soft smile, hoping to convey my unwavering support.

"Whatever happens, I'm with you. We'll face him together," I promised, my voice imbued with sincerity. I didn't know the extent of Derrick's ruthlessness, but I knew Lucas was strong, resilient, and determined. Together, we could forge a path through the shadows.

He finally met my gaze, a flicker of gratitude softening his features. "Thanks. I needed to hear that." His smile was fleeting but genuine, a reminder that beneath the layers of tension and fear, there still existed a bond between us—one forged in the fires of adversity.

As night descended, we settled into a routine. I lit candles that flickered like stars, casting a warm glow throughout the cabin. The shadows danced on the walls, and I felt as though we were encased in a protective bubble, safe from the chaos outside. Lucas shared stories of his past, the laughter breaking through the darkness like a beacon of hope. He spoke of our small town, of the silly pranks we played as kids, of summer nights spent swimming in the lake, and the friendships that had shaped him.

With each tale, the weight of Derrick's threat began to ease, replaced by the comforting familiarity of our shared memories. I found myself laughing, my heart swelling with warmth at the thought of those carefree days. It was moments like these that reminded me why I cared for him so deeply.

But as the fire crackled and the shadows lengthened, the reality of our situation crept back in, an unwelcome visitor. "What do you think he's planning?" I ventured, a knot tightening in my stomach. The uncertainty loomed over us like a dark cloud, and I could feel Lucas's tension return.

"Derrick's not just a brute. He's cunning," Lucas replied, his voice low, almost a growl. "He'll play mind games. He'll try to get inside my head, make me doubt myself." His gaze hardened, a flash of determination igniting behind his eyes. "But I won't let him. I can't."

I nodded, understanding that this was more than just a physical confrontation; it was a battle of wills. Derrick's betrayal had left scars, and the confrontation would reopen old wounds. I reached for his hand, intertwining my fingers with his, a silent promise of solidarity. "You're stronger than he knows, Lucas. We'll face this together."

The night wore on, and as we settled into a tentative peace, I felt the world outside slipping away, the shadows of the forest embracing us. But beneath that serenity lay an undercurrent of tension, a quiet storm brewing in the distance. I couldn't shake the feeling that Derrick was closer than we imagined, lurking just beyond the tree line, waiting for the right moment to strike. The thought sent a chill through me, a reminder that safety was an illusion, and the true battle was yet to come.

The following morning brought a muted dawn, sunlight filtering through the thick canopy of leaves overhead, casting dappled patterns across the cabin's wooden floor. I awoke to the aroma of coffee brewing, mingling with the fresh, crisp scent of pine wafting through the open window. The gentle sound of birds chirping outside was almost melodic, a reminder that life persisted beyond our secluded sanctuary, yet a faint sense of unease clung to the air like a shadow that refused to dissipate.

Lucas moved around the tiny kitchen with a practiced ease, his silhouette framed by the soft morning light. He wore an old flannel shirt, sleeves rolled up to reveal strong forearms, the ruggedness of the fabric contrasting sharply with the tenderness of his demeanor. I admired how he embodied both strength and vulnerability, a man caught in the throes of an impending storm, yet determined to protect what he held dear.

"Sleep well?" he asked, glancing back at me with a playful grin that could light up the darkest of days. I could see the remnants of worry etched into the lines of his face, but he was attempting to cloak it with a semblance of normalcy, and I appreciated his effort.

"Like a log, if that log was constantly worrying about a psychopathic former brother-in-arms lurking in the bushes," I replied, swinging my legs off the bed and letting my feet touch the cool, uneven floor. The moment felt almost normal, a comforting routine despite the gravity of our situation. I couldn't help but smile back, hoping to draw him into the light for just a moment longer.

"Glad to hear I'm not the only one with insomnia," he teased, pouring a cup of coffee and offering it to me. The warmth of the mug seeped into my hands, a small solace against the chill that lingered in my bones. I took a sip, the rich flavor bursting on my tongue, a reminder that even in our isolation, there were moments of comfort.

As we sat together at the small wooden table, the weight of our circumstances settled between us like an uninvited guest. I studied Lucas's profile, the way his brow furrowed as he contemplated our next move. He was a man forged in fire, his past shaping him into someone who wouldn't back down from a fight. But the idea of facing Derrick, the man who had once been his closest ally, sent ripples of tension through him that I could feel even from across the table.

"Are you ready for this?" I asked, my voice steady despite the anxiety bubbling within me. "I mean, confronting him? It's a big deal."

Lucas set down his cup and leaned forward, his eyes locking onto mine. "I have to be. If I don't confront him, he'll keep coming for me. For us. He's relentless. I can't let him think he can just waltz back into my life and take everything I care about." His resolve was palpable, yet the shadows danced in his gaze, hinting at the deeper fears lurking beneath his bravado.

"Do you think he'll come here?" I inquired, trying to gauge just how much danger we were truly in. The idea of Derrick prowling through the woods, just beyond our line of sight, was enough to make my heart race.

"Maybe. But he doesn't know I brought you here. He thinks I'm alone," Lucas replied, his voice barely above a whisper. "That gives us a slight advantage."

I wanted to believe him, but Derrick was cunning, a predator who had played the long game before. "What's your plan?" I asked, curiosity getting the better of my caution.

Lucas leaned back in his chair, rubbing the back of his neck as he considered my question. "I'll lure him out, confront him, and hope that I can talk sense into him. If that doesn't work..." He trailed off, the weight of unsaid words hanging heavy between us. I could tell he had already accepted the possibility that words might not be enough.

The atmosphere shifted as we discussed strategy, the initial warmth of coffee and morning light giving way to an icy sense of dread. I felt as though we were teetering on the edge of a cliff, the ground beneath us eroding with every passing moment. Yet I could see the determination flickering in Lucas's eyes, and it fueled my resolve.

"Whatever you need to do, I'm with you," I affirmed, my heart pounding in my chest. "I'll back you up. You won't face him alone." It was a promise, a pact sealed with the strength of my conviction.

As we prepared for the day ahead, a sudden sound pierced the serenity of our morning—a crack of twigs snapping outside, followed by the unmistakable crunch of footsteps on the forest floor. I froze, my breath hitching in my throat as I exchanged a glance with Lucas, whose expression transformed from determination to steely focus in an instant. The calm of the morning shattered like glass, leaving only the echo of our heartbeats and the sound of the approaching threat.

"Stay here," Lucas ordered, his voice a low rumble, commanding and protective. He moved towards the door, his body a coiled spring ready to unleash its power.

"Wait! What if it's Derrick?" I whispered urgently, panic bubbling beneath the surface. The thought of him finding us here, cornering Lucas, sent a chill racing down my spine.

"Exactly. Which is why I need you to stay put. Just for a moment," he replied, his tone brooking no argument. Before I could protest further, he slipped out the door, leaving me in the silence of the cabin, heart pounding with uncertainty.

Time seemed to stretch, the minutes feeling like hours as I waited, straining to hear any hint of what was unfolding outside. My imagination conjured up images of confrontation—Lucas standing tall against the looming figure of Derrick, the intensity of their history flaring like a match struck in the dark. I could almost feel the weight of that moment crashing against the fragile walls of our sanctuary.

But then I heard it—a sharp, guttural voice breaking through the tranquility. "Lucas! You can't hide forever!" It was Derrick, his tone dripping with the confidence of a man who believed he held all the cards. My heart raced as I moved silently towards the door, peeking out through a crack, desperate to see what was happening.

The sight that met my eyes was electric. Lucas stood his ground, shoulders squared, and hands clenched into fists at his sides. Derrick loomed before him, a stark contrast with a sneer twisting his lips. The shadows of the trees loomed behind them like silent witnesses to the unfolding drama, and I felt an instinctual pull to intervene, to leap into the fray and support Lucas.

"Is this where you've been hiding? In this little cabin?" Derrick taunted, his voice dripping with mockery. "You think I wouldn't find you? You're not as clever as you believe, Lucas."

Each word was a dagger, aimed at Lucas's pride and resolve. I could see the tension in his stance, a ripple of anger coursing through him as he met Derrick's gaze, unwavering. "What do you want, Derrick?" Lucas replied, his voice steady, though I could hear the undertones of pain simmering beneath the surface.

"I want what's mine," Derrick shot back, his demeanor shifting from mockery to menace. "You've taken everything from me, and now it's time to settle the score."

My breath hitched in my throat as the stakes escalated, the palpable tension crackling like electricity in the air. I knew then that whatever followed would change everything, and I wasn't ready to let Lucas face this alone. The weight of our situation bore down on me, and with a rush of adrenaline, I made my decision. I had to step into the light, to be part of this fight, no matter the cost.

The tension hung thick in the air like a storm cloud ready to burst. I stood in the doorway, the fading sunlight casting long shadows behind me, creating a narrow frame around the confrontation unfolding just beyond the threshold. Lucas's face was a mask of determination, but I could see the flicker of doubt in his eyes, like a candle fighting against a gale. Derrick's presence loomed, a predator circling its prey, and I could feel the prickling sense of danger crawl up my spine.

"Everything you have is built on lies, Lucas. You know that, don't you?" Derrick taunted, his voice dripping with venom as he stepped closer, each movement calculated and deliberate. The way he sneered sent a wave of disgust washing over me. "You were never meant to rise above me. You were just my shadow, nothing more."

"Maybe you've forgotten who the real monster is here, Derrick," Lucas shot back, his voice steady but low, a warning held within the calm. "I didn't betray you. You betrayed everyone, including yourself."

Derrick laughed, a harsh sound that sliced through the woods. "Look around you. This little charade, this pathetic little cabin in the woods—it's all a part of your fantasy, isn't it? A way to escape reality? Well, newsflash: reality is coming for you."

Every fiber of my being urged me to intervene, to yell out and stand beside Lucas, but I remained frozen, the weight of the moment pressing down on me like an anchor. Derrick's words hung in the air, heavy with implications. I could feel the walls closing in, the forest whispering its secrets as if it were alive, urging me to act.

"Derrick, you don't have to do this," I finally found my voice, stepping out from the safety of the cabin. The cool evening air rushed to greet me, invigorating yet terrifying. "You're only going to end up hurting yourself more."

Derrick's eyes narrowed, surprise flickering across his features. "And who might you be? Another pawn in Lucas's sad little game?" His disdain was palpable, but I noticed a shift, a momentary falter in his bravado.

"I'm someone who knows that the real game is the one you're playing," I said, my voice steadying with every word. "And it's time to stop pretending you're the puppet master when you're just a scared little boy hiding behind a mask of arrogance."

For a heartbeat, the forest was silent, as if holding its breath. Lucas's gaze darted between me and Derrick, a silent question forming in his eyes. I took a breath, ready to press on, to challenge the chaos that threatened to consume us.

"Enough!" Derrick roared, his temper flaring. "You think you can just waltz in here and save him? He made his choice when he turned his back on me!"

"Choice?" I countered, my heart racing. "Your choices are what led to this! You could have built something together, but you chose betrayal. You chose power over loyalty, and now you're alone. Is that what you wanted?"

The two men stood before me like titans clashing, and I felt the tremors of their animosity reverberating through the ground. Derrick's expression twisted, and for a moment, he looked almost human, the mask of malice slipping just enough for me to see the vulnerability beneath. But it was gone as quickly as it had come, replaced by an anger so deep it threatened to consume him.

"You're right about one thing," Derrick spat, his voice lowering to a menacing whisper. "I'm not alone. I have others who will do my bidding. And they're coming for you."

A cold wave of dread washed over me. The reality of Derrick's threats struck hard, and I glanced at Lucas, whose expression had hardened, the resolve returning like a fortress being rebuilt.

"You think you can intimidate us? You're mistaken," Lucas said, taking a step forward, defiance radiating from him like heat from a fire. "You might have allies, but I have something you'll never understand. I have people who stand by me, who believe in me, and I won't let you take that away."

Derrick's laughter rang out, harsh and mocking. "People? You think they can protect you? You're both fools, living in a fantasy. I will destroy everything you love. You can count on that."

Without thinking, I reached out, grabbing Lucas's arm. "We need to get out of here!" My instincts screamed at me to run, to leave before the threat escalated. Derrick was dangerous, and the darkness that surrounded him was thickening by the second.

"Not yet," Lucas said, his voice calm, but his grip on my hand tightened. "This is our fight. I won't let him walk away thinking he's won."

As if summoned by our defiance, the forest seemed to shift. A rustle in the underbrush drew our attention, and the hairs on the back of my neck stood on end. The world felt charged, like the calm before a thunderstorm, and I knew something was coming—something terrible.

"Lucas," I whispered urgently, fear creeping into my voice. "We need to go now."

But Derrick only smiled, a wicked gleam in his eyes. "Oh, but it's too late for that. You don't get to leave that easily." He raised a hand, and in that instant, I knew he was summoning whatever dark forces he had at his disposal.

With a sudden, bone-chilling howl, shadows erupted from the forest, writhing like smoke come to life. They lunged toward us, dark tendrils reaching out, grasping, and pulling at the very essence of our safety. Lucas stepped in front of me, the determination in his stance radiating an almost palpable energy, as if he were a shield against the encroaching darkness.

"Get behind me!" he shouted, and I obeyed instinctively, my heart pounding as adrenaline surged through my veins. The shadows swirled around us, hungry and chaotic, a nightmarish storm that threatened to engulf everything we had fought for.

"Lucas, we can't fight this!" I yelled, panic spilling from my lips. The darkness pressed closer, a suffocating presence that felt almost sentient, an entity that thrived on fear and despair.

But Lucas remained undeterred, his eyes locked on Derrick. "I won't let you win!" he shouted, voice steady despite the chaos. With a fierce determination, he surged forward, ready to confront the very darkness that Derrick had summoned.

In that heart-stopping moment, as shadows lunged and reality twisted, I felt a surge of fear and hope mingling within me. Would Lucas's bravery be enough to push back against Derrick's impending onslaught?

And just as I prepared to reach for him, to fight beside him, a piercing scream shattered the air—echoing not from Derrick but from the depths of the forest. The sound was filled with anguish, reverberating through the trees, and I knew then that we were not alone in this battle.

As I turned, my heart racing with dread, I glimpsed a figure emerging from the shadows—a figure whose presence shifted everything I thought I understood about this fight. The trees seemed to part, revealing something far more terrifying than I could have ever imagined, and in that moment, everything I believed about loyalty and betrayal hung precariously in the balance.

Chapter 19: The Confession

The flames flickered in the hearth, casting playful shadows that danced along the walls of the dimly lit room, each flicker a brief glimpse into the tangled emotions swirling between us. Lucas sat across from me, the weight of his unspoken thoughts hanging heavily in the air. He was always the strong one, the one with the steady gaze and the ability to keep his emotions at bay. But tonight, beneath the soft glow of the firelight, that facade began to crack.

I watched him, my heart aching at the turmoil I could see just beneath the surface. His fingers absently toyed with the fraying edge of his jeans, a habit I had come to recognize as a sign of his anxiety. The room felt charged, as if the very walls were holding their breath in anticipation of his next words. When he finally spoke, his voice was barely above a whisper, laced with the kind of pain that seemed to echo from some dark corner of his past.

"It wasn't supposed to happen like this," he said, his eyes fixed on the flames as if they held the answers he sought. "I thought I was doing the right thing. I was trying to help... but it all went wrong. So wrong."

I leaned in closer, drawn by the raw honesty in his voice. "What do you mean?"

Lucas exhaled slowly, his gaze finally meeting mine, and I saw the torment swirling in his emerald eyes. "There was a deal, a chance to turn everything around for my family. But someone... someone I trusted turned out to be a traitor." He swallowed hard, the pain etched in the lines of his face. "In my arrogance, I thought I could handle it. I thought I could protect everyone. But it backfired. People got hurt. Lives were ruined."

Each word felt like a dagger, piercing through the armor he had built around himself. My instinct was to reach out, to hold him, to reassure him that he wasn't alone. "You were trying to do the right thing, Lucas. Sometimes... things spiral out of control, no matter how good our intentions are."

He shook his head, his expression hardened by regret. "But the aftermath was mine to bear. I should have seen it coming. I should have known better."

"Stop it," I said, my voice firm but gentle. "You're not to blame for someone else's betrayal. You can't carry the weight of the world on your shoulders."

His hand twitched toward mine, and I took the opportunity to grasp it, intertwining our fingers. The warmth of his skin sent a rush of comfort through me, anchoring him to the present, away from the shadows of the past that threatened to engulf him. "You don't understand," he murmured, his voice cracking slightly. "Every day, I relive it. Every choice, every moment. I see their faces... the ones I couldn't save."

"Lucas, look at me." I pulled him from the abyss of his memories with a steady gaze. "You are not a monster. You're human. You make mistakes, just like everyone else. But you have a chance to do better now. You're not alone anymore."

His grip on my hand tightened, a silent acknowledgment of the truth I laid before him. The fire crackled, filling the space between us with a comforting sound, and for a moment, the world outside faded into oblivion. It was just us, locked in a moment that felt both fragile and timeless.

"Promise me you won't shut me out again," I said softly. "I can't bear the thought of you carrying this burden alone."

"I promise," he replied, his voice low but resolute. Then, as if drawn by an invisible force, he leaned in, capturing my lips with his in a kiss that felt like the dawn breaking after a long, stormy night. It was filled with everything we had yet to say, every secret and every fear intertwining in a beautiful, chaotic dance. In that kiss, I felt the warmth of his heart and the strength of his resolve. It bound us tighter, sealing our shared confessions in a way words never could.

But as I melted into him, a chill skittered down my spine, an echo of an unsettling feeling that we were running out of time. I could almost sense Derrick's presence looming like a dark cloud on the horizon, always just out of sight, yet undeniably close. The tension in the air thickened, and the kiss that had ignited my spirit also ignited a flicker of fear deep within me.

"What if Derrick finds out?" I whispered, pulling back slightly to look into his eyes, searching for reassurance.

"We'll figure it out," Lucas said, his voice steady, but I could see the flicker of uncertainty in his gaze. "I won't let him hurt you. Not again."

The promise hung in the air between us, laden with the weight of our unspoken fears. We both knew that Derrick was a force to be reckoned with, a shadow that crept closer with each day that passed. He would stop at nothing to reclaim what he believed was his, and the thought sent a jolt of adrenaline through my veins.

Lucas stood, his determination igniting a fire in his heart that mirrored the one in the hearth. "We need to be proactive. We can't wait for him to make the first move. We have to take control of this situation."

I nodded, the firelight casting a warm glow around us, even as a storm brewed just outside. The world was shifting beneath our feet, and as the flickering flames reflected in Lucas's eyes, I felt a sense of empowerment begin to rise within me. Together, we would confront the shadows of our past and take the fight to Derrick before he could claim another victim.

Our journey was just beginning, and I was ready to face whatever challenges lay ahead, hand in hand with the boy who had captured my heart.

The warmth of the fire enveloped us, but my mind raced with the shadows of uncertainty lurking just beyond the flickering light. Lucas's revelation had cracked open a door to his past, and I could sense the raw edges of his guilt hanging in the air like smoke. As we pulled apart from our kiss, the lingering warmth of his lips still tingled on mine, but I couldn't ignore the chill creeping into my bones.

"What do we do now?" I asked, my voice barely above a whisper. The question hung in the space between us, heavy with implication.

"We prepare," Lucas replied, a flicker of determination sparking in his eyes. "We can't let Derrick catch us off guard."

I nodded, feeling the swell of adrenaline rise within me. It was time to stop reacting and start taking control. I had been on the sidelines for too long, watching while the storm brewed, waiting for the inevitable crash. "What's the plan?"

Lucas leaned back, a thoughtful expression settling on his features as he considered our next move. "First, we need to gather information. Derrick's movements, his associates—everything. I have some contacts who might know what he's up to."

"Contacts?" I raised an eyebrow. "Like the ones who sell questionable information for a price?"

A wry smile tugged at his lips, a glimmer of mischief illuminating the seriousness of our situation. "Exactly. You'd be surprised what people are willing to sell when it comes to the underbelly of this town."

"Great," I said, rolling my eyes. "Just what I've always wanted—an inside scoop from the shady corners of society. Remind me to send my gratitude to Derrick for this delightful adventure."

"Don't worry, I'll make sure to get you a souvenir," he shot back, laughter spilling from his lips. The sound was a welcome reprieve from the tension that had settled over us, a reminder of why I was in this fight to begin with. Lucas was worth every moment of uncertainty, every risk we had to take.

As we began to formulate our plan, the fire crackled energetically, casting an inviting glow around us. I pulled a notepad from my bag, scribbling down ideas and strategies as Lucas paced, his mind clearly working through the various angles of our approach. We had to think several steps ahead, as if playing a high-stakes game of chess, and I could feel the thrill of the challenge igniting a fire of my own.

"Let's start by tracking Derrick's usual haunts," Lucas suggested, tapping his chin in thought. "If he's out there, flaunting his power, he'll have his entourage with him."

"Ah, yes," I said, my tone dripping with sarcasm, "the notorious gang of ne'er-do-wells who love a good public spectacle."

"Exactly! If we can blend in, maybe we can overhear something useful. A slip of the tongue can be quite revealing."

I couldn't help but chuckle at the image of us donning disguises—perhaps oversized sunglasses and trench coats, ready to infiltrate the local watering hole of bad decisions. "What about the whole 'secretive spy' vibe? We could really pull off the double agent thing."

Lucas smirked. "You think I'd look good in a fedora?"

"Only if you promise to carry a martini and say something cliché," I quipped, meeting his playful banter with my own.

The mood shifted as the laughter subsided, and a weight settled back into the room. I could feel the undercurrents of danger creeping closer. "But seriously," I said, my tone sobering. "If Derrick catches wind of our plans..."

Lucas interrupted, his expression resolute. "Then we won't let him. We'll be smarter than he thinks. We have to be."

I glanced at the fire, the flames licking the logs with fervor, and nodded. "Alright, we'll gather intel, stay low, and keep our eyes open. But what happens if we find something? What's our next move?"

His gaze sharpened, a new intensity filling the space between us. "We confront him. But not without a plan. We need to know what he's after and how to counter it. I won't let him hurt you again."

His fierce protectiveness sent a thrill through me, but I could also sense the storm of emotions roiling beneath the surface. Lucas was a warrior at heart, but I worried about the cost of the battle ahead. "And if confronting him means putting us both in danger?"

"We'll figure it out," he replied, his voice steady. "Together."

There was something in his unwavering commitment that anchored me, a promise wrapped in determination. Just then, a soft knock echoed from the front door, interrupting our planning session. My heart raced at the unexpected interruption, a surge of anxiety rushing through me.

"Who could that be?" I asked, glancing toward Lucas, whose brow furrowed with concern.

"Stay here," he said, moving toward the door with a quiet caution that belied his usual confidence. The shadows of the evening cloaked him as he approached, creating an almost cinematic tension in the air. I could feel my heart pounding in my chest, my instincts on high alert.

He opened the door slightly, peering out into the darkened hallway. A moment passed, the silence stretching painfully, until I heard a voice.

"Lucas? It's me."

The familiar tone of Madeline broke through the tension, a wave of relief washing over me. I stepped closer, catching a glimpse of her through the crack in the door. "What are you doing here?"

"Something's happened," she said, urgency coloring her words. "We need to talk. Now."

Lucas exchanged a quick glance with me, his expression shifting from caution to concern. "What is it?"

Madeline stepped inside, her eyes darting between us as if she were afraid of being overheard. "It's about Derrick. He's making moves, and they're not just business-related. He's come back to settle a personal score."

My stomach twisted at the implication, the reality of our situation settling heavily upon me. "What do you mean?"

"There are whispers that he's looking for someone to make an example of. He's become more unpredictable, and I don't think it's just about the deal."

The weight of her words settled like lead in the pit of my stomach. Lucas and I shared a tense glance, the unspoken fear hanging between us. Derrick was no longer just a shadow in the background; he was now a looming threat, a predator with a vendetta.

"Who's he targeting?" Lucas asked, his voice low, but the intensity behind it was undeniable.

Madeline took a deep breath, her eyes shining with an intensity that mirrored our own. "I don't know yet, but I heard his name mentioned—yours, Lucas."

The name hung in the air like a death sentence, a chilling reminder that our lives had been irrevocably altered. I could feel the walls of our carefully constructed sanctuary beginning to crumble, the firelight flickering as if in sync with my rising panic. The game had changed, and we were now players in a deadly round of chess, each move critical, each moment heavy with consequence.

I grasped Lucas's hand tighter, the warmth anchoring me as I prepared to face whatever storm awaited us, knowing that together, we might just weather it all.

Madeline's urgent words hung in the air like an ominous cloud, the reality of her revelation dawning on us both. Lucas's expression hardened, his jaw tightening as he processed the implications. "Derrick is targeting me?" he echoed, disbelief etched across his face.

Madeline nodded, her voice steady but laced with concern. "Yes. I overheard him talking to some of his associates. He's not just angry about the deal anymore; he wants revenge, and you're at the top of his list."

I felt the blood drain from my face. The very mention of Derrick's name sent a chill creeping down my spine, conjuring memories of his cold gaze and the ruthlessness that simmered beneath his charming exterior. "What does he plan to do?" I asked, my voice steadier than I felt.

Madeline shook her head, frustration pinching her features. "I don't know specifics. But I have a feeling it's not going to be pretty. We need to figure out a way to protect ourselves—and each other."

Lucas's eyes narrowed, a fierce determination igniting within him. "If he wants to make an example of me, then he'll have to go through me first."

"Lucas, wait," I interjected, grasping his hand firmly. "This isn't just about you anymore. Derrick's not afraid to hurt people to get what he wants. We have to think this through."

"Thinking hasn't done us much good so far, has it?" he shot back, the tension in his voice palpable. "We've been reactive instead of proactive. I'm not going to stand by while he tries to intimidate us."

Madeline stepped forward, her eyes fierce with resolve. "Then we fight back. We gather intel, but we also prepare ourselves. If Derrick thinks he can waltz back into our lives and throw threats around, he's got another thing coming."

"Right," I said, my heart pounding with adrenaline. "What's the plan? We can't just sit here and wait for him to make the first move."

"We need to reach out to the people in our circle," Lucas suggested, his mind racing. "There might be others who have faced Derrick's wrath. We can gather information and rally support."

"That sounds like a good start," Madeline agreed, a spark of hope igniting in her eyes. "But we also need to think about how to protect ourselves. If it comes to a confrontation, we need to be ready."

"What about the people he associates with? If we can leverage their connections, maybe we can get a step ahead of him," I proposed, the gears in my mind starting to turn.

Lucas nodded slowly, clearly appreciating my input. "You're right. If we can get someone close to Derrick to talk, we might learn more about his plans."

Madeline's brow furrowed in thought. "There's someone I know who might have information. A friend of mine used to work for Derrick's father. If we can reach out to him, he might have insights into Derrick's motivations."

"Let's do it," Lucas replied, his determination returning. "We'll reach out tonight. The sooner we gather intel, the better."

As the three of us launched into an improvised strategy session, the fire crackled, the warmth providing a false sense of security against the dark reality we faced. I could feel the energy shifting, urgency infusing our plans as we turned our attention toward the night ahead.

Madeline pulled out her phone, tapping out a message to her contact. "I'll keep this discreet. If he responds, we can meet somewhere neutral," she said, glancing up at us.

"What about Derrick? If he has people watching us..." I started, but Lucas interrupted.

"Then we'll have to be careful," he said, his voice low. "But we can't let fear dictate our actions. The more we hide, the more power we give him."

The weight of his words settled heavily upon my shoulders. The stakes were higher than ever, and each decision we made felt monumental, like stepping onto a tightrope with no safety net.

"Let's split up for a bit," Madeline suggested. "We can cover more ground that way. I'll go check in with my contact and see what I can find out. You two can brainstorm other ways to gather information."

"Sounds good," Lucas agreed, his focus returning to me. "Let's meet back here in an hour."

"Be safe," I said, squeezing his hand as we parted. There was a mix of apprehension and determination in the air, the weight of our choices settling in as I watched Madeline slip out the door, leaving us alone once more.

Once the door clicked shut, the atmosphere shifted again, thick with tension and unspoken fears. "What if this backfires?" I asked, my voice barely a whisper.

"It won't," Lucas said, stepping closer, his eyes locked onto mine. "We'll figure it out, together."

I nodded, trying to dispel the gnawing anxiety twisting in my stomach. "You're right. Together."

But deep down, the doubts lingered. Could we really outmaneuver Derrick? He was a force of nature, unpredictable and dangerous. As I looked into Lucas's eyes, I felt a flicker of hope, but it was accompanied by a shiver of fear.

The hour dragged on as we strategized, our plans morphing and shifting as we threw ideas around, each one tinged with urgency. Lucas's intensity was captivating, but the stakes felt too high, the danger too real.

Suddenly, Lucas's phone buzzed, and he glanced down at the screen. His expression shifted, concern flickering in his eyes. "It's Madeline."

I leaned closer as he read the message, his brow furrowing further. "What is it?"

"She met with my contact," he said, his voice low. "But Derrick's already onto them. They were followed."

Panic surged through me, a tidal wave crashing over my carefully constructed composure. "What? Are they okay?"

"I don't know. She didn't have time to elaborate. But we need to act fast."

Before I could respond, the door swung open, and Madeline burst in, breathless and wide-eyed. "We need to go. Now."

"Why? What happened?" I asked, my heart racing.

"There are people coming. Derrick's men. We can't stay here."

The words sent a jolt through my system, adrenaline flooding my veins as I glanced at Lucas, who was already moving into action. "Let's go!" he urged, his voice cutting through the panic.

We sprinted toward the back door, the urgency propelling us forward. Just as we reached for the handle, a loud crash resonated from the front of the house, echoing through the air like thunder. The unmistakable sound of shattering glass followed, sending shards of fear slicing through my heart.

"Quick!" Lucas urged, pulling me toward the back, but I hesitated, looking back toward the source of the noise.

"Did they—"

A voice cut through the chaos, rich and mocking. "Running away already? I thought we had unfinished business."

Derrick's silhouette loomed in the doorway, a dark figure framed by the chaos behind him. He stepped forward, his smile chilling, and I felt the world narrow around me, the realization that our confrontation had come sooner than expected crashing over me like a wave.

"We're not done yet," he taunted, his eyes gleaming with menace.

In that moment, every plan we had made felt irrelevant. All that mattered was the fight that lay ahead, and I knew that nothing would ever be the same again.

Chapter 21: Descent

The cold air wrapped around me as Derrick led us through the decaying corridors of the abandoned warehouse. Each step echoed in the vast emptiness, the sound swallowed by the crumbling walls that loomed like silent sentinels. The smell of rust hung heavy in the damp atmosphere, mingling with the faint scent of something far less savory—maybe remnants of the past, like echoes of old machinery or the ghosts of dreams long abandoned. Shadows clung to the corners, twisting into shapes that made my heart race. I could feel the oppressive weight of Derrick's malevolence pressing down on me, a palpable force that wrapped around my throat like a noose.

Lucas walked beside me, his demeanor tense but resolute. There was something in his eyes—an unwavering determination that made my chest tighten with admiration. But as we followed Derrick deeper into the bowels of this forsaken place, the bravado that usually colored Lucas's words was missing, replaced by a cautious silence that hinted at his own trepidation. I caught glimpses of fear etched into his features, and it tore at me, knowing that he was in this situation because of me, because of my insistence to confront the chaos that surrounded us.

Derrick's laughter sliced through the heavy air, sharp and mocking. He turned to Lucas, his eyes glittering with a deranged delight, as if he were a conductor orchestrating a symphony of despair. "You thought you could escape me, didn't you? You thought I'd just disappear into the shadows after all I've sacrificed? Oh, Lucas, you truly are naive." His voice dripped with contempt, each word laced with a venom that made my skin crawl.

"Derrick, this isn't you," Lucas said, his voice steadier than I felt. "We can talk about this. You don't have to go through with whatever twisted plan you've concocted. There's still a chance to—"

"To what? To reason with me?" Derrick spat, cutting him off. "You're the reason for my suffering, the reason I'm trapped in this hell. Everything I've done, every dark turn I've taken, it's all led me to this moment—to make you pay. I've waited for this. I've savored every second, and now, it's time for the curtain to drop."

I could see the way Derrick's fingers twitched, his energy crackling in the air like a live wire. It sent a shiver of dread through me, coiling tight in my stomach. As much as I wanted to believe Lucas could pull us from this nightmare, I knew Derrick was unpredictable, a volatile storm waiting to erupt. My mind raced, searching for a way out, a plan, anything to shift the balance of power that had tilted so dangerously in Derrick's favor.

Derrick moved closer, his expression morphing into something I could only describe as deranged joy. "You remember those nights, don't you? The ones where we laughed, where you pretended to be my friend while all the while you plotted your escape? Every time you turned your back, I watched. Every time you thought you could be free, I tightened the chains. And now," he leaned in closer, eyes wide with manic intensity, "now you'll see how I've transformed that pain into power. You'll witness your downfall, and I'll be the one to bring you to your knees."

A cold sweat broke out along my skin, but I couldn't let fear take root. I was determined not to be a bystander in my own life, not anymore. "You think you're powerful, Derrick? You think that you can control us with fear?" I felt the words slip from my mouth before I had the chance to filter them, but as soon as I spoke, I could see the flicker of surprise in his eyes. "Power isn't about control. It's about making a choice. And you've made yours—now it's my turn."

He scoffed, taken aback by my sudden defiance, but I could see a spark of curiosity igniting behind his fury. "And what choice is that, sweet girl? To stand against me? How foolish."

"Foolishness is a luxury you can't afford, Derrick," Lucas chimed in, his voice low and dangerous. "You've convinced yourself that you're the hero of this story, but you're just a villain hiding behind a mask of pain. And I'll show you how that mask can shatter."

Derrick faltered, if only for a heartbeat, his facade cracking just enough to expose the insecurities beneath. But then he regained his composure, the smirk returning as he shook his head in disbelief. "You really think you can change anything? This is the end of your story. I've already decided the outcome."

My heart raced, an urgent pounding that echoed the tumult of emotions surging through me. I knew that every moment counted; I had to find a way to break free from this web he had woven. "You're wrong, Derrick. The only person you're trapping is yourself," I shot back, my voice gaining strength. "You're consumed by your hatred, and that's the real prison. We may be here now, but this won't end with your victory. You can't escape the consequences of your actions."

He recoiled slightly, as if my words had struck a nerve. I seized the moment, bolstered by a rush of adrenaline, as a plan took shape in my mind. "Lucas, if you can distract him for just a second—"

Before I could finish, Derrick lunged, fury lighting up his features like a wild flame. But Lucas was quick, darting sideways just as Derrick reached for him. The chaotic dance intensified, each movement a fragile balance between fear and resolve.

I steeled myself, drawing in a deep breath as I prepared to act. If I wanted to break free from this nightmare, I needed to seize control, to reclaim my narrative before Derrick could tighten his grip. The tension hung heavy in the air, thick with the promise of confrontation, and I steeled myself for what was to come.

The air was thick with tension, swirling like the dust motes that danced lazily in the shafts of dim light streaming through cracked windows. Derrick's laughter echoed, a jarring sound that ricocheted off the rusty metal beams and faded into the gloom. He circled us

216

ALINA FORD

like a predator, each step deliberate, as if savoring the thrill of his impending victory. Lucas and I stood back to back, the weight of our situation heavy on our shoulders. I could feel the heat radiating from Lucas, a fierce energy that grounded me even as fear clawed at my insides.

"Do you remember when we used to talk about our dreams?" Derrick taunted, his voice laced with mock nostalgia. "You were going to be someone special, Lucas. A hero, even. Look at you now. A washed-up shadow of your former self. All that potential wasted." He leaned closer, his breath hot and rancid. "And you, my dear," he said, turning his gaze on me with a predatory glint. "You're just the icing on the cake, aren't you? A pretty little distraction to keep him from facing reality."

I clenched my fists, fighting the urge to shrink away from his gaze. "You think I'm just a distraction? You're the one who can't move on from the past. You're stuck in this cycle of bitterness and rage, Derrick. It's exhausting just watching you." The words tumbled out before I could censor them, a spark of courage igniting within me.

Derrick's expression flickered, irritation sparking in his eyes. "You don't know anything about me. You're just a child playing dress-up in a world you can't comprehend." His smile, if it could be called that, twisted into something sinister. "But you will. You'll learn all too soon."

Lucas stepped forward, his presence imposing as he challenged Derrick. "Enough with the theatrics. This isn't a play, Derrick; it's our lives. If you think you can just waltz in here and dictate how this ends, you're sorely mistaken."

Derrick's lips curled into a smirk, amusement dancing in his eyes. "Oh, but you're wrong, Lucas. This is exactly how it ends. I have all the cards, and you... well, you're just playing at a game you've already lost."

As he spoke, I felt the ground beneath us tremble ever so slightly, a reminder that this warehouse was more than just a backdrop for his twisted fantasy. The walls felt like they were closing in, the air thickening around us, almost as if the very structure itself was holding its breath in anticipation of the chaos to come. My heart raced, adrenaline coursing through my veins, pushing me to act before the inevitable spiraled beyond our control.

"Let's talk about choices, then," I interjected, my voice steady despite the tremor in my hands. "You've made yours, Derrick. You've chosen this path of destruction. But you're not invincible. We're not without options. I refuse to let you manipulate us any longer."

Derrick's face contorted with rage, and I knew I had struck a nerve. He lunged forward, but Lucas was ready, stepping in to block Derrick's advance. "We're not afraid of you, Derrick," Lucas growled, his voice low and fierce. "This ends now."

Suddenly, I spotted a glimmer of light reflecting off something metallic on the ground near Derrick's feet—a discarded piece of machinery. In that fleeting moment, I made a split-second decision. "Lucas, go!" I shouted, grabbing the makeshift weapon and hurling it toward Derrick with all my strength. The metal clanged against the concrete, startling him.

In the chaos, Lucas charged forward, pushing Derrick off balance, and I darted to the side, my heart pounding in my chest. It was a reckless move, but desperation has a way of blurring the lines of caution. Derrick stumbled, momentarily thrown off guard by the unexpected turn of events.

"Do you really think this changes anything?" he sneered, regaining his footing and straightening. "You're still trapped, and now you've only made me angrier."

"Let us go, Derrick," Lucas said, his voice low and firm. "This isn't who you are. You don't have to do this."

Derrick paused, the darkness in his eyes flickering for just a moment, and I seized the opportunity. "You have a choice, Derrick! You can step back from this edge before it consumes you. You can let go of the past!"

For a heartbeat, I saw uncertainty cross his features, a crack in the facade he had built around himself. But then, it vanished, replaced by a simmering rage. "You think you can talk me down? You think words can save you? You're both fools." He lunged again, this time with a fervor that made my skin crawl.

I ducked just in time, feeling the rush of air as he narrowly missed me. Lucas was right there, and together, we moved as one, a synchronized dance of survival against a backdrop of looming despair. My mind raced, searching for an escape route, a way to break free from this nightmare.

"Think, Lily!" I urged myself, forcing my mind to focus amidst the chaos. I needed to distract him, to throw him off balance again. "Derrick, you're stronger than this. You can still change!"

His laughter rang out, hollow and chilling. "Change? You think I haven't embraced who I am? You think I haven't savored the power I've claimed? You're about to learn just how wrong you are."

The moment hung in the air, charged with a dangerous energy, and I felt the world narrow to this one point in time. I glanced at Lucas, who nodded slightly, a silent agreement passing between us. We would stand together, no matter the outcome.

Suddenly, a loud crash reverberated through the warehouse, causing Derrick to momentarily divert his attention. The wall to our right had given way to a small section of broken bricks and debris, exposing a glimmer of moonlight. The light beckoned to me like a siren's call, a reminder that freedom was not far away.

"Lucas, this way!" I shouted, urgency fueling my every word as I sprinted toward the opening. Derrick's furious cries echoed behind us, but the sense of impending escape drove me forward, pulling Lucas along with me.

As we rushed toward the opening, the world felt alive around us, a cacophony of sounds and emotions swirling together. Hope blossomed, fragile but fierce, urging me to push harder, to break through the confines of this oppressive space. The air grew cooler as we neared the breach, the promise of freedom tantalizingly close, while behind us, Derrick's rage turned into a chilling determination.

"Run!" Lucas shouted, and I didn't hesitate. Together, we plunged into the uncertain night, leaving behind the darkness of the warehouse and the haunting specter of Derrick's obsession. We raced into the world beyond, the weight of our past trailing behind us like a shadow, but with every step, I felt the chains of fear begin to break. Freedom was out there, waiting for us to grasp it, and this was only the beginning.

The moonlight spilled through the jagged opening we had made in our frantic escape, illuminating the world beyond the warehouse in a silvery glow. The cool night air felt like a balm against the sweat that clung to my skin, a refreshing reminder that freedom was within reach. I could hear Derrick's furious shouts behind us, each word laced with the venom of his twisted obsession, but the sounds faded into the background as adrenaline surged through my veins.

"Keep running!" Lucas urged, his voice low but urgent as we sprinted away from the warehouse. I could feel the thrum of his heartbeat matching my own, a rhythm of determination that spurred us forward. The darkness enveloped us like a comforting cloak, but the shadows held secrets—fearful and dangerous.

"Where do we go now?" I gasped, glancing over my shoulder. The warehouse loomed in the distance, a hulking beast in the night, and I could barely make out Derrick's silhouette as he emerged from the breach we had left behind. "We can't just run forever."

"There's a shortcut through the alley!" Lucas shouted, his eyes scanning our surroundings. "If we can make it to the street, we can find help."

Without hesitation, he veered toward a narrow passage that snaked between two dilapidated buildings, their brick façades weathered by time. I followed closely, heart racing as I navigated the debris scattered across the ground—crumpled cans, shattered glass, and the remnants of a life once vibrant. The alley seemed alive, filled with whispers and shadows that flickered just beyond the edge of my vision.

As we darted through the narrow space, I felt a flicker of hope igniting within me. Perhaps we could outsmart Derrick after all. But that optimism was short-lived as the sounds of his pursuit grew louder behind us, like thunder rumbling in the distance.

"Faster!" Lucas urged, and I could feel his determination propelling us forward. The alley twisted and turned, leading us deeper into the heart of the town, where the familiar streetlights flickered like distant stars, casting erratic patterns of light and shadow. I could almost taste the safety of the main road, where people bustled about, blissfully unaware of the chaos unfolding in the shadows.

Just as we reached the end of the alley, a loud crash echoed behind us. I turned to see Derrick barreling through the debris, his face a mask of rage, eyes burning with an insatiable hunger for vengeance. "You think you can escape me? You're wrong! You're mine!" he bellowed, the sound reverberating off the walls like a sinister chant.

I exchanged a glance with Lucas, the urgency clear between us. "We can't let him catch us!" I shouted, and with that, we burst into the open street, gasping for breath as we slowed, momentarily disoriented by the brightness of the lights.

The street was bustling with life; people walked by, their laughter and chatter blending into a backdrop of normalcy. I grasped Lucas's arm, desperation clawing at me. "What if he catches up? What if no one believes us?"

"Then we make them believe us," Lucas said firmly, his gaze locked on a nearby diner that glowed like a beacon in the night. "In there. We'll find a way to get help."

We raced toward the diner, the heavy scent of fries and grilled burgers wafting through the air, a stark contrast to the adrenaline-fueled panic coursing through us. As we pushed through the glass door, the cheerful jingle announced our arrival, but the warmth of the interior did little to quell the chill of fear that lingered in my bones.

"Two shakes and a stack of pancakes, please!" an old woman behind the counter called out, oblivious to our frantic expressions. The clatter of dishes and the murmur of conversations enveloped us like a comforting embrace, but I couldn't shake the feeling of impending doom looming just outside.

"Excuse me!" I shouted, turning to the patrons gathered at the nearest booth. "We need help! There's a man—he's dangerous!"

Several heads turned, but the chatter continued, a dissonant symphony that drowned out my plea. Panic began to rise in my throat. Were we truly alone in this fight? My heart sank at the thought of Derrick catching up to us while these strangers remained indifferent.

Lucas grabbed my hand, squeezing it tightly. "We can't lose hope. We need to get to the back—there's a phone. Someone will listen," he urged, pulling me toward the far end of the diner.

We maneuvered through the maze of tables, the warmth of the diner's lights creating a stark contrast to the cold dread that clung to me. I could hear Derrick's angry shouts filtering through the din, his pursuit relentless and unyielding.

"There! The restroom!" I pointed to a door at the far side, the light flickering overhead. "If we can lock ourselves in, we can call for help."

Lucas nodded, and together we dashed toward the restroom, hearts racing as the sounds of Derrick's footsteps grew louder. Just as we reached the door, it swung open, revealing a disheveled man with wild eyes who stumbled out, narrowly missing us.

"Outta my way!" he grunted, clearly oblivious to the chaos unraveling around him.

I pushed through the door and slammed it shut behind us, locking it just as Derrick's shadow fell across the small window in the door. His face was a mask of fury, and I could see him pounding against the door, his fists striking the wood with a force that made the walls shudder.

"Let me in!" he shouted, his voice a low growl. "You can't hide forever! This isn't over!"

I stepped back, my heart racing as I frantically scanned the tiny restroom, searching for a means of escape. The window was too small to fit through, and the cramped space offered little in the way of options. Lucas fumbled for his phone, only to curse under his breath as the screen blinked out. "No signal! He's blocking us!"

"We have to think fast," I said, the walls closing in on me, the air thick with fear. "If we can't get help, we need a plan to fight back."

Suddenly, the sound of breaking glass shattered the tension, and I turned to see the man from before stumbling back into the restroom, clutching a beer bottle, his face pale with shock. "What the hell is going on?" he slurred, eyes darting between us and the door.

"Get out! He's dangerous!" I shouted, and just as I spoke, Derrick's voice rang out, louder now, filled with rage.

"I will end this, once and for all!"

Panic flooded through me. This was it—the moment of truth. We were backed into a corner, and the only way out was to confront the chaos Derrick had unleashed.

The man's eyes widened as he registered the urgency in my voice. "You really think you can fight him?"

"Watch us," Lucas snapped, determination igniting in his gaze. "If we have to stand our ground, then we will."

But just as Derrick's fist struck the door again, the handle rattled violently. My breath hitched in my throat, and I exchanged a glance with Lucas, knowing we had mere seconds to decide our fate.

"I won't let him win," I murmured, adrenaline pumping through my veins. "Whatever it takes, we will stop him."

As the door splintered under Derrick's relentless assault, we stood ready to face the storm, hearts pounding in sync with the impending chaos that threatened to unravel our lives. In that moment, a single thought echoed in my mind: We would not be mere victims in this tale. We would fight back.

Chapter 22: A Desperate Gamble

The night air bites at my skin as we stumble into the open, the chaos of the warehouse fading into a distant echo. Each breath I take is sharp, laced with the crispness of early autumn, invigorating and disorienting all at once. I can still feel the weight of fear coiling in my stomach, a reminder of the shadows we've escaped but not entirely left behind. The moon hangs high, a silver sentinel overseeing our flight, casting eerie shadows that dance in the corners of my vision, making me wonder if we are truly alone.

Lucas's grip on my hand is firm, his warmth radiating against the chill. I can sense the adrenaline coursing through him, matching my own—a chaotic symphony that drowns out every rational thought. We dash across the gravel lot, the stones crunching underfoot like shattered glass, amplifying the sound of our escape. The world around us feels surreal, a stark contrast to the stifling atmosphere of the warehouse filled with threats. I can hardly believe we've made it this far, yet the danger still looms, hovering just out of sight like a predator waiting for the right moment to pounce.

"Where to?" Lucas breathes, his voice a mix of urgency and determination. I glance at him, his features illuminated by the moonlight—strong jaw, eyes blazing with resolve. He looks like someone who could take on the world, and at this moment, he's all I have. My heart swells with an unexpected warmth; even in this madness, I can't help but admire his courage.

"Over there!" I point to a narrow alley that runs alongside the warehouse, cloaked in darkness. It seems to lead away from the chaos and toward an unknown safety. "We can hide there, catch our breath."

He nods, and we sprint toward the alley, the shadows swallowing us whole as we duck into the narrow passage. The scent of damp earth and distant smoke envelops us, mixing with the stale odor of the warehouse. The alley is a world apart, filled with the soft patter of rainwater trickling down a nearby drain and the distant hum of the city—a strange lullaby in the midst of our nightmare.

As we lean against the cool, damp brick wall, I can feel Lucas's heart pounding beside me, a steady reminder that we are alive and still fighting. I close my eyes for a brief moment, drawing in the sounds and scents, grounding myself in the reality of our situation. We've evaded Derrick, but how long until he realizes we're gone? The thought sends a shiver racing down my spine, and I glance at Lucas, hoping he can sense my unease.

"What's the plan now?" he asks, brushing a hand through his hair, the movement both charming and disheveled. It reminds me that underneath all this chaos, we are still just kids trying to navigate a world that has become all too perilous.

I take a deep breath, willing my mind to focus. "We need to get to the old mill on the outskirts of town. If we can make it there, we can find a way to warn the others." The old mill has always been a place of refuge for us—a relic of our childhood adventures. It stands at the edge of town, a dilapidated structure that seems to hold our secrets within its crumbling walls.

"Are you sure it's safe?" Lucas's brow furrows, but I can see the flicker of trust in his eyes. He knows the mill as well as I do, a place filled with echoes of laughter and shared memories.

"Safe enough. It's far enough from Derrick's reach, and we can use the back entrance to slip in undetected. We can figure out our next move from there."

With a determined nod, we start moving again, sticking to the shadows, our footsteps muffled against the damp ground. Each step feels like a heartbeat, thumping in rhythm with my racing thoughts. I can't shake the feeling that we're being watched, the hairs on the back of my neck prickling with unease.

Just as we near the street corner, a sharp sound slices through the stillness—a low growl echoing off the walls. Lucas freezes beside me, his eyes widening in alarm. "What was that?" he whispers, his voice barely above a breath.

I strain to listen, my pulse quickening. It's not just our imaginations running wild; something lurks in the darkness, a presence that feels all too familiar and threatening. Suddenly, a figure emerges from the shadows, and my heart drops into my stomach.

"Lucas!" I hiss, tugging him back, but it's too late. The figure steps into the light, revealing Derrick, his expression a mask of triumph. "Did you really think you could escape me?"

The chill of dread courses through me as I instinctively draw closer to Lucas, who stands his ground, jaw clenched in defiance. "We're not afraid of you, Derrick." His voice is steadier than I feel, a beacon of strength amid the encroaching darkness.

Derrick chuckles, the sound low and menacing. "Brave words from a couple of kids playing a dangerous game. But you don't understand the stakes." He steps closer, and I catch a glimpse of the glint of something metallic in his hand.

"Run!" I shout, pushing Lucas ahead of me as I make a desperate bid for escape. My heart races, a drumbeat of fear and adrenaline propelling me forward. We bolt toward the old mill, the sound of Derrick's laughter echoing behind us—a reminder that this nightmare is far from over.

The mill looms ahead, its silhouette cutting against the starry sky, a ghost of our past. I know it's our only hope. We can't let Derrick catch us, not now when we are so close to finding a way to end this madness. I can feel Lucas's presence beside me, a lifeline as we navigate this treacherous terrain, and I pray with every ounce of my being that we'll find safety within those weathered walls.

The mill stands before us, a crumbling fortress draped in shadows, its weathered wood exuding an air of resilience against the encroaching night. I push the door open with a creak that reverberates like a warning through the silent structure. Lucas hesitates for just a moment, glancing back at the darkness we're fleeing, but I pull him inside, urgency pulling us deeper into the musty interior. The scent of damp wood mingles with the faintest hint of nostalgia, reminding me of afternoons spent exploring this place long before it became a refuge from danger.

We slip into the belly of the mill, the dim light filtering through cracked windows casting eerie patterns on the floor. Dust dances in the air, caught in the beams of moonlight, and for a moment, I allow myself to revel in the memories of laughter and play, of innocent adventures with friends who knew nothing of the shadows stalking us now. But that moment is fleeting; the past is a luxury we can't afford.

"Where do we go from here?" Lucas's voice cuts through the stillness, bringing me back to the present. His expression reflects a mix of fear and determination, and I can't help but admire his bravery. It's the kind of courage that could turn the tide, if only we could harness it properly.

"There's a back room," I reply, recalling the old layout of the mill. "We can barricade ourselves in there and figure out our next steps." My heart races at the thought of being cornered again, but this time, it feels different. The mill holds secrets, and perhaps it can offer us the solace we desperately need.

We navigate through the familiar labyrinth of rusting machinery and decaying wood. I brush my fingers along the rough surface of a beam, feeling the history of this place pulse beneath my touch. It's alive with memories, and I cling to that thought, hoping it can shield us from the reality outside.

As we reach the back room, I glance at Lucas, whose expression has shifted from apprehension to something more resolute. "We'll make it through this," he states, his voice stronger now, like a lifeline thrown into turbulent waters.

"Right," I agree, feeling a flicker of hope. "But we need to be smart. Derrick won't give up easily."

With a swift motion, we push a heavy crate against the door, its weight grounding us against the impending storm. We huddle together, the shadows wrapping around us like a thick fog, creating a cocoon that both protects and isolates. I can feel the heat radiating off Lucas, and despite the circumstances, my heart flutters in a way I haven't allowed myself to acknowledge before.

"Do you think we lost him?" he asks, breaking the silence that has settled around us like a heavy blanket.

I lean closer, straining to listen for any sign of pursuit, but the mill stands eerily quiet. "For now," I reply, my voice a whisper. "But he'll be looking for us. We can't let our guard down."

As if on cue, a distant sound breaks through the stillness—a low rumble, followed by the faintest vibrations in the floor beneath us. My heart leaps into my throat. "What was that?" I ask, panic rising like bile.

Lucas's brow furrows, his eyes narrowing in concentration. "I don't know, but we should check it out. If Derrick's coming, we need to be ready."

Against my better judgment, I nod, knowing that remaining hidden could be just as dangerous as confronting whatever lurks beyond the door. "Okay, let's move quietly," I whisper, urging him forward.

We ease the crate away from the door, its weight feeling insurmountable, as though the very act of revealing ourselves will draw the attention of whatever horrors await. I push the door open just a crack, peering out into the dim corridor. The air feels charged, as if the mill itself is holding its breath, waiting for something to happen.

What I see sends a chill spiraling down my spine. Derrick's men, shadows of intimidation, are moving through the space, their voices hushed but urgent. "They can't have gone far," one of them says, his tone dripping with frustration. "Search every inch. They have to be here."

I pull back, closing the door softly, my heart pounding in rhythm with my frantic thoughts. "They're looking for us. We need a plan, and fast," I say, adrenaline igniting my senses.

"Do you think we could sneak out the back?" Lucas suggests, glancing around the dim room as if trying to decipher the safest route.

"The back door is probably locked, and if we go out there, we'll be exposed." I consider our options, my mind racing. "What if we set a distraction? Draw them away from the main area so we can slip out unnoticed?"

Lucas's eyes light up with a spark of mischief. "Like throwing something to make noise? I might have just the thing." He pulls out a small, worn-out baseball from his pocket, a remnant of happier times when the world seemed less complicated. "If we throw this far enough, it might buy us a few moments."

I can't help but chuckle at the absurdity of it all. "Who knew that a baseball would become our weapon of choice?"

"We're living in a horror movie, so I'd say it fits," he retorts, his grin infectious.

"Okay, but we need to time this perfectly. As soon as we hear them shift, we make our move," I say, my heart racing with the thrill of the impending gamble.

Lucas nods, the seriousness returning to his expression. "On three, then?"

"On three."

We hold our breaths, listening intently to the muffled voices outside. I grip the doorknob tightly, my fingers sweaty against the cool metal. The moment stretches, time seeming to warp around us.

"One..." Lucas starts, his voice barely above a whisper.

"Two..." I add, the anticipation crackling in the air.

"Three!"

I push the door open and Lucas hurls the baseball down the corridor, its trajectory spinning with the promise of chaos. The sound it makes as it strikes the floor reverberates through the mill, a sharp crack that slices through the tension like a knife.

"Go!" I shout, and we bolt, hearts racing as we make our escape into the unknown, leaving the ghosts of the past behind us as we dive into the uncertainty that lies ahead. The thrill of the chase ignites something deep within me, and for the first time, I feel like we just might stand a chance against the shadows closing in.

The thrill of our escape electrifies the air as we dart from the mill's shadowy interior into the open night. The stars shimmer overhead like watchful eyes, and the chill of autumn nips at our skin, grounding us in the reality of what we've just done. Each pounding step on the gravel feels like a countdown, a race against the inevitable return of Derrick and his men. The quiet murmur of the night surrounds us, but it's deceptive; danger lingers just beyond the edges of our perception.

"Where now?" Lucas pants, glancing over his shoulder as if expecting Derrick to leap from the shadows at any moment. His breath billows out in puffs of white, and for a fleeting moment, I find comfort in the mundane reality of our shared breath.

"The back road should lead us to the edge of town," I suggest, my voice steadying as I visualize the winding paths that crisscross through the woods. "If we can get there, we can find cover until we figure out our next move."

Lucas nods, determination etched into the lines of his face. "Let's go, then." With his hand gripping mine like a lifeline, we plunge deeper into the night, weaving through the trees that stand sentinel along the path, their leaves rustling softly in the wind as if whispering secrets.

As we move, the woods envelop us, a sanctuary that feels both familiar and alien. The smell of damp earth and decaying leaves surrounds us, mingling with the faint sweetness of pine. I can almost hear the echoes of our laughter from past escapades hidden among these trees, but now those memories feel like ghosts haunting the corners of my mind, reminding me of a time when life was uncomplicated and carefree.

"Did you ever think we'd be doing this?" Lucas's voice breaks through my reverie, tinged with disbelief and a hint of amusement.

"Running for our lives? Not exactly on my bucket list," I quip, forcing a smile despite the tension coiling in my chest. "But I guess we can add it now. It's a good conversation starter, right?"

He chuckles softly, the sound a welcome reprieve from the weight of our situation. "Yeah, like 'So, what did you do last summer? Oh, you know, just evaded a criminal mastermind.'"

The laughter fades as we press on, but the camaraderie between us feels like a buoy in an unforgiving sea. Just as I'm about to suggest a faster pace, the tranquility of the woods shatters—a crash echoes behind us, branches snapping and voices rising in urgency.

"They're coming!" I hiss, adrenaline surging through my veins. "We need to move—now!"

Without another word, we sprint through the underbrush, the sound of our pursuers growing louder, more insistent. The branches claw at my arms, and I can feel the sharp bite of panic creeping in as the darkness closes around us like a shroud. My heart thunders in my chest, each beat a reminder of the stakes.

Suddenly, I spot a narrow path veering off to the right. "This way!" I shout, yanking Lucas in the direction of the trail that seems to plunge deeper into the heart of the woods. The path is overgrown and winding, barely visible in the moonlight, but it promises the possibility of concealment.

We rush down the trail, our breaths mingling with the rustling of leaves, the sounds of pursuit fading momentarily as we navigate the treacherous terrain. Just as we start to feel a flicker of hope, the ground shifts beneath me, a sudden drop that sends me tumbling down an embankment.

"Hold on!" Lucas yells, reaching out for me. His hand brushes against mine, and I grasp it tightly as I roll to a stop at the bottom, my heart racing. The air is thick with the scent of damp moss and pine needles, and the impact has left me breathless, but I can't linger.

"Are you okay?" Lucas calls down, his voice strained with concern.

"Yeah, just my pride bruised," I manage to reply, pushing myself up and brushing off dirt and leaves. "Let's keep moving."

With a steadying breath, I look around. We're in a small clearing, the trees forming a natural barrier that offers some respite from the chaos above. I can hear the sounds of Derrick's men above us, their voices a low rumble of frustration as they try to track us down.

"This might buy us a moment," Lucas murmurs, glancing around as if gauging our options. "But we can't stay here long."

"Agreed," I reply, scanning the area. The moonlight spills into the clearing, illuminating a cluster of rocks that could provide cover if we can get there quietly. "We should head for those rocks. They might shield us if they come this way."

With our plan set, we creep toward the stones, the sounds of the searchers growing louder as they descend the path above. My heart pounds in my chest, a steady reminder of the ticking clock. Each moment stretches into eternity as we huddle behind the rocks, trying to remain unseen.

"Do you think they'll find us?" Lucas asks, his voice barely a whisper.

I shake my head, forcing myself to be brave despite the gnawing fear. "Not if we're careful. Just keep quiet."

Time drags on, each heartbeat echoing in my ears, the tension palpable as we wait in silence. I focus on the sounds around us—the rustling leaves, the distant hooting of an owl, the very faint sound of water trickling somewhere nearby. It's almost calming, but the looming threat reminds me of our precarious situation.

Suddenly, a loud crash reverberates through the trees, a sound that could only mean Derrick and his men are closing in. I feel a jolt of fear shoot through me. "We need to move, now!"

As I speak, I catch sight of a flash of movement just beyond the tree line—a figure, silhouetted against the moonlight. My heart sinks as recognition washes over me.

"Derrick," I whisper, panic clawing at my throat. He's closer than I thought, and if he sees us now, there's no escaping.

Lucas's hand tightens around mine, and I can feel the heat radiating from him, grounding me in the chaos. We hold our breath, waiting, hearts pounding in unison as Derrick's figure draws nearer. The tension is thick enough to slice, and in that moment, time seems to stand still, teetering on the edge of dread and uncertainty.

Then, out of the shadows, I see movement behind Derrick—a second figure, cloaked in darkness, its intentions unreadable. I can't make out their features, but an instinctive chill runs down my spine. The air shifts, a tension palpable as if the forest itself is holding its breath.

"Get ready," I whisper, steeling myself for whatever comes next. We're about to plunge headfirst into the unknown, and I have no idea what lies waiting in the shadows, but I know we must be ready for anything.

The moonlight flickers, and just as I prepare to make a move, a loud shout echoes through the trees—Derrick's men have found us. I feel a surge of adrenaline as I glance at Lucas, the weight of the moment crashing down around us, and together, we brace for the storm that's about to erupt.

Chapter 23: Final Stand

The sun dipped low on the horizon, casting an amber hue over the landscape, a bittersweet farewell to the day as shadows stretched long, creeping like anxious fingers across the ground. The air was thick with tension, almost electric, vibrating with the unresolved energy of the confrontation that loomed just beyond the city's edges. I stood between two worlds: the familiar chaos of the city behind me, filled with its cacophony of sirens and distant laughter, and the quiet, oppressive stillness of the wilderness ahead. My heart pounded in my chest, each beat a reminder of the stakes at hand.

Derrick appeared like a specter emerging from the twilight, his silhouette dark against the fading light. There was a wildness in his eyes that sent a chill down my spine. The man I once thought I knew had transformed into a stranger, fueled by a rage that crackled in the air like static. His fists were clenched, and his jaw was set with a determination that felt both terrifying and strangely heartbreaking. He had been a friend, a mentor even, but that was before the darkness had swallowed him whole. Now, standing before us, he embodied every twisted aspect of betrayal, his intentions as sharp as the blade concealed within his coat.

"Lucas," I whispered, my voice trembling. He turned to me, his eyes reflecting the dimming light, filled with a resolve that steadied my fraying nerves. I could see the weight of the moment pressing down on him, yet there was a fierce determination in his stance that gave me courage. This wasn't just about survival; it was about confronting the demons that had haunted him for far too long.

As Derrick took a step closer, his voice was a low growl, rich with venom. "You think you can escape me? After everything I've done for you?" The accusation hung in the air, thick and suffocating, as if the world had paused to witness this moment.

Lucas straightened, the air around him shifting with the force of his presence. "You've done nothing for me, Derrick. You've only ever looked out for yourself." Each word was deliberate, carved from the stone of his conviction. I could feel the tension coiling like a spring, ready to snap.

Derrick laughed, a harsh, bitter sound that echoed off the trees, mocking the gravity of the situation. "You've become soft, Lucas. You think you can protect her? You're nothing without me."

I could see Lucas's muscles tense, his breath hitching for a moment as he fought against the tide of Derrick's provocations. "I'm stronger than you think. You've underestimated me."

In that instant, the world felt impossibly small, as if it had contracted to the space between the three of us. I could see the myriad emotions playing across Lucas's face—fear, anger, determination—and I understood that this was his moment of truth. For me. For us. Derrick had unleashed a monster within Lucas, one that had been lurking beneath the surface, waiting for the chance to break free.

Derrick lunged, the movement swift and desperate. Time slowed as I watched, my heart in my throat, unable to look away. Lucas sidestepped with an agility that belied the weight of the moment, his body reacting with instincts honed through years of survival. He didn't just evade; he countered, striking back with a fluidity that was both beautiful and terrifying. It was a dance of violence, each movement sharp and precise, fueled by an urgency that resonated in my bones.

"Enough!" Derrick roared, his frustration bubbling over as he charged again. The ground trembled beneath us as they clashed, a symphony of grunts and the dull thud of bodies colliding, echoing in the stillness of the evening.

I felt rooted to the spot, a spectator to their struggle, the world around us fading into the background. My hands curled into fists, nails biting into my palms, a surge of helplessness washing over me. I wanted to leap in, to intervene, but I knew this was Lucas's battle, one he had to face alone.

In that fleeting moment of vulnerability, as Derrick swung wildly, I saw something shift. His fury blinded him, turned his focus inward until he was lost in the storm of his own making. Lucas seized the moment, a glint of resolve sparking in his eyes. He disarmed Derrick with a deft maneuver, wrenching the weapon from his grasp and tossing it aside, where it clattered to the ground, a metallic echo in the gathering dusk.

"You've lost, Derrick," Lucas declared, his voice steady but laced with the weariness of a man who had fought too long and too hard. Derrick staggered back, disbelief etched across his features as he processed the reality of his defeat.

The confrontation left the air charged, an electric pulse coursing between us. I stepped forward, the instinct to comfort Lucas overpowering my initial fear. His chest heaved with exertion, and for a moment, I saw the boy I loved, stripped of pretense, laid bare in his vulnerability. I reached for his hand, grounding myself in the warmth of his touch, the connection between us a silent vow.

Derrick's shoulders slumped, a man brought low by his own darkness. The fire in his eyes flickered, dimming as he grasped the futility of his anger. "You think you've won? This isn't over," he spat, his voice laced with bitterness.

"It is for you," Lucas replied, the strength in his voice unwavering. The finality of his words hung in the air, a statement that felt like both a relief and a heavy burden. Derrick was defeated, but the scars he left behind would linger, etched into the fabric of our lives like an indelible mark.

As Derrick turned away, disappearing into the shadows that had once consumed him, I exhaled a breath I didn't realize I was holding. The confrontation had transformed us, forcing us to confront the monsters we'd been fighting for so long. We stood together, united in our victory yet aware of the path ahead, a road fraught with uncertainty but illuminated by the flicker of hope. Together, we had faced the darkness, and though it would take time to heal, we emerged stronger, ready to face whatever came next.

As Derrick staggered back, the raw fury that had once seemed invincible now lay crumbling at his feet, mingling with the dust of the old dirt road that wound toward the darkening trees. His breath came in ragged gasps, and for the first time, I caught a glimpse of uncertainty flickering in his eyes. The man I had known, once confident and commanding, was now a mere shell, emptied of the bravado that had fueled him for so long. I couldn't help but feel a pang of sympathy amid the chaos, a strange sorrow for someone who had chosen the path of destruction over redemption.

"Get away from me!" he spat, his voice a raw whisper of desperation. The venom in his words cut through the silence, sharp and biting, yet they lacked the potency they once held. I wanted to believe that this was the last we would see of him, but deep down, I knew his shadow would linger, a reminder of the darkness we had faced. Lucas stepped forward, the glint of determination in his eyes shining brighter than ever.

"It's over, Derrick. You can't control this anymore," Lucas asserted, his voice steady, resonating with the authority of someone who had reclaimed their power. I could see the tension in his shoulders easing, the burden of fear lifting as he embraced the victory we had fought so hard to achieve.

With a final, defiant glare, Derrick turned and fled, retreating into the gathering dusk like a wounded animal seeking refuge. The moment he disappeared from view, I let out a breath I didn't realize I had been holding, a mixture of relief and disbelief flooding my senses. We were alive, standing on the precipice of a new beginning, yet the battle was far from over. The air crackled with an energy that felt both exhilarating and terrifying, and I was acutely aware of the weight of the night pressing down upon us.

"What now?" I asked, my voice breaking the fragile silence that had settled around us. Lucas turned to me, and the warmth of his gaze melted away the remnants of fear clinging to my heart.

"Now we figure out how to move forward," he replied, his smile a mixture of triumph and vulnerability. It was a new era, one filled with uncertainties, but with him by my side, I felt a flicker of hope ignite within me.

As we began our trek back toward the city, the darkness wrapped around us like a cloak, each rustle of leaves a reminder of the world we had left behind. The familiar sights began to loom in the distance, streetlights flickering to life, illuminating the path we had walked so many times before. Yet tonight felt different—charged with the knowledge that we had faced our fears and emerged stronger.

"I can't believe we did it," I said, my voice barely above a whisper, almost afraid to disrupt the magic of the moment. Lucas chuckled softly, his eyes sparkling with the remnants of adrenaline.

"Did you really think Derrick would have the last word?" he replied, his tone light but laced with an undercurrent of seriousness. "He's always underestimated us, especially you."

His words hung in the air, and I couldn't shake the feeling that our fight wasn't just against Derrick. It was a battle for our identities, our choices, and the paths we would forge. The city felt different now, as if the very fabric of it had shifted beneath our feet, weaving our fates into a shared tapestry.

As we approached a small café, its neon sign casting a welcoming glow, I could feel my stomach rumbling in agreement with my mind's insistence on celebration. "How about we treat ourselves?" I suggested, nudging him playfully. "I could use a victory latte."

He grinned, the tension of the confrontation easing away with every step we took toward the door. "You read my mind. Let's go celebrate like it's the end of the world."

Inside, the café hummed with life, a stark contrast to the quiet chaos outside. The scent of freshly brewed coffee mingled with the sweet aroma of pastries, enveloping us in a warm embrace. We found a cozy corner booth, the plush seating inviting us to sink into it like old friends. As we placed our orders, I couldn't help but feel a sense of normalcy returning, a thread of familiarity woven back into the fabric of our lives.

"Do you think Derrick will come back?" I asked, my curiosity piqued despite my earlier resolve to push thoughts of him aside. Lucas leaned back, his expression contemplative.

"Maybe," he said, his gaze thoughtful as he stirred his coffee. "But we'll be ready. We've faced him once; we can do it again if we have to." His confidence reassured me, filling the space between us with an unspoken understanding that we were stronger together.

Just then, the bell above the café door jingled, and I glanced up, my heart momentarily skipping a beat. A figure stepped inside, the shadow falling across the entrance revealing a familiar face. It was Jess, her eyes wide as she scanned the room before landing on us. Relief washed over her features, and she made her way over, her energy infectious.

"There you are! I was worried sick!" she exclaimed, collapsing into the seat beside me. "You wouldn't believe the rumors swirling around town. I thought you two had vanished into thin air."

"Just a minor adventure," Lucas replied, his grin brightening the room. "Nothing we couldn't handle." Jess raised an eyebrow, skepticism written all over her face.

"Minor? Please. You guys have a flair for the dramatic," she teased, a grin spreading across her lips. "But seriously, I'm glad you're okay."

As we laughed and exchanged stories, the sense of camaraderie enveloped us, and I felt the weight of the world lift. With each sip of coffee and every shared joke, the future began to unfurl before us, vibrant and full of possibility. The scars of our battles would remain, but they would serve as reminders of our resilience, each one a testament to the strength we had found within ourselves and each other.

The café buzzed around us, a backdrop to our renewed hopes and dreams. And as we sat there, surrounded by friends and laughter, I understood that while darkness would always linger in the corners of our lives, it was the light of connection, courage, and love that would guide us forward.

The hum of laughter and the rich aroma of coffee surrounded us, but I could feel a tension simmering beneath the surface, like a pot just waiting to boil over. Jess leaned forward, her eyes bright with concern and curiosity. "Seriously, you guys need to fill me in on what happened out there. I thought I was going to lose my mind while waiting for you to show up."

Lucas exchanged a glance with me, a silent agreement passing between us. The thrill of our recent victory was still fresh, but the shadows of our confrontation loomed large, and I wasn't quite ready to relive it all in detail just yet. "It was a bit dramatic, to say the least," Lucas admitted with a wry smile, stirring his coffee absentmindedly.

"Dramatic? That's like saying a hurricane is a little rain," Jess shot back, crossing her arms with playful indignation. "You've got to give me more than that. Did you at least kick his butt?"

"Something like that," I replied, feeling the corners of my mouth lift into a grin. "Let's just say Derrick won't be bothering us anytime soon."

"That's the spirit!" Jess exclaimed, her relief palpable. "But you know, he's not the type to give up easily. What if he decides to come back with reinforcements?"

The question hung in the air, and I could see Lucas's expression shift as he considered her words. "If he does, we'll be ready for him," he declared, his voice steady. "We've got each other's backs, and that counts for a lot more than any number he can muster."

As the chatter around us buzzed with life, I felt a sense of warmth bloom within me, wrapping around my heart like a cozy blanket. We had faced darkness and emerged, not unscathed, but stronger. I watched Lucas as he spoke, his resolve shining through, and I knew that together we could navigate whatever storm lay ahead.

Just then, the café door swung open again, and a gust of wind rushed in, sending a few napkins fluttering like startled birds. My gaze flicked to the entrance, and my heart plummeted at the sight of a familiar figure—Max, Derrick's loyal right hand and a man whose loyalty to his friend seemed as fierce as a wolf's. He stepped inside, scanning the room with an intensity that sent shivers down my spine.

"Damn it," I muttered under my breath, my heart racing. "What's he doing here?"

"Who?" Jess turned, her brow furrowing as she followed my gaze.

"Max," I replied, my voice low. "He's with Derrick."

Lucas's expression hardened, his easy demeanor shifting to one of vigilance. "Stay close," he murmured, his body positioning itself protectively between me and the doorway.

Max's eyes locked onto us, a predatory gleam flickering within them. He sauntered over, a smug grin plastered on his face, his presence as unwelcome as a storm cloud on a sunny day. "Well, well, if it isn't the dynamic duo," he drawled, his tone dripping with sarcasm. "I heard you had quite the adventure. I thought I'd drop by and see for myself."

"Lucky us," I shot back, forcing a lightness into my voice despite the knot of dread tightening in my stomach. "What brings you to our little celebration?"

He leaned on the table, his eyes glinting with malice. "Just came to deliver a message from Derrick," he said, the smile never reaching his eyes. "He's not done with you yet. Not by a long shot."

Lucas shifted slightly, his body taut as he glared at Max, the tension palpable. "Tell him to stay away from us. He has nothing to prove," he replied, his voice firm.

Max chuckled, a sound devoid of humor. "That's cute, Lucas. But you don't get to call the shots anymore. Derrick's angry, and you know what they say about a cornered animal." He leaned in closer, lowering his voice. "He's got nothing to lose."

"Then he's even more dangerous," Jess interjected, her voice strong and defiant. "But that doesn't mean we'll back down."

"Oh, I'd love to see you try," Max taunted, pushing away from the table with an exaggerated flourish. "Just remember, you've made some powerful enemies." With that, he turned and walked away, his footsteps echoing in the quiet café.

As the door swung shut behind him, I felt a chill settle in my bones. "What does he mean by 'powerful enemies'?" I asked, the question hanging in the air like a fog that refused to lift.

Lucas's jaw tightened, his gaze distant as he stared at the door, contemplating Max's parting words. "It means Derrick is more desperate than I thought. He's willing to go to extreme lengths to prove a point."

"Great, just what we needed," Jess huffed, crossing her arms. "It's like a bad movie we can't turn off."

"Let's not panic," I said, trying to inject a sense of calm into the swirling chaos. "We've faced Derrick, and we can face whatever comes next. We have each other, and we're stronger for it."

Just as I finished speaking, the café's lights flickered, plunging us momentarily into darkness before they returned to their normal glow. The sensation was disconcerting, a hint of something lurking just beyond our reach. I exchanged worried glances with Lucas and

Jess, a silent agreement that this moment felt charged, brimming with a sense of impending conflict.

But the world outside seemed to hold its breath, and I couldn't shake the feeling that something was about to unfold. "We should get out of here," Lucas suggested, his voice urgent. "I don't want to be around if Derrick sends someone else."

As we made our way to the door, a low rumble echoed through the ground beneath us, a tremor that felt like a warning. I paused, looking back at Lucas and Jess, the fear reflected in their eyes mirroring my own. "What was that?" I asked, my voice barely above a whisper.

Before anyone could answer, the door burst open with a force that sent a chill racing down my spine. A figure stood silhouetted against the night, and I felt my breath hitch in my throat as recognition hit me like a punch to the gut.

It was Derrick, and behind him, a shadowy group emerged, their faces obscured but their intentions clear. A primal fear surged within me, and I took a step back, heart pounding, the world around us spinning into chaos as the realization dawned: this fight was far from over.

Chapter 24: A New Dawn

Days turned into weeks, and I could feel the warmth of spring creeping into the city, melting away the remnants of winter's chill. Lucas and I walked through the bustling streets, hand in hand, relishing the newfound freedom that hung between us like a vibrant banner unfurling in the wind. The scent of fresh coffee wafted from nearby cafés, mingling with the sweet notes of blooming flowers that burst into color all around us. It was as if the city itself had taken a deep breath, shaking off its winter coat to reveal a landscape alive with possibilities.

"Do you remember when we first came here?" Lucas asked, a playful smile dancing on his lips. His eyes sparkled with mischief, and I couldn't help but return his smile, feeling the corners of my mouth lift in a way that made my heart flutter.

"Vaguely," I replied, feigning indifference while the memory flickered in my mind like a firefly in the dusk. "Wasn't that the time we got lost trying to find that awful pizza place? The one with the weirdly shaped slices?"

"Oh, it was definitely a crime against pizza," he laughed, the sound rich and warm, wrapping around me like a cozy blanket. "But we made the best of it. Just like we always do."

There was a soft sincerity in his voice that sent a shiver of comfort through me. We had grown so much since those chaotic days when our lives felt like a tangled mess of fear and uncertainty. Now, we were standing on the edge of a new beginning, the sun illuminating the path ahead, promising warmth and adventure.

As we wandered through the crowded streets, the city pulsed with life around us—families laughing, street performers showcasing their talents, and the sweet strumming of a guitar blending into the hum of conversation. I spotted a small park just off the main road, a hidden gem cradled among the towering buildings, where vibrant tulips swayed gently in the breeze, their colors a riot of reds, yellows, and purples.

"Let's sit," I suggested, tugging him toward a sun-drenched bench that looked inviting enough to keep us there for hours.

He chuckled and nodded, settling beside me. "I could use a break from all the excitement of city life. Not that there's ever a dull moment with you around."

"Flattery will get you everywhere," I teased, nudging him playfully with my shoulder. We both knew I had a penchant for the dramatic, and he enjoyed every moment of it.

The warmth of the sun seeped into my skin as I watched a little girl chase butterflies, her laughter ringing like music in the air. It was a stark contrast to the world we had navigated just weeks prior, where shadows loomed like storm clouds. Lucas intertwined his fingers with mine, grounding me as the memories washed over us. The threats, the fear, Derrick's looming presence—they all felt like a distant echo now, fading into the background as we focused on the beauty of the moment.

"What's on your mind?" Lucas asked, tilting his head, his expression softening.

I hesitated, my thoughts momentarily tangled in the comforting peace we had found. "I was just thinking about how far we've come," I said, looking down at our joined hands. "It feels... surreal."

He nodded, his gaze penetrating mine, as if searching for something beneath the surface. "Surreal is a good word. But I think we deserve this, Em. We fought for it."

The intensity in his eyes sent a thrill coursing through me, a reminder of our shared struggle and the resilience that had carried us through the darkest nights. It was strange how love could blossom from adversity, transforming pain into something vibrant and alive.

Just then, a commotion caught our attention. A man in a suit was rushing past, his phone glued to his ear as he barked into it, oblivious to the world around him. I couldn't help but chuckle. "He looks like he's got a lot on his plate."

Lucas chuckled, and for a moment, we watched the world swirl around us. "You know, it's moments like these that remind me how ordinary life can be beautiful," he mused. "Like those people over there."

He gestured to a couple seated on a nearby bench, sharing a sandwich and giggling like schoolchildren. Their carefree spirits reminded me of us, before the world had thrust its darkness upon us. "We could be like that, you know. Just enjoying the little things."

"Exactly!" I exclaimed, my enthusiasm bubbling over. "What's stopping us? We can have our own picnic! We could grab sandwiches and sodas and just... be."

Lucas raised an eyebrow, an amused smile spreading across his face. "You mean we can live dangerously? In a park, no less?"

"Absolutely! Life is too short to miss out on picnics!"

He laughed, the sound echoing in the sunlit space, and stood up. "All right, Miss Adventurer. You've convinced me. Let's do it."

With that, we set off, hand in hand, toward a nearby deli that promised the best sandwiches in town. As we walked, I felt the weight of the past lift a little more with each step. The future was still uncertain, but it no longer felt like a looming threat. Instead, it shimmered with the possibilities of laughter, love, and spontaneous adventures.

Inside the deli, the air was filled with the mouthwatering aroma of fresh bread and spices. We quickly ordered our sandwiches, and as we waited, I watched Lucas chat with the cashier, his easy charm lighting up the small space. He was in his element, a magnetic presence that drew people in, and I couldn't help but admire him.

"Your order will be ready in a minute!" the cashier called, grinning at Lucas as he leaned casually against the counter.

"Thank you!" he replied, flashing a smile that could melt glaciers.

"See? You're a natural," I said, nudging him playfully.

He shrugged, a devil-may-care grin plastered on his face. "What can I say? I'm just here to spread joy and sandwiches."

As our sandwiches were handed over, we made our way back to the park, the sun dipping lower in the sky, casting a golden hue over everything. It felt like we were in our own little bubble, a world untouched by the storms we had faced. Sitting on the grass, we laid out our makeshift picnic, the sandwiches and sodas becoming our humble feast.

"This is perfect," I declared, taking a hearty bite of my sandwich. The flavors burst in my mouth—savory turkey, crisp lettuce, and a touch of tangy mustard.

"See? I told you it was a good idea," he replied, his eyes twinkling as he took a large bite of his own.

We fell into a comfortable rhythm, teasing each other and laughing, the worries of the world melting away like the last remnants of winter. Each moment felt precious, each laugh a promise of what was yet to come. As the sun dipped below the horizon, painting the sky in shades of pink and orange, I felt a renewed sense of hope—a sense that our lives were no longer defined by what had tried to tear us apart but rather by the love we had fought to preserve.

The laughter and chatter from the park melted into the backdrop of city life, creating a symphony of sounds that wrapped around us like a comforting embrace. As Lucas and I finished our impromptu picnic, we leaned back on the grass, gazing at the sky above, where clouds drifted lazily, their shapes morphing into fantastical creatures. I felt a sense of calm wash over me, an exhilarating thrill that everything was finally aligning.

"Look at that one! It's definitely a dragon," I pointed out, squinting against the sun.

Lucas chuckled, following my gaze. "A dragon? That looks more like an angry potato to me."

"An angry potato? How dare you!" I feigned indignation, a smile breaking through my mock frown. "What kind of dragons are you familiar with? I'll have you know that in my world, dragons are majestic and fierce."

"Potatoes can be fierce," he replied with mock seriousness. "Just ask the French fries."

We both burst into laughter, the sound bright and carefree, resonating through the park like a joyful melody. But as we lay there, a moment of quiet settled in, filling the space between our laughter with something deeper, a shared understanding of what it meant to heal. The weight of our past lingered, but it was no longer the dominant force in our lives.

As the sun dipped lower, casting elongated shadows, I felt a slight chill in the air, the transition from day to night a gentle reminder that change was inevitable. I turned to Lucas, who was propped up on one elbow, watching me with a look that made my heart race. "What's on your mind?" I asked, catching the intensity of his gaze.

"I was just thinking how this feels right," he said softly, his thumb brushing over my hand. "All of this—the park, the food, you. It feels like we're finally starting fresh."

I nodded, the simplicity of his words echoing the complexity of our journey. "It's almost surreal. I keep expecting something to go wrong, like a plot twist in a cheesy romance novel."

"Or a rom-com where the couple runs into a series of ridiculous mishaps," he added, a grin spreading across his face. "I can see it now: 'Two lovers, one angry potato, and a pigeon with a vendetta.'"

I burst out laughing again, imagining the scene he painted—a pigeon swooping down and wreaking havoc as we tried to enjoy our peaceful evening. "Honestly, if that happens, I'm leaving you. I refuse to be part of a disaster movie."

"Smart move," Lucas said, pretending to take notes in the air with a serious expression. "Always protect yourself from rogue birds."

Just then, as if the universe had decided to play along with our banter, a pigeon landed nearby, cooing loudly and eyeing our leftover sandwich like it was the treasure of a pirate ship. We both exchanged glances, bursting into fits of laughter at the perfect timing.

"See? This is what I'm talking about!" I exclaimed, waving my hand at the pigeon. "Disaster strikes at any moment. We need to flee!"

Lucas laughed, his eyes twinkling with mischief. "Fleeing from a pigeon? I'll never live that down. But I'd follow you anywhere."

His sincerity tugged at my heart, and as I watched him, I felt the softness of my affection for him swell, blossoming into something deeper, richer. The laughter faded, replaced by a comfortable silence that spoke volumes.

Eventually, we decided to pack up our makeshift picnic, carefully wrapping the remaining sandwiches to take home. As we gathered our things, the sky transformed into a canvas of deep oranges and purples, the sun casting a final glow over the city. It was as if the universe was blessing our new beginning with the most beautiful farewell to the day.

"Ready for our next adventure?" I asked as we stood to leave, our fingers still intertwined.

"Always," he replied, and the word held a promise.

We strolled back through the streets, the city illuminated by streetlights flickering to life, casting a warm glow that felt almost magical. Each step felt lighter, the world around us buzzing with energy and potential.

"I have a surprise for you," Lucas said suddenly, pulling me to a stop.

"Oh? What kind of surprise?" I asked, curiosity piqued.

"Not telling," he said, his lips curling into a playful grin. "But I promise it's worth it."

I rolled my eyes, knowing he would drag this out as long as possible. "You know I'm terrible at waiting, right? The suspense is killing me."

"Is it really suspense if you're so eager?"

"Touché," I conceded. "But still, I expect a dramatic reveal."

Lucas laughed and led me to a small alleyway filled with murals and street art. "Close your eyes."

"What? Why?" I protested, but he merely raised an eyebrow.

"Trust me," he said, and I could hear the sincerity in his voice.

With a reluctant sigh, I closed my eyes and let him guide me forward. The world fell away, sounds dimming as I focused on the rhythm of his footsteps beside me.

"Okay, now open," he instructed, his voice laced with excitement.

I opened my eyes, and the sight that greeted me took my breath away. The alley was adorned with an explosion of colors, vibrant murals that told stories of love, hope, and resilience. Each stroke of paint seemed to dance under the streetlights, breathing life into the bricks. In the center, a larger mural depicted a phoenix rising from the ashes, its wings outstretched in a triumphant display of rebirth.

"It's... beautiful," I whispered, stepping closer to take it all in.

"I thought it might resonate with us," Lucas said, his voice softening. "A reminder that we're rising, too, just like that phoenix."

I turned to him, my heart swelling with gratitude and affection. "You know, this is one of the most thoughtful surprises I've ever had. It's perfect."

His smile widened, lighting up his features. "I'm glad you like it. I figured we could make a tradition of finding places like this, places that speak to us."

I couldn't help but smile back, the idea blooming in my mind like the flowers of spring. "I'd love that. Each mural can tell our story, marking the moments that define us."

"Exactly. And someday, we'll have our own story to add to it."

With the backdrop of the mural glowing behind us, I felt an electric spark of possibility. The world was wide open, filled with adventures waiting to unfold, and there was no one else I wanted by my side but Lucas. As I turned to him, my heart racing with a mixture of hope and excitement, I knew that we were no longer just surviving. We were truly living.

The vibrant colors of the mural still danced in my mind as we meandered through the streets, our laughter mingling with the city sounds that felt almost like music to my ears. The atmosphere was alive with potential, and each moment unfolded like a well-crafted story, one that we were eager to write together. Lucas led me to a quaint café tucked away on a side street, its outdoor seating adorned with string lights that twinkled like stars against the early evening sky.

"Let's get some coffee," he suggested, his eyes sparkling with mischief. "You can fuel your caffeine addiction while I marvel at how you've managed to charm the entire city into being your personal backdrop."

I rolled my eyes playfully. "Please, I'm just here for the coffee. You, on the other hand, are the one who looks like he just stepped out of a romance novel. If there's a swoon factor, you've got it covered."

He feigned a modest shrug, his grin widening. "I appreciate the compliment, but let's be honest; I'm really just here to bask in your glow."

We found a cozy corner table, the scent of freshly brewed coffee wafting through the air, mingling with the sweet aroma of pastries that made my stomach growl in anticipation. I scanned the menu, my eyes landing on a decadent chocolate croissant. "I think I need this in my life," I declared, my voice filled with conviction. "And possibly two coffees to wash it down."

Lucas chuckled, leaning back in his chair. "You've got a one-track mind when it comes to food. But who am I to judge? Bring on the pastries!"

As we placed our order, the barista shot us a knowing smile, clearly entertained by our banter. The café buzzed with chatter, the walls lined with photographs that told stories of countless patrons who had sought refuge here, much like we had. With each sip of the rich, velvety coffee, I felt my worries dissipate, the warmth spreading through me like a gentle embrace.

"So, what's next for us?" I asked, my curiosity getting the better of me. "Now that we're not running from shadows and you've embraced your inner phoenix, what are we going to do with this newfound freedom?"

Lucas leaned forward, his expression turning serious, but the spark of mischief lingered in his eyes. "Well, I was thinking we could start with some serious adventure planning. I mean, the world is our oyster now—though, I've never really liked oysters."

"I'd rather have chocolate croissants," I quipped, taking a bite and letting the flaky pastry melt in my mouth. "Now that's a worthy adventure."

"Perhaps we can travel," he continued, ignoring my interruption with a playful roll of his eyes. "See new places, meet new people. Maybe even go on a quest for the best chocolate croissant in the world."

I laughed, imagining us traversing the globe in search of pastries, our culinary journey a delicious backdrop to our love story. "I'm in! But if we encounter any angry potatoes along the way, I'm out."

Lucas feigned shock. "How could you abandon me in the face of adversity? We'd have to join forces to take down the potato menace!"

"Right, right. My bad! But I think we should probably steer clear of anything with wings—at least for now."

Our laughter echoed through the café, and for a moment, it felt like nothing could touch us. But as the evening wore on, the conversation shifted to the reality that lingered in the corners of our minds. I couldn't shake the feeling that Derrick's influence hadn't vanished completely; it merely lay dormant, waiting for the right moment to resurface.

After finishing our pastries, we left the café, the cool night air wrapping around us like a gentle reminder of the reality we'd fought to escape. Lucas paused, his expression contemplative as we stood at the intersection of two streets, the glow of the streetlights illuminating his features.

"What if he comes back?" I asked, the question lingering like a shadow over our newfound happiness.

Lucas's jaw tightened slightly, a flicker of determination in his eyes. "We won't let him. We've faced worse, Em. We can handle anything together."

I nodded, grateful for his unwavering strength, but uncertainty gnawed at me. Just as we were beginning to feel whole again, the past seemed to linger like a stubborn ghost, haunting us with its unresolved threats.

"Promise me we'll stay vigilant," I said, my voice steady yet laced with vulnerability. "I don't want to live in fear, but I also don't want to be caught off guard."

"Promise," he replied, his voice low and serious. "We'll keep an eye out, and if anything happens, we'll face it head-on."

Our resolve felt like armor, but just as I started to relax, a distant sound broke through the quiet night—an engine revving, sharp and aggressive. I glanced around, my heart racing as the sound grew louder, a dark shape speeding toward us down the street.

"Lucas," I whispered, the unease curling in my stomach like a serpent.

Before he could respond, a sleek black car skidded to a halt just a few feet away from us. The driver's window slid down, revealing a face I recognized all too well—a sharp jaw, cold eyes, and a smirk that sent chills racing down my spine.

"Miss me?" Derrick's voice was like ice, slicing through the warmth of our moment.

My heart dropped into my stomach, the world around us fading into a blur as dread filled the air. Lucas instinctively moved closer to me, his body shielding mine as he took a protective stance.

"What do you want?" Lucas demanded, his voice low and fierce, radiating an intensity that I knew all too well.

"Just wanted to catch up," Derrick said, leaning back in his seat, an unsettling calmness in his demeanor. "You know how it is—can't let old friends drift too far apart."

I exchanged a glance with Lucas, my pulse racing as a wave of panic surged through me. This wasn't just a casual reunion; this was a threat.

As Derrick's gaze flicked between us, a twisted sense of satisfaction danced in his eyes, and I felt the weight of the past crashing down, threatening to engulf us once more. Just as the tension reached a breaking point, Derrick leaned forward, his voice dripping with malice.

"Oh, I hope you're ready for what's coming. It's going to be quite the ride."

With those chilling words, he pressed down on the gas pedal, the car roaring to life as it sped off into the night, leaving us standing in the fading glow of the streetlights. The laughter and warmth we had shared moments ago vanished, replaced by an icy grip of dread.

As I stood there, breathless and trembling, the reality settled over us like a thick fog. Derrick was back, and this time, it felt different—more dangerous, more insidious. The fight wasn't over; in fact, it had only just begun.

Milton Keynes UK
Ingram Content Group UK Ltd.
UKHW031153251124
451529UK00001B/80

9 798227 503763